Cowboys & Kisses

Teens of Black Falls, Texas— Book One

A Young Adult Novel

Sasha Summers

Cowboys & Kisses: Teens of Black Falls, Texas- Book One

Copyright © 2014 Sasha Summers

ISBN-13 ISBN (Print) 978-1-939590-30-5
ISBN-13 (ebook): 978-1-939590-29-9
Library of Congress Control Number:

Inkspell Publishing
5764 Woodbine Av.
Pinckney, MI 48169

Edited By Deb Anderson

Cover art By Najla Qamber

PRAISE FOR SASHA SUMMERS

"Summers is a fantastic writer and, if you have not read her work yet, you definitely should." Marissa - For The Love of Film and Novels

"Miss Summers is able to really capture the emotion of the piece and we feel for the character." - Dan Wright, Author

"I can assure you, you're in great hands when reading a book by Sasha Summers." Viviana, Enchantress of Books

"Ms. Summers is an amazing writer, trust me on this. One of the best I have read, actually." - Jean Murray, Author

"Honestly, I have not read anything by Sasha Summers that I did not love and I look forward to more works by her." - Holly, Full Moon Bites Reviews

"A sweet story about family, growing up, and a love that heals all wounds." BookKins.com - BookKins Reviews.

"Sasha Summers writes character that move into your heart and stay there. You cry with them, get mad at them and cheer for them." - Jolene Guinther Navarro, Author

SASHA SUMMERS

DEDICATION

To my amazing daughters:
Summer and Emma
Love fearlessly, dream endlessly,
& believe in yourself unequivocally

1 CHAPTER ONE

"It needs a little TLC," my father said as he put the truck in park.

A little TLC? What the hell is he thinking? I glared at the back of his head. *Oh, wait, he isn't.*

"Um, yeah, Dad." Even Dax, my twin brother, sounded pissed now. Good, maybe he'd cross over to my side—the dark side. "You could say that."

This was not Grandma's yellow house with pretty white lace-looking trim. This house was grey. And dirty. And old. And pathetically sad. Now it was *way* more haunted house than Grandma's house.

Not Grandma's house anymore. My house. I felt sick. *He's officially trying to drive me crazy.* I glared at my father, but he was staring at the house—grinning like an idiot.

That was when I noticed the scaffolding covering the far wall. It looked like someone was scraping the paint off the house—which meant Dad knew the house was in bad *bad* shape.

We all climbed out of the truck. I was relieved to see Mom and Dax were just as thrown by the whole shack thing as I was. This was a big deal—a real shock. Well, not for Dad obviously.

"What?" He shrugged, glancing at our expressions. He looked irritated.

Like you have any right to be irritated.

"It'll be just like new in no time," he said, all calm and cool and smug.

You are such a prick.

"I'm sure it will," Mom said, pushing my irritation closer to anger. When had she become his biggest cheerleader? And why? Like his mid-life crisis needed a cheerleader?

I looked pointedly back at the house and crossed my arms over my chest. *My life is a bad joke.*

The wind picked up, kicking up dust. The lone chain holding up one corner of the front porch swing squeaked miserably—which was fitting. Yep, *so* haunted house.

"At least you'll have something to do. School doesn't start for a few weeks," my dad continued.

"Yeah, Dax," I said softly to my brother.

"This isn't a solo kind of project." Dax shot me a look. I couldn't tell if he was mad at me or Dad, but since I hadn't done anything to him—recently—it had to be Dad. With good reason.

"You think *I'm* going to make this place less of a dump? That I'll sweat my ass off fixing up a pile of crap we're being forced to live in? Since we have nothing else to do, I mean." I heard how nasty I sounded, but I just didn't care. "Thanks, but I'll pass."

I'd been talking to Dax, but I made sure every syllable was loud enough for my dad to hear. We didn't talk— hadn't talked in almost five months now. I found talking loudly to other people allowed me to get my point across just fine.

I could tell it had this time. My dad stared at me, the muscle in his jaw working—a dead giveaway he was pissed. *Good.* I wanted to fight.

I raised my eyebrows at him, daring him to say something. Anything. I wanted him to know this was all his fault.

My mom put her hand on Dad's arm, tugging on him. He closed his eyes, took a deep breath, smiled at her, and turned to greet the moving truck as it pulled up the driveway.

Anger, hot and hard, choked me. When Mom's pale blue gaze met mine, I didn't back down. I hated to see the disappointment in her eyes, but she was *wrong*. *This* was wrong and I wasn't going to pretend it wasn't. I raised my chin just a little and stalked back to the truck. *Not caving. Not apologizing. Not my fault—just my problem.*

I grabbed my bag out of the truck bed, unaware the soft fabric snagged on the metal corner of the truck latch. I heard the rip of fabric and froze. *Perfect.* It wasn't bad, just a little tear. *Calming down now.* I counted backward from twenty and took a deep breath before swinging the bag over my shoulder. I kept my head down as I climbed up the steps onto the front porch.

I walked to the broken swing, pulling on the chain. I'd spent hours on this swing when I was little—snapping beans, shucking corn, trying to needlepoint with Grandma, reading Reader's Digest stories out loud… I tugged harder on the chain. It squeaked, but held tight.

At least the view was familiar. Massive oak and cedar trees ran the fence lines. Acres of fields, row after row of round hay bales, and then? More fields… Not much else. No houses, just the faded dirt road, a few dilapidated barns, and…nothing.

Because this is Hell and no rational person would choose to live here.

I turned the front door handle and pushed it open, bracing myself…

Okay. Not so bad.

It looked clean and mostly empty. One lone rocking chair sat in the corner, an odd box here and there.

Thank God.

I poked around a little, memories popping up.

Grandma's sewing kit in the bottom of the hall closet. The bottom kitchen drawer full of extra ketchup, sugar, salt and pepper packets. Making pie with the peaches and apples from Grandma's orchard. I'd made some good memories here...but that was because I hadn't been living here. I could *leave* then, go home... Now *this* was supposed to be home, my home. There was no escape.

That hot, hard knot started to form in my throat again.

I wandered up the stairs, noting the colored patches on the wall, where family photos had hung for years. On the landing, more blank walls and empty spaces. I kept going, heading to the room where I'd slept when I was little. *Guess it is my room now.* Down the hall, last door on the right, and up a flight of steps: Dax's and my old playroom. The only room we could get loud and not get in trouble since it was at the other end of the house from everyone and everything. Just the way I liked it. I stood in the doorway. It seemed smaller now.

It felt weird for it to be so *bare.* My footsteps echoed off the wooden floors. A few dusty boxes were stacked on one side of the room. I walked to the window, peering down at the fields and the valley in the distance. Maybe it was because I knew this view was going to be the view I had to see for the next year, but it wasn't as nice as I remembered it.

Everything was so...so brown. Rocky. Cactus everywhere. It wasn't green. No rolling grasses. No steady wind. This wasn't north Texas. This was...

My hands fisted and my chest ached. *This is home now*, I heard my dad's words...almost a threat. He'd said it over and over again. *Like he can brainwash me into believing it or something.* This might be his hometown and his house. But this was his choice...not mine.

I kicked one of the boxes against the wall, letting my frustration out.

Something thumped back.

I jumped, freaking out as the thumping kept going—

faster and faster—from behind the box. The house had been empty for almost six months. Out here, in the middle of nowhere, it was possible that something got inside. A skunk, a raccoon, a…a snake…

I swallowed, glancing at the bedroom door. Dax and my parents were in and out, unloading boxes. "Dax?" I called out. "Dax!" He was into nature, kind of. He could take care of it.

"Anytime you want to help, Allie." Dax's voice floated up the stairs. "Whenever you're done having a temper tantrum."

Temper tantrum? Really? His tone rubbed me the wrong way. *Fat chance.* I kicked the door shut.

The thumping went crazy. *Crap.*

I almost opened the door when I heard Dax yell, "Wimp!" *I'm not a wimp.* I could do this. Without help. I was stronger than him, more physical than he ever was. *He* was the wimp. I *would* so do this.

I reached forward, pulling the box back fast—like ripping off a Band-Aid.

A tiny bird stared at me with sparkly black eyes. Its chest rose and fell so rapidly it looked like it was about to pop.

I laughed. "You scared the crap out of me." The bird cocked its head at me, hopped, and flew to the window—straight into the glass with a sickening smack.

"Oh, stop…" I stared at the stunned bird lying on the floor. "Wait, wait, okay?" It shook itself and flapped its wings, preparing to fly again. "Seriously, chill." I took a step forward, not sure what to do. The bird flew up, hovering in front of the window, pecking on the glass. "Yeah," I agreed. "I get it. You want to go outside."

It settled on the windowsill and stared at me. I stared back. *Now what?* I couldn't catch it. I didn't want to hurt it trying.

"Can you *herd* birds?" I wrinkled my nose. It blinked at me. "I think you're going to have to go out that way." I stared at the window.

If I could open it *and* somehow get the screen off *and* not scare the bird even more, the little guy would be free. Easier than trying to get it down the stairs and out the front door.

I slid along the wall toward the window, holding my arms against my body. "I'm not going to hurt you," I explained to it. "I'm going to get you out of here. This is my...my room now." It blinked. "I know, I'm super thrilled too." *Stupid bird.*

I reached out, slowly twisting the window latch. The bird hopped off, flitting across the room to perch on the edge of one of the old boxes. I pushed the window, hoping it would slide right open.

It didn't. It was old, the wood dry and sticking in the grooves. "Of course not." I shook my head, gripped the window more securely and tugged. The window barely moved, moaning loudly. "*So* haunted house," I grumbled.

The bird chirped from the box in the corner.

"Thanks for the help." I sighed, fighting with the window.

Suddenly, the window slipped up an inch, then jammed on something. The wood frame splintered in my grip, a thick splinter gouging into my finger. "Ow! Ow, crud, crap, darn it," I bit out, staring at the bird before I realized I didn't have to keep my language PG. "Shit." I pulled out the splinter and sucked on my finger. "Son of a bitch." I turned back to the window, fueled by months of frustration and anger...and now pain.

"Open, dammit!" I shoved, putting all of my weight behind it...shattering the glass pane and sending shards onto the side yard below. With most of the glass gone, I pitched forward, one arm windmilling forward and knocking the screen out before I could catch it. I caught myself on the window frame, grabbing frantically. A sharp burst of pain radiated along my palm and up my arm. "Shit!" I yelled, pulling my hand back. A nasty gash throbbed, oozing blood. "Perfect. Just perfect!"

"Allie?" I heard my mother call me from outside.

"What?" I bit out. The bird flew out the window, its wings ruffling my hair as it escaped. "You're welcome," I called after the bird.

Dax was laughing. "What did you do *now*?"

I lifted my other hand off the window. The remaining wood and glass fell around me on the floor, the crash echoing in the empty room. I shut my eyes and stood, furious and bleeding. There wasn't a sound from outside, just footsteps on the stairs. *Perfect.*

I heard a squeak in the hallway—the same board that told Dax and me when Grandma was almost to our room so we needed to pretend we were sleeping. Which meant I was about to get an audience for this. *Stupid bird.* I squeezed my eyes tightly shut, waiting.

Footsteps on the steps...

"You okay?"

I didn't know that voice. I opened one eye, hesitant. Then both.

I didn't know this...this *cowboy*. This *really* cute, golden-tanned, copper-eyed cowboy taking up the doorway space. His light brown hair brushed the doorframe as he walked in...because he was tall and broad and so freaking cute. I stared at him like a complete idiot, while he stared at my hand.

"No, she's not. Okay's not a word we use to describe her." Dax followed Cute Cowboy Guy into my room, looking at me with a mixture of amazement and frustration.

"Cut your hand?" Cute Cowboy Guy came forward. He took my hand, lifted it close, and inspected the gash. He sucked in his breath, a sharp hissing sound. "You did a good job on that. Might need stitches."

I stared at my hand in his. His hands were rough and big, but his touch was gentle. Gentle or not, why was he in my room? Why was I letting him touch me? *Snap out of it,*

Allie. "Who the hell are you?" I pulled my hand from his, wincing.

"Nice," Dax muttered. "Allie, this is Wyatt, our new neighbor. He came by. To *help.*"

New neighbor? "Oh," I said, giving him a quick head-to-toe inspection. His faded jeans were ripped along his left thigh, and the sleeves of his plaid snap-front shirt were rolled up to his elbows. And his face…well…he was way too good-looking. Way *way*–

Wyatt smiled. He had a really good smile, white teeth, dimples. "Nice to meet you." And a Texas twang.

I looked at him but didn't say anything. It might have been nice to meet him if I wasn't bleeding all over the floor of a bedroom in the middle of Hell. But—as much as I hated to admit it—even bleeding on the floor, he was pretty easy to look at.

My mother came into the room then, her small medical bag in hand. "What happened?" Her voice had that edge to it, the *why do you do what you do?* exasperation that only I brought out so well.

"There was a bird," I mumbled.

My mother probed around the cut, making me wince. "A bird?" she asked, clearly not believing me.

"Yes. A *bird,*" I repeated. "I tried to let it out. The damn window stuck." She looked at me, one eyebrow rising.

"It was a starling," Wyatt said, pulling my attention back to him.

I cocked an eyebrow in question. My mother did too.

"The bird. I saw it fly out the window." He smiled a slow, easygoing smile. "It was a starling."

"Oh," I answered coolly. I had to work at the tone though—because he was backing up what I was saying. And that might be the only reason Mom would believe me. I glanced at him from the corner of my eye.

"They're pests. Build nests in your eaves, in your light fixtures, cause damage." He was watching me, still smiling.

"Some target practice will fix that."

"Shoot it?" I narrowed my eyes and frowned. "I hope it doesn't decide to live at your place."

Wyatt shrugged. "It wouldn't for long."

Not so interesting after all. I leveled my best bitch-face at hunky cowboy.

"Allie...I need to stitch it." My mother spoke softly, thoughtfully. I watched her cover the cut with a clean gauze pad, knowing this would go on the list of Allie's Screw-ups. "I'll be right back." Her big blue eyes—Dax and I both got her eyes—bore into mine for just a second, and then she left. Mom was a veterinarian and had patched me and Dax up many times. It was a lot easier than having to go to the emergency room.

"Broom unpacked?" Wyatt asked, following her from the bedroom.

Dax looked at me with an elevated eyebrow. "It's been less than an hour and you're breaking windows. What's the deal, really?"

I shook my head at him. "You wouldn't understand. You didn't have any real friends so you didn't leave anything behind." I shot him a smug smile, knowing I was being hateful and not caring.

"Seriously? You think your freaks will miss you? All of *this* charm and charisma?" Dax snorted.

Wyatt came in carrying a broom, dustpan, and trash bag. He glanced between Dax and me and said, "You should sit, keep that hand elevated."

He started sweeping, ignoring me altogether. Which was fine. I didn't want to be the center of attention, no matter what my family might think.

I sat on one of the large boxes, holding my injured hand. Why did this sort of thing happen to me? Some sort of cosmic target? Or just plain karma? I deserved this...all of it. I sighed, catching Wyatt's glance my way.

He smiled at me. I frowned at him, closed my eyes, and leaned back against the wall. Dax said something and

Wyatt laughed. I peeked at them. Not at Dax so much, just Wyatt. I knew his type: all nice and polite for the adults but a real prick with his friends. He had that look, that cocky, arrogant look.

But Mom was gone and he *was* still sweeping up my mess, which was a surprisingly decent thing to do…

Not buying it.

He was too good-looking to be a nice guy. In my experience, that never happened. And Wyatt was beyond good-looking. He was seriously smoking-cowboy-hot. If you were into that sort of thing. Which I wasn't. Hot guys don't faze me.

Most of the guys I hung out with were athletes, the ripped, self-absorbed, say-whatever-they-need-to-say-to-get-in-your-pants-and–tell-all-their-friends types. None of them had anything to tell about me. Dating and boys hadn't been important. Correction—*isn't* important.

Wyatt was no different. I could tell. I didn't know what he was after—yet. But no one did something for free. Coming in, acting concerned over my hand, sweeping my floor, wearing tight jeans that hugged his thighs, with a leather tag on the butt… Now I couldn't stop staring at his butt.

My mother reappeared with her big medical bag just as the boys were finishing up. Except for the missing window and my bloody palm, there was no evidence of my latest mistake. "Thanks, boys." My mother smiled. "If you can give us a little privacy now, I need to fix up her hand."

I tried to act like I was enthralled with the contents of my mother's bag as they left the room. I hated needles and my mom knew it. I appreciated that she'd made them leave.

She asked softly, "You're not trying to hurt yourself, are you, Allie?"

I stared at her. *Seriously?* "I didn't break the window *or* cut myself on purpose, Mom. I told you."

My mother had one of those faces that said everything

even when she wasn't actually saying anything. She didn't exactly believe me. "What happened?"

I tried to ignore the pain, from the stitches *and* from my mom. "Nothing." I stared at my hand.

She sighed. "You're going to have to get a handle on your temper. Maybe we can find you someone here you can talk to, okay?"

"Awesome," I ground out. She didn't want to hear what I had to say, she just wanted to fix me, to make me a smiling, happy, obedient teenage daughter. As long as I *acted* like nothing was wrong, no one had to acknowledge that something *was* wrong.

"I think everything is off the truck, so now we can unpack. Once your room is more like what you're used to, it'll feel more like home." She snipped the thread and smiled at me, a sad, awkward smile. "Just give it a chance. Please. School doesn't start for a while so you'll have time to get situated."

I looked at her, feeling angry all over again. *Feel more like home?*

"You done?" Dax asked from the other side of the door.

"Yep," I said.

My bedroom door opened and Dax and Wyatt came in, carrying my bed. "This is your room?" Dax asked.

I glanced at my mom. She nodded. "Yeah," I murmured.

"Over here?" Wyatt asked, indicating the space under the window. He had really light eyes, more honey-colored than brown—kind of startling beneath his crazy thick eyelashes.

I blinked, breaking the hold those eyes had on me, and nodded. "Under the window, in the closet, in the backyard—I so don't care."

"Thanks, boys," my mother said and smiled at them. "She really shouldn't do anything with her hand like that." She left, patting Dax on the shoulder as she went. *He gets a pat on the shoulder, I get stitches and impatient sighs. My day just gets better and better.*

Dax waited until Mom had left before he said, "I'm impressed. Slicing yourself open to get out of work. That's real dedication, sis." He was teasing, I knew it. But Wyatt obviously didn't.

"She just got stitches," Wyatt said, leveling a disbelieving look at Dax.

I shrugged. "He's a jerk. You'll get used to it."

Dax stared at me, his eyebrows high. "And you're such an angel, right?"

I used my innocent face, the one I used on teachers to turn in papers late without losing points. The one that got me off the hook when Lindie and I did something we both *knew* we shouldn't have done...

God. Thinking of Lindie *hurt.*

My eyes grew hot, burning. My throat felt tight. "No. No angel here." I shook my head.

"Allie?" Dax sounded worried...regretful.

I glanced at him, managing to pull it together. They were both staring at me. *Great.*

Dax cleared his throat. "I'm sorry..."

I shook my head and reached up to smooth my hair—which pulled my stitches. "Shit." I grabbed my hand, wincing. Dax and Wyatt both winced too, catching me off guard and making me smile.

And that's when something really strange happened. Something that made my stomach knot and my lungs feel empty. Wyatt stared at me. Not a little, a lot. His eyes were intense, crazy, stare-into-your-soul, go-in-for-the-kiss stare. He froze completely, a full-bodied statue, which was weird and kind of cool, so I kind of...sort of...stared back.

Because, seriously, he was really gorgeous... *Holy crap. Is it hot in here?*

"She doesn't do that often," Dax whispered loudly to Wyatt. Wyatt blinked, the muscles of his jaw rigid.

I blinked too, looking away. *What was that? What just*

happened? And what had Dax said? "What?" I asked.

Dax shook his head at me. "You're clueless."

I glanced at Wyatt, but he was snapping the bed frame together.

"Going for more boxes," Dax announced as he left.

I felt nervous, which was weird. There was some hunky cowboy putting together my bed—so what? It wasn't like I'd never had a hot guy in my room before. Well, okay, I hadn't...not alone. But it was no big deal. He was just some guy...working in my room.

Why was he helping out? Why was he so *hot?*

Wyatt looked at me then and smiled—all dimples and white teeth.

2 CHAPTER TWO

I had to bite my lip to keep from smiling back.

"You okay?" he asked.

I nodded.

"Need anything?"

I shook my head, holding my breath.

He finished assembling the bed frame and stood up. I admit, I totally checked him out. Again. He was so…tall. And broad. And ripped. He was probably an athlete. He looked like an athlete. Another strike against him. Athletes only loved two things: sports and themselves.

He pulled the box springs onto the frame then plopped the mattress down on top. He pushed the whole thing under the window. His arms flexed. I swallowed.

"Good?" he asked, glancing at me. I nodded. He grinned. "Big change? Moving here?"

I frowned. "You have no idea."

He laughed. It was a nice laugh. He *seemed* like a genuinely nice guy. A nice guy that was insanely hot.

Oh, he's good. I'm not falling for it. My frown turned into a scowl.

Dax backed into the room, three boxes stacked high in his arms. "Mom said we're going out to eat."

Thank God. I needed to get out of here. "Okay." I practically ran from the room and down the stairs. *What the hell?*

I was obviously more stressed out than I thought. I needed to find a hobby, fast. Boys were a waste of time. And a cowboy? *Not* my type—no matter what he looked like. I was so not going to hook up with this guy just because he was *here*. And freaking gorgeous...and I was lonely. I'd never been one of those annoying clingy girls that needed a guy around. I wasn't going to become one now.

"Hungry?" my dad asked as we came down the stairs. I ignored him; he wasn't talking to me—he didn't talk to me.

Dax and Wyatt were right behind me. "Starving," Dax answered.

"Wyatt, is anything open?" my mother asked.

"Yes, ma'am, Peggy's will be open. It's mostly burgers, but they're good."

Did he just say *ma'am?* He was *so* not my type.

"Care to join us, Wyatt?" my mother asked. "You've been such a help today."

I held my breath.

"No, thank you, Dr. Cooper."

"Big date?" my dad asked, grinning.

I glanced at my father. *You are such a loser.* I looked at Wyatt then. He had plans, of course he did. Probably a group of redneck friends waiting for him somewhere. And a girlfriend. He had to have a girlfriend. A boots-and-jeans-wearing girlfriend that—

Wyatt shook his head. "No, sir, but..."

"Well then, let's go." My dad smiled, trying for the I'm-a-cool-guy thing. I sighed and rolled my eyes. *Oh God.*

"Well..." Wyatt glanced at me; I saw him. "Okay. Thank you." He went out the front door.

"I'll ride with Wyatt," Dax offered, following Wyatt out.

Could this day get any longer? I went to the bathroom, ran a brush through my long blond hair, and put on some lip gloss. I frowned at my reflection. It didn't matter what I looked like. I wasn't trying to impress anybody. I tugged my hair into a sloppy knot and wiped off the lip gloss, careful with my bum hand. I plugged into my iPod as soon as I climbed into the truck, so there was no mistaking my *don't talk to me* attitude.

Ten minutes later we were pulling into a very full parking lot. There were more trucks than cars; half of them were jacked up on huge tires, and half of those were covered in layers and layers of dried mud.

Wyatt and Dax got out of a clean white truck, laughing and talking. A clean white truck with three bumper stickers that caught my eye. One was a Trophy Hunter Association sticker; no surprise there. A military sticker: Semper Fi. But the last one? Pink. I read it again: I Support Second Base.

Seriously? Either he was really into baseball or he was a dick. Was it supposed to be funny? Somehow I hadn't pegged him as a healthcare advocacy type. So what were the stickers for?

Yep, total prick.

My dad interrupted my mental tirade. "I remember this place. They have great malts."

My mother smiled at me, saw my face then turned back to my father. "Sounds good."

I followed them inside, wishing I was anywhere but here. I knew it was my imagination, but I swear everyone watched us walk in. I let my gaze drift around the room. Families, a few old guys in cowboy hats, and two tables of teenagers. *Great.*

"Sit with us?" Dax asked me. Wyatt's eyebrows went up in question.

"Us?"

Dax looked pointedly at the tables full of teenagers. "Wyatt's friends."

I glanced at Wyatt. He smiled at me, warm-copper eyes

waiting. *No thanks, boob boy.* No introductions. No new friends. New house. New room. New school. New life. No more new anything. I shook my head.

Dax looked frustrated. "Come *on.*"

I sighed. "I'm not stopping *you.*"

Wyatt nodded, his grin dimming just a little.

"I'll order for you?" my mother asked.

I nodded and found us a table, sat in the chair and leaned against the wall. I tore open the white paper straw wrapper and winced, the simple action pulling my stitches.

"How are you feeling?" my mother asked as she joined me at the table. I shrugged.

"I'll put the screen back on for tonight so we don't get a bug infestation overnight. We'll have to see if the hardware store carries glass tomorrow." My dad dumped some sweetener into his tea without looking up.

I glared at him. *Who are you talking to? The table? Mom? The air?*

I stirred my water with the straw. *Hey Dad, I hurt my hand. It was an accident. Mom had to give me stitches. If you care. Which you don't.*

There was a shout of laughter from Dax's table so I looked over. They were all laughing and smiling. Dax was grinning, which made me want to grin—but I didn't.

Wyatt's copper gaze found me. I frowned at him then turned back to my water glass.

"We need to find someone who can help out around the place, Davis." My mother was looking at her cell phone. "I'll have to open the clinic no later than Wednesday. And you'll be flying out on Thursday."

He was leaving? Of course he was. He always left. That was part of his job: Mr. Corporate Security Investigator. Gone at least three weeks out of the month, longer if his case was Super Important. It didn't matter we'd moved where *he* wanted to be, were living the life *he* wanted, he still wasn't planning on being around.

"I'll ask around at the hardware store in the morning,"

Dad answered. "After this month, things won't be so tough."

My mother smiled, a real smile, and they stared at each other. It was weird, this new connection between them. I guess it was nice, they were my parents, but it was an adjustment. The last five years, they'd both been so busy with their careers that they were practically single. Now, they were acting like…a couple or team or something. "I can't wait," she said softly.

Dad smiled at her, a sweet smile that made his whole face relax. *Huh.* "Me too," he said.

Her smile grew as she reached across the table, taking his hand in hers.

Okay, enough. I shook my head. "What's happening now?" I asked her, curious in spite of myself.

I made the mistake of looking at my dad. His brows lifted, his hazel gaze darting to me before he stood and made his way to the counter, waiting to collect our food.

Mom watched him, sighed, then said. "He's cutting back on the travel. Once a month, unless some emergency comes up."

I blinked. That was…unexpected.

Dad brought the food to our table and the two of them started talking about all the repairs that needed to be done, so I zoned out. I didn't care. That was their thing. I put my earbuds back in and turned on some music.

I took a bite of the burger. So, one good thing came out of tonight. Awesome burger. I took another bite—at the same time Wyatt looked at me. He smiled.

I took a huge bite, knowing I'd look revolting—but that was the goal. I was really good at pushing people away.

So why was he smiling, with the white teeth and the adorable dimples? Apparently I needed to work harder at making the whole new girl mystique wear off quickly. I didn't want a thing to do with Wyatt or his dimples.

***

I was exhausted. I couldn't find my sleeping pills. Without sleeping pills, I dreamed. Dreaming was bad. Dreaming led to nightmares…or memories…whatever… I didn't get much sleep. But the sun spilled into my room— no curtains or blinds to keep it out.

"Heard you last night," Dax said from my doorway, tossing two apples back and forth.

I pushed up onto my elbows, not quite awake. "What?"

"Rough night?" he asked.

I yawned. "Kept you up? So you're here for an apology?"

He shook his head. "You're *so* rude." He bit into an apple, adding, "Do you *want* everyone to hate you? Really?"

"I get enough lecturing from Mom and Dad."

"I'm not lecturing. I'm curious." He threw an apple to me. "I don't get it."

"So?" I flopped back onto the bed. "Feel free to close the door and leave me alone."

"Allie… There are nice people here, ya know? Would it have killed you to try last night? I mean, Wyatt's a nice guy."

"I don't give a shit."

"I know you miss Lindie. I miss Lindie too. But she would kick your ass if she saw the way you were acting."

"Shut up, Dax. Shut. Up." I stood, the anger appearing so fast I could barely contain it. "*You* don't know what Lindie would do." I poked him in the chest, my voice rising. "She was *my* best friend, not yours." I pushed him back, slamming the door in his face.

"I'm sorry, Allie." I heard him through the door. "I'm sorry."

"Go away." I hit the door, wishing I could hit something more substantial. "Leave. Me. Alone."

Everyone was *sorry*. I hated that word. It didn't change anything. It was my fault. All of it was my fault. And now I was stuck, *here*, alone. And Lindie was…

I heard the squeak of the board. He was leaving. He was going. I was alone. No one would bother me or check on me. No one.

I need to get out of here.

No car. No phone. No one to call.

I pulled off my PJs and dug through my suitcase for my running clothes. I dressed, pulled my hair into a ponytail, grabbed my iPod, stopped in the kitchen for a water bottle, and took off.

I ran, letting angry music rage in my ears. Every time I felt winded, I thought of Lindie running beside me—smiling, red-faced, and shaking her head. "Keep up, you pansy." She'd poke at me until I found the energy to keep going. She knew me, how to keep me going.

And she could *run*. For hours straight and never get tired. She was on the track team, long distance running. She rarely made it off the bench during soccer season, but the coach kept her around because she was a one-woman powerhouse of motivation. She'd get a little too intense if she forgot her ADD meds. That was one of my responsibilities, making sure she remembered them every day.

Thinking about her like this didn't hurt so much. It was like she was with me, running beside me like she used to. But she wasn't. And just like that my heart was twisting and my lungs were on fire.

I'm sorry, Lindie. I'm so freaking sorry.

An hour later, I was still running, my lungs desperate for a break. I stopped and pulled off my t-shirt. I was drenched; my sports bra was soaked through. But there wasn't much of a breeze to cool me off.

I took a long sip of water and leaned against a tree, hoping to get my bearings. *No luck, no idea where I am.* I finished off my water. *I'm screwed.*

I pushed off the tree and started back, trying to retrace my steps. It would have helped if I'd been paying attention when I started, but no. All the trees looked the same; so did the cactus. I kept on walking, hoping…searching for some guidepost or landmark. I was going to take a long, cold shower. Maybe take a nap. If I ever reached civilization again.

There was rustling in the trees. Something was there. Every girl-stranded-in-the-woods horror movie sprang to mind. There were *actual* dangers out here, too. Snakes. Javalinas. Coyotes. Turkeys. Foxes. Skunks.

Music?

Music was coming…this way.

I stopped, still very aware that something was lurking in the bushes, and turned. It was the country. I was on my property, wasn't I? So whoever was coming would not be some cannibalistic chainsaw-wielding serial killer, right?

The rustling in the bushes stopped; maybe *it* was hiding from whatever was coming?

Shit. What's coming?

Wyatt's truck was driving across the field, making a beeline straight for me. I stopped, so relieved I almost smiled. Almost.

"Hey." Wyatt smiled as he pulled up alongside me, all gorgeous.

I glanced down at the sweaty t-shirt I held. I could only imagine what I looked like. *Not that it matters how I look.*

"How'd you get out here?" He tipped his beaten up baseball cap back.

I shrugged, trying not to notice how tan his forearm was as he rested it along the open window. "I went for a run."

He nodded, brown eyes sparkling. "Lost?" His smile was hard to resist. *But I will resist it.*

I bit my lip and nodded.

"Need a ride?" he asked.

Now, I *knew* that I did. But I didn't want his help. I didn't want to ride in his truck with the boobies sticker on it. "You can point me in the right direction."

He stared at me for a minute, shook his head, and said,

"I was headed to your house."

"Oh…" I had to go with him, boob stickers and all. What other choice did I have? Let the thing in the bushes get me? My eyes met his. *Holy crap.* "Sure." I walked around the truck and climbed in.

He waited for me to close the door. "You run every day?" I nodded. "Dax said you're an athlete." I glanced at him. "Soccer mostly?" I nodded again. He grinned, shaking his head. "You talk a lot."

I couldn't help it. I smiled…and laughed a little too, damn him. His honey-copper warm eyes fixed on my face, making my stomach knot and my heart go crazy. *Wrong. No way. None.*

I rolled my eyes and looked out the window. We drove on in silence.

I don't know why he got to me. *Did* he get to me? No, he didn't. I was bored. He was there. And, so far, nice. And hot…really, really hot. *Whatever. I don't like it.* I frowned, thankful he didn't say anything else.

His truck bounced over a few hills, skidded around a windmill, across a massive field, and through a gate. I saw Dax walking, looking supremely pissed and overheated. *Awesome.*

Wyatt pulled up alongside him. "Hey."

Dax glared at me, then nodded at Wyatt. "Hey, man."

"Ready to go?" Wyatt asked.

Dax nodded, opening the passenger door. "Scoot over," he said.

I could tell he was really mad, so I did, very aware that I was in my sports bra and sweaty…wedged next to Wyatt, feeling dirty and sticky. I prayed I didn't stink. Because *he* smelled just as good as he looked. *Of course he did.*

"Allie." Dax sighed and I looked at him. I knew that look—a Dax-sermon was coming.

I held up my hand. "I needed to get out of there. I screwed up. Again. Got it." I didn't want to fight, for a change.

"Okay," Dax murmured, sounding surprised.

Wyatt's forearm brushed across my thigh as he changed gears, totally distracting me...and knocking the air from my lungs.

"Thanks," Dax said to Wyatt.

"You...you sent him out looking for me?" I asked, further humiliated.

Dax shrugged. "Not really. We were going to the hardware store for Dad so I asked him to keep an eye out on the way over."

Wyatt's arm brushed my leg again, catching my attention. His forearm was tan, muscled—I could see the flex of muscles as he shifted gears again.

"You going to take the job?" Dax asked Wyatt. "My parents are kind of desperate." I looked at Wyatt.

"I don't know." Wyatt looked at me, then Dax. "I could definitely use the money."

"Then do it." Dax nodded. "You should know, the list keeps growing. But you've seen the place, so you know what you're getting into." He laughed. Wyatt nodded.

List? Job? My parents... What were they talking about? Then I remembered Mom saying something about hiring someone to help out around the place. *Oh no...*

"Wait," I managed, dreading the answer as soon as I asked the question. "What job?"

His warm gaze rested on my face. "Your dad wants me to work out at your place, get it fixed up."

I blinked, aware that his thigh was now pressed along mine. "Oh," I mumbled.

He smiled a small smile, then shifted gears as he picked up speed. I shivered when his arm brushed over the top of my thigh.

"Work on him, Allie. If he's there, it'll make things a lot easier." Dax punched me on the shoulder.

I glanced at my brother, then back at Wyatt. "Um...whatever."

Dax sighed. "Way to sell him."

"He either wants the job or he doesn't," I argued, glancing at Wyatt again. Wyatt laughed. "Do you?" I asked.

He nodded, looking at me. *Did he just look at my mouth?* I saw the muscle in his jaw tighten, and looked out the front windshield.

"Cool." Dax leaned back against the seat.

No, it is not cool. It is the exact opposite.

"Saving for anything special?" Dax asked.

More boobie stickers? A new speaker system?

I saw Wyatt's jaw muscle tighten, then relax. "Nothing special," he said.

We pulled into the hardware store parking lot. Wyatt held the door open for me, so I slid out on his side and pulled on my t-shirt. He smiled at me. I didn't smile back.

"What are we getting?" Dax asked. "Besides a new window." He shot me a look. I glared at my brother.

"How's your hand? Feeling okay?" Wyatt asked without a hint of sarcasm. I looked at him, skeptical. But...dammit...he was being sincere. I nodded, frowning.

Dax led the way but Wyatt opened the door for me, waiting for me to go through. I did, glancing at him as I went by. It was strange, the whole chivalry thing.

We worked our way down the list my dad had put together, giving me plenty of time to study Wyatt. And I did. I couldn't help but notice how his shoulders flexed under his worn white t-shirt. I mean, he was loading sheets of plywood onto the cart, so his muscles just kind of demanded attention. Just like his butt.

I swallowed. His faded jeans looked like they were glued on. It was too nice a view not to enjoy it.

Dax noticed, his eyebrow shooting up. I glared at him. "I'm going to look at paint," I announced before I stalked off. *What is wrong with me? Why do I care about his butt or his muscles?*

I stared at the paint samples, pulling a few cards and comparing colors. I didn't know what I wanted to do with my room, if it even needed to be painted, but I did know space was a good thing.

"Need some help?"

I turned. "No, thanks." I recognized this guy. He'd been sitting at the table in Peggy's with Dax and Wyatt. He wore a nametag on his Black Falls High School football t-shirt. Levi. He was cute. And he knew it.

"You sure?" he asked. "I work here. I'm not just trying to get your number or anything."

I shot him a look. "Yeah, the *nametag* kind of gave away the whole working-here thing. Unless you just wear a nametag around all the time?"

He laughed. "Right." I turned back to the paint samples, putting the cards back. "You're Dax's sister? Allie?" he asked.

I nodded, not looking at him. *Hint. Hint.*

"I'm—"

I glanced at his nametag. "Let me guess. Levi?"

"Right." He laughed. "Welcome to Black Falls. How you liking it so far?"

Dax and Wyatt came around the corner, pushing the now full flatbed lumber cart. I was saved. Wyatt and Levi shook hands and thumped each other's backs. I shook my head, stepping back a little.

Levi eyed the cart. "Working on something?"

"Got lucky. Mr. Cooper hired me to fix up the place," Wyatt said.

Dax laughed. "Say good-bye to the rest of your summer."

"It's a lot of work," Wyatt agreed.

"Oh." Levi looked at me, a long, head to toe look that almost made me laugh out loud. "He need any more help?"

I shook my head and started to walk away, but Levi stopped me.

"Hey, Allie." He shot Wyatt and Dax one of those wish-me-luck looks and followed me down the aisle. I sighed. This couldn't be good. "I was wondering if maybe you'd want to go to the bonfire. Next Friday night. Fourth of July. After the rodeo."

Bonfires. Rodeos. Hell...

I saw Dax over the corner of Levi's shoulder. He was making that face, a pleading face. The be-nice-and-I'll-owe-you-big-time face. It took everything I had not to sigh, loudly, in irritation.

"You...and your brother. Come with me, meet everyone," Levi said.

Both Wyatt and Dax were watching, waiting. "I'm not sure," I managed.

I saw Dax's shoulders slump, saw him shake his head. He mouthed "Please"... *Dammit.*

"Wait. You mean *next* Friday?" I said it fast, before I could regret it. "Sure."

Levi's smile was pretty killer. Not as warm as Wyatt's, but it was nice. *I'm comparing Wyatt to Levi because...?*

"Pick you guys up at eight?"

I nodded, still trying to figure out what the hell I was thinking—or doing.

"Cool." He looked a little *too* happy.

I nodded again and turned, walking out of the hardware store before I could change my mind.

Five minutes later Dax and Wyatt were loading everything into the back of the truck. Dax was all smiles, but I didn't say a thing. It was only as we were pulling into the grocery store parking lot that I understood his interest.

"Will Molly be at this bonfire?" my brother asked, looking at Wyatt. Wyatt grinned, nodding.

Dax smiled again, climbed out of the truck and slammed the door. He had a certain spring in his step that meant something was definitely up. I slid out on Wyatt's side again—he was holding the door—and cocked an eyebrow.

"Molly?" I asked him softly.

Wyatt nodded. "Molly."

"Oh." I walked into the store, considering this new

development. I waited until Dax had pushed the cart ahead and turned back to Wyatt. "And Molly is…"

"Really nice, Allie."

It was the first time he'd said my name. It made me feel… I sucked in a deep breath. *Nothing. He doesn't make me feel anything. Nothing!* I stiffened. "Good. I guess."

"Levi's a good guy too." His brown eyes locked with mine. "In case you were wondering."

"I'm not." I shook my head, a little lost in those warm eyes, and walked straight into someone.

3 CHAPTER THREE

"Excuse me," I mumbled at the middle-aged woman I'd plowed into.

"It's okay, honey." The woman smiled. "Well, Wyatt, how are you? How's your summer been going?"

"So far so good, Mrs. Neilson." He was all manners. "This is Allie Cooper. She'll be in the senior class, too. Allie, this is Mrs. Neilson, our high school counselor."

"Allie Cooper." Mrs. Neilson looked at me with a new expression on her face. An expression I knew all too well. "Allie, we're happy to have you here. Just know my door is always open, if you need to talk."

"Thank you," I whispered, hoping she'd stop there but suspecting she wouldn't.

"I know you've been through quite a bit the last few months. Death is always hard. But it's even harder when it's someone young." I saw her glance at Wyatt then. He nodded a little, looking extremely uncomfortable.

"Does Mom like the oil- or water-packed tuna?" Dax interrupted, holding out two cans of tuna for my inspection.

"Water," I said, taking the other can. "I'll put this back." The relief in my voice was obvious but I didn't care.

I took the can and hurried to the end of the aisle. I had no clue where the tuna belonged, but I was not going to stand in the middle of a grocery store for a five-minute therapy session. I took a few deep breaths and I walked, slowly, down each aisle.

Tuna was on aisle five. I put the can back and headed, carefully, back in the direction I'd come from, looking for Dax. He was with Wyatt, standing in the middle of the frozen food aisle. Mrs. Neilson was nowhere to be seen. *Safe.*

Wyatt looked amused, Dax not so much. "Get lost?" Dax grumbled as I walked up. "'Cuz it's such a big store."

I shook my head.

"Here." Dax thrust the list at me.

I shrugged and took it, eager to get out of here. "Whiner."

Wyatt laughed, making it hard to hold back my smile. I managed it, but it was close.

I noticed the sky as we were standing in the check-out line. The checker followed my gaze. "About time. It's getting a little too dry around here."

"We need it," Wyatt agreed, bagging the groceries.

I decided not to get worked up over the black clouds. I was not going to freak out every time it rained. It was…stupid. Instead, I watched Wyatt. He was quick to do stuff—whether or not someone asked him for help. He stepped up, without thinking about it. Which was weird, wasn't it? I mean, did he always have to be so…helpful? What was he hoping to accomplish? I mean, it was sort of cool, sure, but weird too.

Dax was clearly developing a guy-crush on Wyatt because he started bagging our groceries too. I shot him a look, but he just smiled.

We paid and loaded the truck as the first drops of rain started. By the time we left town, the rain was falling so heavily it was hard to see through the windshield. Trying to visualize my happy place wasn't gonna happen. I stared at my hands, focusing on the calming techniques the counselor had taught me.

The roads were slippery, making the truck hydroplane twice, but Wyatt got it back under control. The feel of the car slipping... I pressed myself back against the seat and closed my eyes. Counting backwards from fifty wasn't working. I kept starting over...

I tried not to react to every little jerk and tug, but ended up fisting my hands in my lap.

"We're here," Dax said softly, putting his hand on my arm.

I opened my eyes and nodded. I hated the sympathy on my brother's face. And Wyatt...he looked confused...worried, too. I needed to get out of the car, rain or no rain. "We going in?"

Wyatt nodded, opening the door. He took my hand, steadying me in the mud. I took three bags of groceries and ran to the front door.

I kicked off my running shoes inside the door and carried the plastic shopping bags into the kitchen. Dax and Wyatt joined me, in their sock feet, with the rest of the groceries. We were all dripping.

"I'll go get some towels," Dax offered, shaking the water from his shaggy blond head as he left the room.

My nerves were still shot. The rumbling thunder and slight shake of the old house wasn't helping. Instead of pressing myself into the corner of the room, I started unpacking the bags. Wyatt and I worked together. He handed me stuff. I put it away...until one loud boom made the lights go out. I didn't mean to make the strange little sound that ripped from my chest, but it slipped out anyway.

There was one window over the kitchen sink, but the covered porch didn't let in much light. The dark didn't really bother me; it was the storm, the rain, the thunder... My heart was racing as I turned, barely able to make out Wyatt.

His hand brushed mine, making me jump. There were rough calluses on his fingers, rough against my palm. His fingers wrapped around mine and I held tight, letting him lead me from the kitchen. The living room was brighter; a whole wall of windows illuminated the room in a gloomy gray...*and* showed just how brutal the storm was. Limbs bent beneath the punishing wind. Rain pelted against the glass, making me back up, wishing for someplace safe.

Wyatt didn't let go of my hand. His thumb brushed over my knuckles. I moved behind him, wishing I could lean against him—rely on his strength.

"Allie?" he whispered, almost like he was going to scare me or something. I looked up, staring at him even though I couldn't see him clearly. He was staring down at me.

The lights flickered, then came back on. He was still looking at me...

Holy shit.

I yanked my hand away and ran out of the room. I didn't need his sympathy. I didn't want it.

I bumped into Dax as I ran up the stairs to my room. I slammed the door behind me, welcoming the anger. The next crack of thunder wasn't as bad because someone, probably Wyatt, had hammered wood over the broken window. If I didn't lie on my bed or look out the massive window above it, I could avoid looking outside. And then I wouldn't have to see the rain or the storm...and I wouldn't be reminded of that rainy night and that God-awful storm...

***

Thump.

What was going on?

Thump.

I rolled over.

Thump.

I opened one eye and peered out the window.

Thump.

The sun was already up, shining bright and hot. I

blinked.

Thump.

Wyatt.

Thump.

Wyatt was whacking wood posts into the ground.

Thump.

With his shirt off. I rested my chin on my hands, staring. *Oh. My. God.*

Thump.

He was... He looked...

I don't like him. I don't like him. I don't—

Thump.

Dax knocked on the door before sticking his head in. "You up?"

Maybe not. Wyatt. Looking like...*that?* This had to be a dream.

Thump.

"Earth to Allie." Dax attempted to control his amusement.

I tore my attention from the half-naked dream sweating outside my window and rolled onto my back. "I'm up...I think." My chest felt heavy, hot, and my stomach was tight.

Thump.

"Need a tissue?" Dax asked. "You've got a little drool *right*...there." He pointed to the corner of his mouth.

"Shut up." I sat up, rubbing a hand over my face, and glared at my brother. "What the hell is he doing? I was sleeping." I tried to sound pissed. It was a lame attempt to distract my brother, but I didn't have a choice. He'd give me so much shit if he knew I was...

I was what? Getting hot and bothered by a farm boy?

"Get dressed. I've got something to show you." He winked. "Daylight's a-wasting," he said as he pulled the door shut.

"You did *not* just say that," I called after him, smiling at his retreating laughter. *Daylight's a-wasting? Really?* Dax was going a little too native for me.

Thump.

I turned back to see Wyatt straighten, stretch. My mouth went totally dry. He shifted the sledgehammer, his arms flexing in the rising sun. He rolled his neck, his shoulders rippled, and his stomach was…

I blew out a breath and jumped up, tugged on running clothes, and headed for the kitchen. Mom had left a note. Dad had left this morning and she'd be home later. She wanted my help at the clinic, if I was up for it. I dropped the note on the table and grabbed a banana.

"Allie?" Dax called out.

I pushed through the back screen door. "What?"

Dax waved me forward. "Come on."

I went, trying not to stare at Wyatt. He was jaw-droppingly hot this close. And way more ripped than I'd imagined, lean and long and… He smiled at me, wiping his face on a large blue bandana before hanging it back on the fence.

I nodded at Wyatt, forcing myself not to stop and stare, and asked Dax, "What's up?"

Dax smiled. "Get in the truck."

I waited, hoping Dax would get in first, but no… He waited, putting me beside Wyatt again. I slid across the seat, just in time to see Wyatt pull his t-shirt on. Good. I *didn't* really want to sit next to him half-naked or anything. I felt my heart pick up as he climbed into the truck, his thigh pressing against mine. *Yes, the shirt was a good thing.*

We drove away from the house, stopping at the end of the fence line. Wyatt parked and Dax pointed. A wide path cut through the tall waving grass.

I leaned forward. "I didn't see this yesterday."

"It wasn't here yesterday." Dax laughed, getting out. I climbed out after him, totally confused. "Wyatt mowed it for you."

Wait, what? My heart was really going crazy now. *He did this for me?* I couldn't *not* look at him now. He was still in the truck. His eyes traveled over my face, quickly, before he looked out his window.

I kept staring at him. He looked at me then, his forehead wrinkling. He looked…cautious.

"Th-thanks," I managed.

He nodded and smiled the kind of smile that made time stand still. For that second, it was just me and him and that freaking amazing smile. That smile was for me…

I didn't want that. Did I? I didn't want anything to do with those honey-colored eyes or that super-hot, amazingly capable body. I swallowed and turned back to the path. A distraction…something to break the tension…

"Up for a race?" I blurted out, glancing at Dax, then Wyatt.

Wyatt was out of the truck before Dax answered.

"You're in boots," I pointed out.

"Then you might be able to beat me," he answered.

I narrowed my eyes and glanced at Dax. Dax held his hands up. "I think I'm going to watch this time." He shook his head. "Ready?"

I glanced at Wyatt. He winked. I laughed. *Dammit.*

"Go!" Dax yelled.

And we were running. I don't know how he made it as far as he did. The grass was slick and he *was* in boots. But he made it all the way down the hill before he slipped and went down. I glanced back at him, lying in the grass, and turned around.

"Break anything?" I asked, offering him my hand.

He took my hand. "Nope."

I helped him up, nervous. He stared down at me, took a step closer… *Dammit.* His hand squeezed mine, pulling me closer. I froze, pulling my hand from his. "Next time, wear running shoes." I ran off, following my newly created track. I didn't look back. I was too freaked out. My heart was going crazy and I felt…I felt happy. But I didn't deserve to feel happiness. *Dammit.*

I wasn't a good person. I'd done horrible things. That

night…that night with Lindie… I felt a familiar coldness seep into my chest. It should have been me, not Lindie.

It's my fault. My fault.

I ran until my lungs were on fire, then headed back to the house. I ignored Dax and Wyatt, refusing to slow down until I was inside. I tore off my running clothes and jumped into the shower, turning the water as hot as I could get it. It burned, making my eyes ache. *No crying.*

"No crybabies allowed, Allie." I could *hear* Lindie…remember how she'd tried to calm me down when I'd broken my wrist during a game. It had been bad, requiring three pins, but Lindie wouldn't let me cry. *"Tough it out, Allie. Don't let anyone see you cry. Especially not the boys. It's nothing. You're fine."*

We both knew it wasn't fine. My hand was lopsided, hanging at an awkward angle, and I was close to passing out. I managed to brace it on the coach's clipboard, while Lindie kept talking, trying to distract me until my mom had pulled up the car and we'd driven to the ER. Even there, wanting to throw up and dizzy from pain, Lindie had almost made me laugh. *"You're fine."* She'd shaken her head, acting disappointed in me. *"I don't see what all the fuss is about."*

I smiled at the memory. She'd been the last face I remembered seeing before they wheeled me into the OR. "I'm…I'm trying to be fine," I said out loud, hating the tremor in my voice. "But I wish you were here."

Lindie didn't lie to me. She never had. She wouldn't now. She wouldn't tell me what happened was an accident. She'd tell me it was my fault and tell me to get over it. But I was the reason she wasn't here. I was the reason she was gone forever.

"I'm so sorry…" I pressed my forehead against the shower tiles, letting the water pour over me until it was freezing cold and my teeth were chattering. I turned off the water and stepped out of the shower, shivering. I tugged on the white robe Lindie and I had stolen from the hotel room we'd shared during the playoffs and threw myself on my bed. Newspaper clippings and posters were tacked up on my walls, making me lonelier. Nothing like being reminded of everything that was gone.

My mother's voice traveled up the stairs. "Allie?"

"In my room," I answered. I heard her on the stairs, the squeaky board, and sat up, tugging my robe tighter around me.

"You didn't just wake up, did you?" she asked as she came in the room. "It's almost one."

I shook my head. "I went for a run." Did she know about the path?

She was surprised. "Good for you. Any chance you'd be willing to come down and help me at the clinic?"

I wrinkled my nose but saw something on her face that stopped me, like she was bracing for my answer—like she knew I'd give her some lame-ass excuse when there was no reason not to help her except that I didn't want to. She was here too, just like Dax and me, dealing with redneck hell...

I stood up. "Give me a sec to get dressed?" First Dax, now Mom. *I'm losing my bitch-mystique.*

Mom's smile was pretty awesome. So was her relief. "I'll make some lunch for the boys." She paused at the door. "Is it just me, or is Dax becoming Wyatt Two?"

"Not just you." I shook my head. *So not going to happen.* But I wasn't going to say that out loud. Didn't want her to read anything into it.

"He's certainly a good guy. Wyatt, I mean. So sad he has so much responsibility at such a young age. I don't know how he stays so...positive." She pulled the door shut before I could ask her what she was talking about.

What did Wyatt have to be sad about? His ripped body? His booby truck? His mob of cowboy friends? Okay, his job sucked, but at least he had a job. He didn't act sad. If anything, he was way too nice. But...was he really? A *good* guy? Or was he a guy that knew how to play nice until he got what he wanted? What *did* he want?

It didn't matter. As long as he did what my parents needed, what did I care? I didn't.

I tugged on denim shorts and a pink tank top, brushed through my hair and clipped the sides back, and dabbed on a touch of lip gloss. I stuck my tongue out at my reflection. I didn't need to put myself together to go work at Mom's place, but I wasn't going to over-analyze why I was putting a little extra effort into my appearance. *Very little.*

Dax and Wyatt were at the table when I came into the kitchen. Mom was pouring them lemonade and feeding them sandwiches. All in all, the kitchen was pretty quiet— just a lot of chewing.

"Dax says you guys have big plans on the horizon?" Mom asked when I came into the kitchen.

I glanced at Dax. "The things I do for my brother. I have zero interest."

I loved it when my mom looked at me that way, like she was proud of me. "That's sweet of you."

Wyatt stood up, rinsing his plate at the sink. "You don't have to go, Allie. Dax can ride with me."

Wyatt was going? *Interesting...*

"No offense, Wyatt." Dax leaned back in his chair, smiling. "But I don't think Levi would be too happy."

Wyatt nodded, the muscle in his jaw hardening for a minute. "Right. Levi."

Wait a minute. Holy crap...

Wyatt's jaw muscle flexed as he scrubbed the plate— the plate that looked clean.

Does...does Wyatt like me? I swallowed, focusing on the rooster hotpad that hung on a hook by the sink. *No, not possible. Why would he? I've been a total bitch to him—to everyone. Not a chance.* Which was a good thing. He deserved way better.

I glanced over at Wyatt. His intense gaze was waiting for me. He grinned, the whole dimples thing super gorgeous.

Not that he needs to know that's what I'm thinking.

I bit my lip and rolled my eyes. He chuckled, almost making me smile...until I noticed Mom and Dax were watching us closely. *Awesome.*

"I'm not going for some stupid...redneck," I managed, my face hot. Wyatt didn't seem fazed by my pathetic attempt at an insult. "Ready, Mom?"

"Yes." She glanced at Wyatt, a slight smile on her face, all thoughtful—like she was working through what *this* might mean. "You boys need anything before we head out?"

Dax shook his head. "Nah, we're good. Home for dinner?"

"Good point. Food." Mom opened the refrigerator, stared inside, then closed it. "How about Allie and I bring something home?"

My cell phone rang, scaring the crap out of me. It had been confiscated, kept in a drawer. Reception was a nightmare out here, according to Dax. Mom pulled it out of the drawer, stared at the number, and handed it to me.

"Is it Mrs. Duncan?" I asked. Lindie's mom called me at least once a week. I think we both needed to talk to each other, to miss Lindie without really talking about her. Probably not the healthiest thing to do—her calls made Mom and Dad uncomfortable.

"No. It's Sebastian Kramer," she said, watching me closely.

"Your old coach?" Dax voiced my shock.

I nodded, lifting the phone to my ear. "Hello?"

"Allie?" I could hear the smile in Sebastian's voice. "How are you? Where are you?"

I walked out of the kitchen and into the living room to get away from Dax and Mom's whispered conversation. It was so good to hear his voice. "We moved. Ever heard of Black Falls?"

"No." He laughed. "Close to anything?"

"About an hour and a half from San Antonio." I stared

out the picture windows at the field. It looked a little greener. Maybe the rain had helped.

"I can drive that." He paused. "I'm coming to see you, Allie. Your mom around? I have an opening on the team and we need you back, girl."

"I can't." I wasn't ready.

"I think I can convince your mom, Allie. You know how charming I can be."

I forced myself to laugh. "Oh, I know. It's just...*I* can't."

There was a long pause. I could almost hear Sebastian scrambling for an argument. He was very good at making people see that what he *wanted* to happen was what *needed* to happen. His voice was light, but there was an undeniable edge to it. "Ever hear that saying about falling off the horse?"

"I have." I sighed. "A lot."

"You think...you think this is what she'd want?"

My throat suddenly felt tight. "Please don't."

I heard him sigh. "Allie, she was your biggest fan. I know she'd give you grief about passing this up."

"Sebastian..." I drew in a breath, hearing the tremor in my voice. "I *can't.*"

"You *can.*" He kept going, not listening to me. No one ever listened to me. "She'd want you to."

I snapped, finally. "Are you really trying to use my dead best friend to get me to play soccer for you?"

There was a long pause. "No, Allie. I just wanted to remind you that you're punishing yourself—"

"Maybe I deserve a little punishment."

"Oh, Allie, that's crazy, hon. We're talking about your future. Something you love. You're gifted—"

"I have to go, Sebastian. Good luck and thanks for calling." I hung up, tossing the phone onto the couch.

Mom was waiting. "Allie?"

I looked at her. "Ready to go?"

She nodded. "Are you..."

"No. I'm not okay. But I shouldn't be okay. Why does everyone think I should be?" My voice was still shaking. I shook my head and walked out the front door, leaning against the porch railing. I felt sick. The wind blew, making that stupid chain on the stupid swing squeak. I stared at it.

"It's a nice swing," Wyatt said, making me spin around. He stood just outside the door, leaning against the chipped paint siding of the old house.

"It's broken," I snapped. *Barely hanging on, just like me.*

"It just needs new chains." He looked up at the porch ceiling. "Maybe a new eye-hook too. A little work. That's all."

I glanced at him, then the swing, and frowned. "Is that supposed to be some sort of metaphor...for life...or me...or something?"

He smiled a sort of sad smile, and looked at me for the first time. "Nope." There was a question there, I heard it.

My mother's voice reached us through the screened front door. "I asked you not to call." Her voice was soft. "Things are difficult for all of us. Please respect my request."

Had she called Sebastian? Or had he called her? *If he called her, he'd better be apologizing.*

Dax came onto the porch. "You okay?"

"If one more person asks me that—" I bit off, shaking my head.

Dax held up his hands. "Chill."

"You'll what?" Wyatt asked, his tone curious, not antagonizing.

I shook my head, crossing and uncrossing my arms. "I'll...God, I'll go off..." I shook my head again. "Something. Scream," I finished softly.

Wyatt pushed off the wall. "Scream. The world won't end."

4 CHAPTER FOUR

I frowned at him. *What the hell do you know about my world anyway?*

Dax laughed softly. "Um, have you met my sister? Queen of repressed emotion. Well, not *all* emotion. She's got the whole I-hate-the-world thing down."

"Dax?" Mom called from inside.

Dax shot me a look and headed back inside.

My hands fisted reflexively, frustration taking over again. I didn't hate the world. Not really. The world hated me.

No, that wasn't true. The world simply didn't care about me, my thoughts, feelings, dreams, wishes…

I glanced at Wyatt and was completely caught up in the crazy intensity of his eyes.

"What's stopping you?" He hadn't moved…but he seemed closer somehow.

"From?" My tone was harsh.

He shrugged. "Letting it all out."

"I…I can't," I said. *Why do you care?*

"Why not?" Wyatt asked, moving closer.

I shrugged. *Leave me alone.* "What's the point?"

"Might help." He continued to look at me.

"Screaming?" I shook my head, a bitter smile forming. "Can't help."

His expression shifted, revealing so much *raw pain*…it was like someone kicked me in the chest, knocking the air out of me, and leaving me reeling. My heart twisted so tight I almost grabbed my chest.

Where had that come from? What was that about?

Wyatt… What are you hiding?

"Maybe not." He looked away then, his face resuming his normal easy-going expression. "You never know."

There wasn't really anything to say to that so I didn't say anything. I stood there, angry and confused. From the pain in his eyes, the twist of his gorgeous face, he was hurting. Really hurting.

We have that in common.

"If you ever decide you want to," he turned back to me, his voice low, "scream, I mean…I know a place that's good for letting it all out."

I scrambled to think of some snappy come-back. Nothing. Instead, I just stared at him. Whatever he'd been thinking about was gone. He was completely serious about helping me. He wasn't teasing me or talking down to me or making fun of me, which was sort of really nice.

I swallowed. Could he understand? I mean, did *he* have something to "let out"?

Wait…I can't care. And he doesn't care either—not really. It's the whole new-girl thing.

Mom came onto the porch, the screen door slamming behind her. "Let's go."

Wyatt turned, smiling at my mom. "I finished the fence. Dax said he'll help me get some scraping done this afternoon. Once that's done, we can paint."

"Wonderful." She looked stressed out, even though she was doing her best to act normal in front of Wyatt. I blamed my old coach for her present state of mind. *You suck, Sebastian.* "Davis said you'll be picking up some calves?" Mom asked as she walked down the steps to her van.

Calves? Really?

Wyatt nodded. "Yes, ma'am. Sale this weekend. Goats are good, too—eat all the scrub out without having to pay for a lot of feed."

I blinked. *Soon I'll be gathering eggs and milking cows.*

"Really?" My mother smiled at him, opening her car door.

Wyatt nodded again. "Yes, ma'am."

"Sounds like a good idea then. You two be careful on that scaffolding, please," she said before climbing into the car and shutting the door.

I followed, feeling confused. It was like I was living in some parallel universe where cowboys weren't a joke and livestock replaced the family pet. I climbed into the car, knowing he was watching me but refusing to look at him.

And I almost made it. Almost. But right before we turned around in the drive, I glanced back. He was standing on the porch railing, leaning forward to assess the single eye-hook holding the corner of the swing up.

***

We'd cleaned the veterinarian clinic for hours before giving up and focusing on the filing cabinet. That had only made it worse. Not only had the previous veterinarian been clueless about hygiene, but he had also been a complete idiot. The files were in no specific order, not by date or alphabetically, and his handwriting was… What was that old joke about a doctor's handwriting? I didn't know how Mom was going to manage it all. There wasn't a computer in the entire building.

The grungy clinic was a far cry from the lab, her classroom, having every available resource at her fingers—everything she'd left. I couldn't ignore the twist of guilt… *No. It's not my fault, dammit.* I didn't move us here. I didn't take her away from her dream job to bring her here. It was all too easy to really dislike my dad at times like this.

By the time we'd locked up her clinic, she was strangely

quiet and I was pissed—as usual. She should torch the place and start from scratch. I thought about suggesting that, but decided she wouldn't be amused.

The drive home was long and quiet. The sun was setting when we got back to the house.

"They got a lot done," she said, looking out the windshield.

I stared, amazed. "Huh." The front half of the second story was completely scraped.

"They must be exhausted."

"Probably starving." I shifted the bag of fried chicken to my non-sore hand and opened the car door. I climbed the steps to the porch and froze. "He fixed it," I murmured.

My mother glanced at me, then at the newly repaired porch swing. Not only was it hanging by four new chains, it had been sanded and repainted a nice crisp apple-green.

"Looks great," she said. "I'm glad your dad hired him."

I nodded but didn't say anything.

Mom opened the front door. "Let's get them fed so they can go to bed."

I followed her in, trying not to read too much into the swing repair. It was just a swing, for crying out loud. A broken swing, that was all.

The lights in the living room were off. The TV was on, blaring some re-cap of sports scores—not that they were watching it. They were both sound asleep. Dax was sprawled across the couch, snoring softly. Wyatt sat in our recliner, his head cocked at an awkward angle. He looked uncomfortable, like he'd get a crick in his neck.

Mom took the food from me and whispered, "I'll go get dinner ready. You can wake them up."

"Gosh, thanks," I murmured, already making my way to the recliner. I stopped, wondering whether or not I should say something…or if I should poke him…or what. Instead, I cupped his cheek, tilting his head back so that it rested against the headrest of the chair. His cheek was rough, stubbly, and warm. He sighed, leaning into my hand.

"Allie?" Dax sounded as surprised as I felt.

I pulled my hand out from under Wyatt's cheek and stepped back. Too late. His eyes popped open...sleepy...then round and surprised because I was leaning over him, invading his personal space.

My cheeks were burning as I scowled at my brother. "Dinner's here."

I stomped from the room, horrified that I'd been caught. *What the hell is the matter with me? Who the hell cares if he gets a crick in his neck? I don't. Dammit.*

"Allie." Mom didn't look up as I came into the kitchen, which was good because I knew my face was red—I could feel it. "Could you get the tea out of the fridge, please?"

I yanked the refrigerator door open, rattling the empty jam jars on top, and grabbed the pitcher of sweet tea. It sloshed over the top as I put it, hard, on the table. I slammed the refrigerator door, making one jam jar fall off.

Wyatt caught it.

I didn't look at him. Or my mom. Or Dax. I sat at the table and stared at the yellow and white paper box full of fried chicken.

"You boys must be exhausted," Mom said as she sat down at the table.

"Wyatt's a machine," Dax complained. "Seriously. My arms feel like lead."

Wyatt laughed. "I'll try to go easy on you tomorrow."

"Tomorrow?" Dax groaned.

"Believe me," Wyatt passed the chicken to me as he spoke, "you'll be worse off if you don't keep working. Your muscles will tense up."

I took the box, taking extra care not to touch Wyatt. "Muscles? Dax?" I couldn't resist.

"Ha, ha." Dax gave me a look. "Hilarious."

I laughed, reaching for a roll from another box. "I thought so." I didn't mean to look at Wyatt, but...I did.

He was smiling at me in a big way. I frowned, grabbed the roll, and sat back in my chair.

"So," Dax said, "how'd it go for you guys at the clinic?"

My mother's eyebrows went up. "It's…well…"

"I think she'd be better off burning the place down and starting from scratch," I offered, instantly regretting it.

Mom burst out laughing. "You know, I was thinking the same thing."

We all laughed then, whether from relief or exhaustion didn't matter. And it felt good.

"Need help?" Dax asked.

"Yes. Lots and lots and lots of it. But," I shook my head, still smiling, "you're just trying to get out of helping Wyatt."

Dax grinned. "Well…okay, yeah, but if you *need* help…?"

My mother was really laughing now. And for the first time in a long time, she looked relaxed and happy. "Oh, Dax!"

"What?" His tone was all innocence. "I just want to—"

"Get out of sweating your ass off tomorrow?" I inserted. Mom kept laughing.

"There is AC in the office, right?" Dax asked. I threw a roll at him and laughed. "Allie and I can change places," Dax offered, one eyebrow rising high as he took a sip of iced tea.

I stopped laughing then, and glanced at Wyatt.

Wyatt looked at me, shrugging. "I bet Allie can handle it. Even with a bum hand."

"That's cold, man." Dax shook his head, leaning back in his chair.

I smiled shyly, hating the way my cheeks were burning—again. Wyatt winked at me and I felt something warm deep inside of me. I frowned.

"Thank you for dinner, Dr. Cooper." Wyatt stood, cleaning off his plate and loading it into the dishwasher. "I hate to eat and run but I promised to help out at the arena."

Mom was surprised. "You're not done for the day?"

He shook his head, glancing at the clock. "No, ma'am. Rodeo every weekend means the younger ones have to practice in the middle of the week."

"What events do you do?" Mom asked.

"Team roping mostly." He rinsed out his glass. "Sometimes steer wrestling, bull riding... Money's better."

I gnawed my bottom lip. Sports were one thing, but a lot of the rodeo *stuff* was dangerous. "You don't play football?" I asked him. *Random question.*

He nodded. "Sometimes."

"You stay busy." My mom's voice was hesitant, curious. "When do you have time for school work?"

He smiled. "After practice. In the morning, at breakfast. Whenever there's no work to be done."

Bet your grades suck, Cowboy. One flaw, then, at least...

My mom nodded, but didn't say anything else.

"Want to come?" Wyatt asked. I didn't know if he was talking to me or Dax, but I was preparing to say "No" when Wyatt added, "It's just me and my roping partner and a bunch of kids."

"Sure, I'll go." Dax cleaned off his plate and loaded it—just like Wyatt.

I glanced at Mom, hoping she'd come to my defense and get me off the hook. I wasn't feeling my usual, argumentative self—I needed help to turn him down.

"Go." Mom smiled at me. "Get out of the house for a little bit."

"You don't *have* to come," Dax argued, arching an eyebrow in challenge.

I scowled at him. I shouldn't go. I should stay here, find a book to read, or watch some TV or something.

"Ever ride a horse?" Wyatt asked me.

I shot him a look. "Um, *no.*"

Wyatt smiled. "Ever been to a rodeo?"

I sighed. "Of course. Texas. Rodeos. Duh."

He laughed. "It's harder than it looks."

I shrugged. "I believe you."

He pushed off the counter. "Thanks again for dinner, Dr. Cooper. I'll be back at first light."

"You *are* allowed to sleep, Wyatt." Mom smiled.

Dax followed Wyatt to the door, almost slamming into his back when Wyatt stopped in the doorway.

"Coming?" Wyatt asked me, brown eyes sparkling.

I knew Dax and Mom were watching. I knew if I went, it would mean something. And I knew *I wanted to go...*

I shook my head. "Don't break anything." I waved.

The slightest frown creased his face before he smiled. "Night."

Dax, on the other hand, was clearly irritated. He shook his head and rolled his eyes.

When they were gone, I felt like an idiot. Once the leftovers were put away and the dishwasher was loaded, there was nothing to do. *Nothing.*

"Let me check your hand?" Mom asked. She unwrapped the bandage and nodded. "Looking good. I'll take out the stitches in the morning." *Good news.* "Any new college letters?" she asked as she finished covering my hand with a clean bandage.

"No. Not yet."

"You've got time. I know your heart is set on SMU, but try to keep an open mind, okay?" I shrugged. Even if I didn't get accepted to SMU, I was leaving. She had to know that. "The clinic needs computers so..." she sighed, looking tired. She had to be exhausted. The move. The clinic. Dad, being Dad. Dax. Me...

"Good luck."

She nodded and moved to her desk. In no time, Mom became absorbed in her laptop, scouring the Internet, determined to find a deal on computers for the clinic— and some organizational software too, I hoped. *Poor Mom. Talk about a big job.*

I didn't have a computer yet—another confiscated item. Which was fine, since I didn't *want* to check email or know what was happening in the rest of the world. It was enough to know that the world was going on just fine without me.

I grabbed a book and went onto the front porch and the waiting swing.

***

This was all familiar, this dream…

A nightmare. Inescapable…

Nothing I did could change it. Or stop it. I was watching it happen again—like a movie.

Rain. Icy cold. Dark night outside. Loud, hot party inside. I don't remember whose house it was. It didn't matter.

Lindie fighting with her boyfriend, Charlie. The scene. Him leaving. Lindie crying. We did shooters to make her stop crying. Lots and lots of shooters.

Lindie flirting with Zach Haney, Charlie's best friend.

Me feeling sick…wanting to go.

Lindie laughing, getting too cozy with Zach—again. Zach smiling, totally into her.

I hated this—watching them hook up and having to keep it a secret.

They kept laughing.

I wanted to go home but they wouldn't listen. I saw myself lean forward, whispering to her—something I couldn't take back. *I'll tell Charlie about Zach*—something I'd promised never to do.

She almost slapped me but I caught her hand, so angry…she might have hated me. But she got Zach to take us home.

It was raining hard and freezing as I made a beeline for Zach's piece of crap Suburban. His dented tank had heavy-duty clear plastic sheeting duct-taped across the back instead of an actual window. I leaned against the side and threw up—a lot—then climbed into the very back and passed out to the sound of rain on plastic...

Rain on metal.

Screaming.

Screeching brakes.

Impact. My bones hurting. And then I was flying—airborne—out the plastic-wrapped window. Falling...forever.

Hitting asphalt, hard. Pain. Whacking my head. Pain. Rain. Confusion. Cold. Pain.

Lindie?

Something wet touched my hand. That was new.

Suburban... Pain... Eighteen-wheeler... Sliding off the road...

Something sticky was definitely on my hand. I shook my hand.

Lindie. Zach. The drainage ditch full of rushing water... I screamed and screamed...

There was panting in my ear. Heavy panting. Something was...licking my hand?

"Pickett." A familiar voice, soft but firm. "Leave her be."

"Wake her up." That sounded like Dax. "She's having a bad dream."

"Is she?"

"All the time."

"I can carry her up." That other voice...Wyatt.

Was this a dream?

Dax snorted. "She wakes up with you carrying her and she'll probably break your nose."

So I *was* sleeping...on the porch swing. That would explain why I was cold...and uncomfortable.

Wyatt's chuckle was soft. "Guess I better hope she doesn't wake up."

Dax murmured, "You're on your own man. I'll wait here."

My brother—my hero.

But my anger died as the most delicious warmth

wrapped around me. Oh. My. God. Strong arms, a heartbeat, a hot palm pressed against my side. And I was being lifted, held, by those arms.

Wyatt was carrying me. *I like this dream…*

I'm glad I *was* sleeping. If I wasn't, I'd have to wake up. He'd put me down. I'd have to get pissy with him—because that's what I did, acted pissed. Right now, I didn't want him to put me down. And I was way too warm and comfortable to get pissy.

The front door opened. We were going inside, up the stairs…

I burrowed in a little, to breathe against his chest. His really strong, no-give chest. *God, he smells good.* Really *really* good.

I turned, pressing my cheek against him. His heartbeat picked up…a lot. And his arms tightened, holding me more surely. Something about that, the way he was holding me, made my heart thump. Maybe I should admit I was awake?

I heard the floorboard creak. We were almost to my room. Which was good. So why was I feeling panic?

Because he'll put me down and leave…

My hand gripped his shirt front. I needed…wanted to hold on to him, to keep him here, protecting me, holding me. And for some new and bizarre reason, I felt sort of…frantic about it.

"Allie?" His voice was soft, his breath stirring the air by my ear.

I didn't say anything. What was I supposed to say? *I'm awake but don't put me down? You smell really good…and you feel even better?* Yeah, that wouldn't go over very well.

Or would it? What if he was cool with it? What if he stayed? Did I want him to stay? I swallowed.

I was being lowered, slowly. I felt the muscles in his chest and arms and shoulders move against me and felt…breathless and hot and confused and…

I'm so in trouble.

53

My bed was soft beneath my back, but before his arms slipped out from under me I opened my eyes.

He froze, bent over me, his arms under me, looking guilty. "Hey."

"Hi." My voice was husky.

"You were asleep," he said, still not moving.

I didn't loosen my grip on his shirt. "And you thought…"

"I'd get you out of the cold." His jaw tightened.

"Oh." I nodded. "That was…nice of you."

He smiled. *Oh shit. Yeah. Big trouble.*

"I'm a nice guy," he said, still not moving.

"So everyone keeps telling me." Why did I sound so breathless? Why did I feel so breathless?

He glanced at my hold on his shirt. I didn't let go.

When he looked at me, his smile was gone. His eyes stared at me, at my face, my eyes, my nose, my mouth. One of his hands slipped from beneath me, slowly reaching for me. His callused fingertips traced my cheek.

My heart went crazy. My stomach was hot and twisting and quivering. *Holy crap.*

I blew out a deep breath, heard it hitch—knew he heard it too. The muscle in his jaw tightened and he smiled at me. *Holy freaking crap.*

I wanted to smile back. I wanted to touch that way too gorgeous face. *I want to kiss—*

The floorboard squeaked.

"Shit," I hissed, letting go of Wyatt, pushing him away, right as Dax stuck his head in my room.

5 CHAPTER FIVE

"Wake her up?" Dax asked.

I sat up, swinging my legs over the side of my bed. "Yeah."

"Are you bleeding?" Dax asked Wyatt, laughing. "I didn't hear any fighting or furniture being broken."

"No one's bleeding." I paused. "Yet." I glared at Dax, refusing to look at Wyatt. I couldn't. What the hell was wrong with me? My heart was pounding like crazy. I was all hot and bothered. Over a *cowboy?*

I needed to find a hobby. Or a job. Or something.

"Good. Nice to know you can still be civilized when you want to be. Or maybe you were just caught off guard, being asleep and all." Dax smiled.

I continued to glare at him, but didn't take the bait. I didn't have the energy.

"You should have come tonight, Allie." Dax was watching me. "Beats sitting around here alone."

I glanced at Wyatt then, but he seemed caught up in the photos and posters and newspaper clippings I'd tacked up on my walls.

"These all about you?" Wyatt asked.

I stood, standing beside him to look at one of the

articles. It was about our journey to the state tournament and our championship game. The picture was after the game. We were all sweaty and victorious. Lindie was making a goofball face and I was grinning like a complete idiot.

"Not just me." I shrugged. He shifted, leaning closer to me. The hair on my arms and the back of my neck stood up. "My old team," I added.

"Allie was the only freshman to play varsity," Dax chimed in.

"You're that good?" Wyatt asked, facing me.

I knew I shouldn't look at him, but the draw was too strong. And once I was looking—staring—at him, it was kind of hard to miss the curiosity in his bright gaze.

He was curious…about *me?* I swallowed, then shrugged.

"She's *that* good." Dax flopped onto my bed. "She's *amazing.*"

I tore my gaze from Wyatt and put some space between us by directing all my attention on my brother. "Don't be a jerk." I knew he hated soccer. He knew I knew he hated soccer. He'd made sure to remind me my games were a huge time-suck on his weekends.

He frowned at me. "I was being serious."

I frowned back. "You hate soccer."

"I do hate soccer." He nodded. "But you're still an amazing player."

I waited. Dax was really good at dragging out sarcastic punch lines. He had one humdinger of a comment coming, I just knew it… Any time now… I arched an eyebrow at him.

"What?" he asked.

I put my hands on my hips. "I'm waiting."

"For?"

"Since when do you give me compliments?"

"The girls' team could definitely use you," Wyatt interrupted.

I shook my head.

"Come on, Allie." Dax sighed. "You're only hurting yourself." I glared at him.

"Too bad." Wyatt looked over one of the boards the team moms had put together—pictures, ribbons, newspaper clippings, all sorts of memorabilia.

A whimper came from the hallway, drawing my attention to a black and grey dog. It sat, its pointy ears perked up, staring at Wyatt with such concentration I couldn't help but smile. "Who's this?" I asked.

"Pickett," Wyatt said, instantly calling the dog to his side. Pickett sat, his ears perked.

"Pickett?" I asked, squatting in front of the dog. Pickett's ears drooped and his stubby tail began to wag frantically.

"He's friendly," Wyatt said.

I put my hand out and Pickett charged me, knocking me onto my butt and plastering me with wet doggie kisses.

Wyatt hissed and Pickett immediately sat where he was. His brown eyes looked at me, then Wyatt, then back at me again.

I could tell the dog was trying to control himself but I couldn't resist. I rubbed Pickett behind the ears, ending any restraint the dog had. He was up, climbing into my lap.

I laughed, turning my head to avoid dog-kisses, and rubbed the wiggling animal with both hands. "I think friendly's an understatement. Why I haven't seen you before?"

"He's always around. Laying in the shade, mostly. When he's not working," I could hear the smile in Wyatt's voice but didn't look away from Pickett. The dog ran around me, climbing over my legs, its stubby little tail going crazy the whole time. I laughed again as Picket settled onto my lap, staring at me until I rubbed his neck.

"You should get a dog," Wyatt murmured.

I looked at him. "Why?" I giggled, tilting my head back to avoid Pickett's slobbery tongue.

Dax looked at Wyatt then shook his head. Wyatt stared at me like I was missing something. Like I needed to feel any more awkward than I already did.

I stood up, hating the droop of Pickett's ears. "What?" Both of them shook their heads, irritating me. "Dax…" I couldn't think of anything. "Get off of my bed," I snapped.

Dax stood, both hands up. "There's the Allie we know and love."

"You can leave any time." I stepped closer.

Pickett was circling me, trying to get my attention. I smiled, impressed. He wasn't jumping up on me or whining; it was like he was trying to…herd me. But I couldn't stay in full bitch-mode while oohing over a dog, so I ignored him and all his furry cuteness.

"Time to go, Pickett." Wyatt pointed to the door and the dog. "We're in the way."

"You're not in the way," I said before I realized what I was saying. But the look on Dax's face, the slight smile on Wyatt's, was too much. "*Pickett's* not in the way," I amended.

I didn't like the way Wyatt's smile dimmed. Or the way Dax frowned at me. Pickett, however, sat at my feet with his stubby little tail wagging.

"It's late," Wyatt tried again. "Gonna be another long day tomorrow."

Dax shook his head. "You're a slave driver, man," he murmured as he walked out of my room. "And *I'm* not getting paid," Dax continued to complain.

Wyatt laughed softly as he made his way to my door.

"Wyatt," I said, stopping him.

He turned, his brown eyes fixed on me.

"I just wanted to say thank you." And then I remembered what I was thanking him for. "For fixing the swing." He smiled. "So…thank you," I said.

He nodded. "You're welcome." His voice was soft. "Sweet dreams." His gaze traveled over my face before he smiled, slowly. He left, Pickett at his heels, and my heart in my throat.

The picture of Lindie caught my eye. *What am I doing, Lindie? What the hell am I doing?*

Knowing Lindie, she'd tell me to grab him and hold on tight. She said having a boyfriend kept things interesting. She always had a boyfriend—changing them often and still managing to keep them as friends. That was just Lindie. Even if she broke your heart, you couldn't help but still love her.

She used to tease me about how completely unavailable I was and how, when I finally did let a guy in, it would be the forever guy.

Wyatt was *not* that guy.

***

Four days of avoiding Wyatt was hard work. He was everywhere—half-naked, smiling, and...there.

I headed out first thing in the morning, running long and hard, knowing he'd be the first thing I'd see when I rounded the final bend in the track he'd mowed for me. And when I did see him, standing on the rickety scaffolding, a strange bubble of excitement and hope rose up inside of my chest.

I'd pretend I didn't see him, not acknowledge him, and head straight inside for a cold shower. After my shower was breakfast—another exercise in torture since Mom now insisted on making the boys a huge spread. I helped, to hurry things up, making French toast or pancakes, cracking eggs, pouring juice or milk...and aware of where Wyatt was every second he was in the room.

I managed not to make eye contact with him. Or touch him. Whatever *almost* happened the other night, whatever stupid, irrational stuff he made me feel—I had to get over it.

Distance.

Attitude.

Going to work and pulling twelve-hour days at Mom's

almost-respectable clinic...

Mom had been making sandwiches for the boys to take to the arena in the evenings, which was a relief. I'd almost made it through the week without slipping up when Dad came home for the Fourth of July. Nothing like walking into the kitchen to find your parents in a seriously intense lip-lock...first thing in the morning.

"Morning," Mom said to me when they'd finished eating each other's faces. I grunted. "Your father got home late last night," she continued. I grunted again. *Like I could miss your make-out session?* "Since it's Fourth of July and all."

I glanced at her from the corner of my eye. Today was Fourth of July?

Dad was standing beside her, his hand resting on her waist. But he was looking at her with such—

"Morning, Mr. Cooper."

Morning, Wyatt. I pulled the orange juice from the refrigerator and carried it to the table. Five places were set. A plate of bacon was already waiting, a bowl of scrambled eggs, too.

I didn't look up, but I suspected Dad was shaking hands with him. "Wyatt, I can't tell you how impressed I am with the work you've managed the last week."

I couldn't argue with that. But I kept my attention on pouring orange juice into each glass. Much safer. No staring or blushing or...drooling. *Dammit.*

"Dax is helping out, Mr. Cooper," Wyatt said.

Dax snorted. "I'm trying. You'd have more done if you didn't have to show me how to do everything."

I dared to look up, then, at Dax. Not Wyatt. I wasn't that brave...or stupid.

"I appreciate that too, Wyatt." My father's voice was warm, sincere. "I haven't been around to teach the kids what they need to know out here."

Out here. In Hell.

"I appreciate your work, too, Dax." I could hear the pride in Dad's voice.

Screw you. I've done work too. I've helped Mom. Without being asked. But you don't need to thank me. I put the orange juice back in the refrigerator and closed the door carefully, refusing to cave and slam it. *I don't need anything from him.*

Mom turned, offering me a plate piled high with fluffy pancakes. I took it, happy for the distraction of rearranging the table. "Let's eat," she said, smiling as Dad pulled her chair out for her.

What is going on? When did we become a family from a sappy TV movie? We were way more reality-show material...a really messed-up reality show.

I sat, ignoring the fact that Wyatt sat right beside me. Ignoring his yummy smell...the heat that rolled off of him. *Give it a rest, Allie, he's just* sitting *there.* Instead, I watched my parents. The way Mom blushed when Dad looked at her. The way Dad was looking at her. The way he touched her hand when he passed her the syrup.

I was now officially living in another dimension. I stared at my empty plate.

"What time is the parade?" Dax asked.

"Noon," Wyatt said. "Should be pretty big, being the hundredth anniversary."

"I'm excited," Mom gushed.

Mom is gushing?

"I remember the parade," Dad said. "Do you kids remember Grandpa Jack? He used to have a longhorn he'd saddle up and ride at the end of the parade. One year, I rode with him. I was about five."

No snarky comments. No attitude.

Mom laughed. "And I bet you were adorable." Dad winked at her, all smiles.

I looked at my twin, wondering if he was seeing what I was seeing. Oh, he was, all right. His blue eyes went round, and his fork froze halfway to his mouth. He blinked, then looked at me. I shrugged a little, knowing he'd understand. We did have the twin-speak thing—when we wanted to.

He shoveled his eggs into his mouth and smiled. I

sighed. *Dork*. So he wasn't worried about the Twilight-Zone display of affection? This was weird. Different. Wrong. One more thing on the crazy list. I shook my head and turned back to the pancake I'd put on my plate. I poked it.

"There's a dance tonight, too," Dax added. "Before the rodeo, right? You ready?"

Wyatt didn't answer, so I made the enormous mistake of looking at him. Mistake because once I started, I couldn't exactly stop. Even though I really did want to. I *did*. But for some ridiculous reason, I was noticing how golden his skin was. His hair had light sun-streaks. His eyes were a warm look-at-me copper. And dammit, he was looking back at me.

Great. *Perfect*. A week of work…down the drain. My heart was lodged in my throat.

"You team rope?" Dad asked.

I blinked. *Stop staring, Allie*.

"Yes, sir," Wyatt said, his gaze sliding over my face.

I swallowed. *Any time now, Allie*.

"So, a busy day." Mom's voice was soft.

Right. Mom. Dad. Dax. All here, at the table, with me and…Wyatt. *Who I will stop looking at now*. Thank God Mom was too googly-eyed over Dad to see my slip. Dad never looked at me, so no worries there. And Dax…Dax was grinning from ear to ear, his eyes bouncing between me and Wyatt. *Even better*.

"And the bonfire tonight, too? Promise you'll be careful." Mom was trying not to sound worried, I could tell.

Bonfire. Rodeo. Dance. Levi. This day gets better and better.

Dad piped up. "Bonfire?"

Mom placed her hand on his arm. "I told them they could go. They're going together. Wyatt too." As if *he* was safe?

Wyatt shifted in his chair, his knee brushing against mine under the table. I felt goose-bumps. Perfect example of how *not* safe he was. My first instinct was to pull away, but I didn't want to be a total witch. Wait. I didn't? That was my thing. If I was a raving bitch, it was a whole lot easier to keep my distance.

His jeans were in bad shape, the knees ripped out on both legs. When he leaned forward for another pancake, his skin pressed against my bare leg. I shivered. *Not breathing.*

He saw it, my reaction. I saw him see it from the corner of my eye. I frowned at my plate and pulled my leg away.

"So, since it's a national holiday and all, does that mean we get a break?" Dax asked.

"Absolutely," Dad answered. "You boys deserve a day off."

"You all coming to the parade?" Wyatt asked.

"Definitely." Dad was all enthusiasm. "Dance and rodeo too. This town knows how to celebrate, if I remember correctly."

Wyatt sat forward, propping his forearm on the table. My gaze wandered, resting on the way the tendons in his arm shifted as he picked up his glass.

"You going to run today, Allie?" Dax asked.

I didn't jump. I was proud of that. But the grin on Dax's face told me he'd been watching me and he knew I was fixating on Wyatt...on his freaking forearm. I was losing it. "Yeah, I should." I sighed.

"You didn't eat anything." My mom sounded worried.

"I will," I offered, standing up and clearing my plate. We'd all picked up a few of Wyatt's good manners. "When I get back."

"Okay." She was clearly in too good a mood to argue.

I pulled a water bottle from the refrigerator and headed out the front door without a backwards glance. By the time I'd circled the track a fifth time, I was dripping sweat. It had to be over a hundred degrees. The cicadas were chirping loudly. The air seemed to move, like steam rising off a fresh-made pie. And the grass crunched beneath my feet. *We need rain.*

I risked a glance at the house as I passed, but the boys were nowhere in sight. Because they had the day off. I shouldn't be looking at them anyway.

Two hours later I was climbing into the back of Dad's truck. I tried not to wince at the sight of my father in boots, pressed jeans, and a straw cowboy hat—but I don't know if I succeeded.

My mom was still smiling and peaceful. Maybe she was on new medication?

Dax, however, was completely wound up. Instead of his usual grunge t-shirts and baggy jeans, he was wearing the same slim-legged jeans as our father. I was relieved to see he still wore his combat boots and a t-shirt, albeit clean and anti-establishment-message-free.

"Molly going?" I asked quietly as we turned into town.

His panicked look was all the confirmation I needed. "Allie—"

I held up my hands. "Not a word."

He smiled, his easy-going sweet smile. "Thanks."

"Doesn't mean I'm not thinking it, though." That made him laugh.

We parked in the parking lot of the grocery store and climbed out. I had no idea there were this many people in Black Falls, Texas. Or maybe they were all here for the parade? Which was kind of...pathetic. This was the best show around? A bunch of old people in full cowboy get-up. Sixty-something-plus women with way too much makeup on and hair sprayed so stiff it wouldn't move in the light breeze that blew now and again. Kids wearing toy gun belts and riding their stick horses around their parents seated in lawn chairs or sitting on the tailgates or fender wells of pickup trucks.

I crossed my arms over my chest, feeling a little underdressed. I was in shorts and a tank top. And flip-flops. It was hot. Really hot.

There wasn't much room. All along the parade route,

cars and trucks, a few bicycles, and a horse or two lined the street. We ended up wedged between a truckbed full of loud senior citizens and a mini-van with the hatch open. There must have been a dozen screaming kids inside, so I moved closer to the senior citizens.

"Who's this pretty little thing?" one of the women asked.

My mother had already introduced herself and Dad, while I'd tried my best to avoid one of the dirty, screaming kids launching pretzels from inside the van—making gun noises with each throw.

"This is Allie, our daughter." I heard the laughter in Mom's voice. She knew how I felt about kids. "Allie, this is Mrs. Gunter."

I turned, going around the side of their truck to shake the old lady's offered hand. "Nice to meet you, Mrs. Gunter."

"You and your brother are twins?" Mrs. Gunter asked. "You look nothing alike."

I smiled. "I'm fine with that."

Mrs. Gunter laughed. "Oh, you must meet my grandson. That boy will trip over his tongue when he sees you." I honestly didn't know what to say to that, so I just kept smiling.

Dax was laughing uncontrollably.

"Who's your grandson?" my mother asked.

"He's a good boy. Plays football at the high school. Raises steers for FFA. Goes to Sunday School every week."

I wasn't sure why Mrs. Gunter was telling *me* this since my mother was the one who asked the question. It was like she was campaigning for the guy or something. Creepy.

My mother was smiling. "He sounds like a good boy."

Dax was still laughing. Dad was talking to a group of men, several feet away—away from the senior set and the child mafia.

"Levi," Mrs. Gunter said. "Levi Gunter."

"Allie knows Levi," Dax chimed in.

"Oh, Lord, you're *that* Allie?" Mrs. Gunter was all smiles then. "Well, of course you are. Sometimes it takes me a while to figure things out. Too much drinking, I guess." I stared at her. She burst out laughing. "Oh, honey, I'm just playin'." I laughed then, or tried to.

The sirens were the first thing I heard. Fire truck sirens. Loud… I felt Dax's hands rest on my shoulders and didn't shrug him off. *They're just sirens.*

I didn't wig out and run away, or hide in Dad's truck, or go lock myself in the grocery store bathroom. I stood there, counting backward from twenty. I knew Dax's touch kept me anchored. In the here and now—not then.

The fire trucks took hours to reach the other end of Main Street. Okay, maybe not hours, maybe it was ten minutes. It could have only been five minutes. But to me it felt like hours. They threw candy and beads as they passed us, and the dirty dozen scrambled out of the van and into the street after some of each.

Then the floats began. Rather, the farm trailers with all sorts of…interesting decorations. From a taxidermy float, complete with turkey frozen mid-flight and leaping deer, to every small Texas county and their elected peach, pear, apple, FFA, FHA, Rotary Club, or Lions Club beauty queen. I wasn't a fan of the whole pageant thing, but it was obviously important to them. Here they were, at noon on the Fourth of July, in full formal gowns under the scorching Texas sun. But I had to give them credit; they kept on smiling and waving.

Then came the school clubs. The entire street roared as the football team rumbled down the street.

"Is it just me, or is the world shaking?" Dax asked.

I shrugged. "It's football, brother dear. King of Texas sports, even more so in small towns, I guess. I mean, what else are they going to do?"

A squad of prancing, smiling cheerleaders surrounded the team float. "That's one thing that doesn't change,"

Dax murmured. "Big town, small town. Cheerleaders always look the same."

"Are you sure Molly isn't a cheerleader?" I asked.

"Huh." His hands squeezed my shoulders. "Guess not."

"Aw, Gramma, don't chase my date off," Levi yelled over the noise. I stared at him.

"I won't pull out your naked baby pictures yet, sweetie. Don't you worry," Mrs. Gunter cackled.

"I knew I could count on you," Levi yelled back, smiling. "See you later, Allie."

"That's the way to stake a claim on a girl, I guess. Publically." Dax snorted.

"I don't think so," I bit out.

"Tonight's going to be…fun." I heard the worry in his voice.

I could handle Levi and his caveman ways. Dax was crushing on Molly. No way was I going to kill his chances with her. But I sighed and acted irritated as I said, "You *so* owe me."

He laughed. "It's okay, Al, Wyatt and I will be there to protect your honor."

"Great." Wyatt… Levi was easier to deal with. I knew what to do with Levi—but Wyatt? He was a serious problem.

"Why don't you like him?" Dax asked. "Wyatt, I mean." I could tell he was smiling.

"Oh shut up," I murmured.

A group of men wearing weird hats driving super-fast tiny cars flew down the street, making little loops and cutting close to the curbs. The kids loved it. More candy was thrown high, sending kids running in every direction.

Dax tried again. "Wyatt's a nice guy and he—"

"Go get some candy," I interrupted, "or some beads or something." He laughed again.

The next set of floats carried elected officials. They waved. I didn't. It was hot. Seriously melt-your-rubber-flip-flops-to-the-asphalt hot. I kept shifting from foot to foot, trying to ignore the rivulets of sweat running down the backs of my legs. Who has parades in triple digit heat? And why? Isn't this animal abuse or something?

A mariachi band was next, strumming their guitars and singing with a certain flare.

"You should see about joining up with the band," I said to Dax, who squeezed up beside me.

"Yeah." He shrugged. "Maybe."

I shot him a look, but he didn't see me. He was completely focused on the very pretty girl leading the rodeo procession. She had to be Molly.

I looked from her to my brother. *Oh, Dax. You've got it bad.*

I glanced back at the girl whose ass I would so kick if she broke my brother's heart. She rode her pretty little black horse, the silver bells on her horse's harness and saddle-thingy cheery.

I got it. She was pretty. And, knowing Dax, she'd be sweet too. And when she saw Dax...well, her smile told me everything. Dax wasn't the only one that had fallen. *Hard.* So no ass-kicking, at least not right away.

Her little horse side-stepped, prancing a bit. But Molly got the animal under control, passing us with a tip of her black felt hat and another smile in Dax's direction.

"You okay?" I asked. "Still breathing? Not hyperventilating or anything?"

"I don't know, Al. I'm not gonna lie. My heart's going ninety-to-nothing here."

I stared at my brother, floored by his confession. He'd never had a *crush.* Not really. Sure, he thought certain girls were pretty, but that was it—as far as I knew. And even though we fought, I knew Dax pretty well.

"She likes you too," I told him, nudging him.

He looked at the ground, kicking the rocks at his feet. "I don't know..."

"Well, I do," Mrs. Gunter interrupted. "Molly's making

68

doe eyes at you, boy. You just treat her right. She's got three older brothers, all of 'em Marines."

Dax's face went from elated to terrified.

"Marines?" I laughed then. "You know how to pick 'em, Dax."

6 CHAPTER SIX

"There's Wyatt," Mom said.

"You know the Holcomb boy?" Mrs. Gunter asked.

Wyatt was riding a huge tan horse, its white mane and tail bouncing in step. I admit, he looked kind of like a knight in shining armor, if knights wore straw cowboy hats, white button-up shirts, and clean starched jeans.

"He's working out at our place," I heard Mom reply.

"Is he, now…" Mrs. Gunter's voice lowered, making it hard to hear what she was saying. "Poor boy…"

I wanted to listen, but I couldn't bring myself to move. I stood there, glad of the crowd. It was a lot easier to check a guy out when you were a nameless face in the crowd.

Mrs. Gunter was still talking. "Too young…tragedy…"

Tragedy?

"He's been amazing. He works so hard. And he's teaching Dax quite a bit." Mom sounded almost protective of Wyatt. I liked it. *You go, Mom.* I sighed. *Dammit.*

"He's always been such a good boy. Nothing like his father." Mrs. Gunter made some strange clicking sound.

I didn't gossip. I didn't like people who gossiped. But I didn't know much about these people, and Mrs. Gunter definitely was the type who'd know everything about…everyone in her small town. Maybe it was because they were talking about him or I was feeling some sort of bizarre defensiveness on his behalf, but something about Wyatt was off.

Something was wrong. I don't know how I could tell. Maybe it was the way he was carrying himself. He wasn't smiling. And he wasn't looking at the crowd. It was almost like he didn't see anything around him.

I put my fingers in my mouth and whistled loudly. My "Hey, I need you" from across the field whistle.

"Damn, Allie." Dax leaned away from me, covering his ears. "Warning next time, okay?"

I regretted it as soon as I did it—until Wyatt turned and saw me, my fingers still in my mouth. He was just as surprised as I was. Well, maybe not. I don't think anyone was as surprised as I was. *What am I doing?*

But it was worth it when Wyatt winked, a lopsided smile erasing his tension. He straightened up in his saddle, owning it. I smiled back, before I could catch myself.

Dax nudged me, reminding me that it wasn't just Wyatt and me here. No, there were lots of other people around—like Mom and Mrs. Gunter and the dozen nasty kids and my father… My father, who was frowning in my general direction.

"I think you popped my eardrum," Dax moaned, tugging on his ear.

"Sorry," I murmured.

The parade ended and the crowd started to disperse, some heading to their cars, others toward the makeshift market that surrounded the old courthouse in the heart of downtown Black Falls.

"Let's go see what's for sale," Mom said, joining us. "It's peach season. We could try making some jam."

"Yeah, sure, Mom. We could *try*." I shook my head.

"*I'm* not eating it." Dax laughed, draping his arm along Mom's shoulders.

She smiled at him. "Your loss. Allie and I might just win next year's jam contest."

"There's a jam contest?" Dax asked.

"Jam. Pie. Chili. Vegetables. Fruits. Salsa. Ribs too, I think," Dad said. "I think they have a watermelon eating contest too."

"I'm hungry," Dax said, and he and Dad led the way across the parking lot toward the small village of tents and canopies.

Mom slipped her arm through mine. "How're you doing?" she asked softly. "Hating every minute of it?"

"It's so freaking hot." I shook my head. "It's...different."

She laughed. "Isn't it, though?"

***

I stared at my reflection. Why did I care? Why was I getting all dolled up? It was a stupid hick dance. Followed by a redneck rodeo. And then a dumb-ass bonfire.

And yet here I was, wearing the outfit Lindie and I had spent way too much money on for last year's Dallas Rodeo, the best concert—with backstage passes courtesy of her dad. We'd *had* to look our cowgirl best. Who knew dressing like a cowgirl was so expensive? Dad had flipped over his credit card bill. I'd done it to spite him. Thinking I'd wear it once and never again... Until tonight.

Jeans with all sorts of bling and stitching on the butt— complete with faux zebra-skin inset crosses on each pocket. Skin-tight, sleeveless blue shirt with all sorts of silver sequins to emphasize my boobs. Lindie had hated that I had boobs and she didn't...hadn't.

I put on big silver earrings and slipped on the faux zebra-fur belt with a flashy buckle. And boots. Five hundred dollar boots with fancy stitching and intricate cut-outs. Lindie's had been almost twice that, but her parents hadn't batted an eye over the bill.

"Ready? Whoa!" Dax froze. "Going native?" He was wearing his trademark t-shirt, jeans, and combat boots.

What am I doing? I shook my head. "No...no, give me a second to change."

"Dad is already in the truck." He grabbed my hand. "Come on. Besides, Levi will *love* it."

"Dax—"

He pulled me down the stairs. "You look great. Seriously." He tugged me out the door.

"Allie, you look gorgeous," Mom said as I climbed into the backseat of the truck. I thought Dad glanced in the rearview mirror, but it was so quick I'd probably imagined it.

We pulled in to the fairgrounds less than ten minutes later. If I thought the parade route was crowded, it had nothing on this. We made our way to the gate and Dad turned to us. "Here." He held out forty dollars to each of us.

"Cool!" Dax took it. "See ya," he said, running off.

I felt a knot in my throat. I didn't especially want to hang out with my parents but I didn't really want to walk, alone, for the rest of the night. I didn't look at Dad as I took the money. I looked at Mom. "Thanks."

Her smile was strained, her gaze shifting to Dad then back to me. I knew what she wanted. She wanted me to smile at him, be the adoring daughter to his doting father. The way it had been, when I was little and adorable—not the embarrassment I was today.

Whatever.

I took a deep breath and looked at my father. "Thank you."

His surprise was almost comical. Really. But then this look crossed his face, this hurt, vulnerable expression I wasn't ready to deal with. I shoved the money in my pocket and hurried past them inside the fairground gates.

Damn him. All of this—this move, our beyond-screwed-up relationship, his and Mom's bizarro marriage—was all *his* fault. He had no reason to look at me like that. Like I might actually matter to him. Because he'd made it perfectly clear that wasn't true.

I wandered for a while, eyeing a few tables with shirts and bags.

"Funnel cake?"

I turned around to find Levi, funnel cake in his outstretched hand. He had powdered sugar all over his shirt. "Did it attack you?" I asked.

"Had to improvise." He looked at his shirt, then back at me, a huge smile on his face. "Almost dropped it."

I nodded. "Good catch." I eyed his shirt again.

He laughed, offering me the funnel cake again. "It's clean. Shirt too." I smiled, a little, but shook my head. "More for me," he said, shoving a large piece of the fried dough into his still-grinning mouth.

His funnel cake went airborne as two guys suddenly jumped him. One clapped him, hard, on the back. The other shoulder-tackled him. And this time, the funnel cake landed on the gravel at our feet.

"Fifteen second rule?" one of the guys asked.

"Shit, sorry, man," the other guy said, laughing.

Levi punched the laughing guy in the shoulder. "You owe me a funnel cake."

They stopped laughing when they saw me. They went from laughing-idiot guys to standing-straight-and-flexing-impressive-muscles guys in less than five seconds. I almost laughed.

Levi noticed too. But he didn't look happy. He looked pissed. And protective. *Awesome.*

"Allie, this jackass is Dylan." He pointed to the redhead on his right. "And this one's Austin."

I nodded at them. "Hey."

Dylan gave me a head-to-toe inspection. "You're smokin' hot."

"Hey," Austin said, reaching around Levi to smack Dylan on the back of the head. "You'll have to excuse Dylan. Too many concussions."

I did smile then. And they all three stared. I wasn't

smiling anymore. "So…I'm going to get something…to drink." I turned, searching for someplace to buy a drink.

"I'll get it," Austin offered, joining me at my side.

"Man, come on." Levi shoved him, hard, out of the way. "You know she's my date."

"We're not at the bonfire," Dylan said. He took up the empty spot on the other side while Austin and Levi kept shoving each other. "Come on, darlin', we'll get you some lemonade."

"I think I can handle it." I tried to put some distance between us.

Dylan had really long legs. "Of course you *can*. But you don't need to."

"Really—"

"Allie?" Wyatt was walking towards us.

I hated the instant wave of relief I felt. Relief. Excitement. "Hey," I murmured, trying not to act like I was happy to see him. Or breathless.

"Hey." His gaze held mine. "You look…great."

Holy crap, was I blushing? Was I? *I was.* My cheeks were hot.

"She looks hot," Dylan said again. Wyatt sighed, shaking his head.

"I *am* hot," I said. "That's why I'm getting something to drink."

Dylan jumped all over that. "*We're* getting something to drink."

"Back off, guys." Levi didn't sound like he was having fun anymore.

Austin laughed. "Chill, Levi. It's not like she's your girlfriend. Or like Dylan stands a chance with her."

Dylan frowned at him. "Dick."

"Right there, man, winning her over with all that sweet talk." Austin was still laughing.

"Sorry, guys, her dad asked me to find her," Wyatt said, calm and collected. He looked at me, waiting.

I knew that my dad would *never* ask anyone to find me.

He avoided saying my name. He'd all but paid me off to disappear for the evening. If Mom wanted me, maybe she'd send Wyatt. So, Wyatt was offering me an escape—with him. If I took him up on it, I'd have to hang with him.

"We'll see you later then." Levi smiled at me, but he shot a narrow-eyed look in Wyatt's direction. It was one of those throw-down "I'm watching you" looks.

I definitely needed to let Levi know I wasn't interested.

We stood there as the three of them walked off, laughing and talking. "You didn't have to do that," I said when they were too far away to hear us.

He shrugged, his eyes staring into mine without blinking. I swallowed. "Lemonade?" he asked.

"What?"

"Are you really thirsty?"

I shook my head. He smiled then. I smiled back. He froze, his jaw muscle working.

"Are you?" I asked, my voice strangely husky.

"What?"

"Thirsty?"

He shook his head.

Why was I standing here, staring at him? Why couldn't I look away?

"That's the second time you've smiled at me today."

He was counting? Interesting…

No. Not at all interesting.

"How do you know I was smiling at *you*?" I asked, digging deep to snap at him.

His smile grew. "I don't. I was hoping you were."

My heart stopped for just a minute. He'd said that…to me. My heart had never worked so hard.

"Hey Allie." Dax was there, talking to me… *Snap out of it!* "This is Molly." Introducing me to Molly.

It was hard, way too hard, to look away from Wyatt and his magnetic gaze, but I did it. "Hi," I said, forcing myself to relax and smile. If Dax liked this girl, I would be on my best behavior—around her, anyway.

"Hi Allie." She had huge brown eyes. "It's nice to meet you." And kind of an adorable accent. "You look so pretty."

"Thanks." *I* felt like I was playing dress-up, but... "Nice to meet you."

"Hey Wyatt." Molly's gaze bounced back and forth between Wyatt and me. *So she's smart, too.* Or Dax had been talking about things he knew nothing about...which was entirely possible. "You ready for tonight?" she asked him.

Wyatt nodded. "And willing."

Molly laughed. "I'm worried. Annemarie Cummings, from El Paso, is here."

Wyatt's eyebrows went up. "Well, don't let that get you worked up."

"Who's Annemarie Cummings?" I asked, trying to keep up.

"She's a world-class barrel racer, Allie. Tough competition. Firefly and I have cut our time, but..." Molly shook her head.

I had no idea what they were talking about. But competition, that I knew well. It was never easy going up against someone better than you. "Wyatt's right. Don't let her get in your head. This is your field...arena...your turf," I finished lamely.

She smiled, shrugging a little. "You're right." But she didn't sound convinced.

An awkward silence fell. Awkward since I was determined not to look at Wyatt but was aware of his every twitch and breath. And awkward because my brother was staring at Molly like he was going to grab her and kiss her any minute now. I wasn't against making out, but it might not be the best thing to do here, in front of the whole town. Especially since her Marine brothers were around somewhere.

"You're going to have to fill me in on...everything," I said, hoping to distract...everyone. "I don't know all the rules and stuff."

Molly shrugged. "Barrel racing is easy. As far as rules go, that is. You blow through the gate and fly around the barrels without knocking them over."

"And if you knock one over?" I asked.

"They add five seconds to your time," Wyatt said.

"Fastest time wins," Molly finished.

Dax nodded. "Got it."

"Guess you have to have a solid relationship with your horse, huh?" I asked as we headed slowly toward the stage on the far side of the fairgrounds.

Molly smiled. "Firefly's my baby. My dad didn't want him, said he was too small. But I knew he'd do right by me. And he has. We've won some pretty big purses—for the small circuits."

I smiled back at her, hoping I looked impressed. I had no idea what a pretty big purse meant; it was all about the winning part of things for me. Trophies and medals didn't hurt, though.

"Wyatt's up on two events tonight. Bulldogging and team roping." Molly shook her head. "Just don't get poked."

"Poked?"

"Steer wrestling," Dax explained.

"Oh." I frowned. It might not be bull riding, but... "Bulldogging?" My gaze found Wyatt and he nodded at me, his brown eyes way too curious.

"You and Hank still going to try for Regionals?" Molly asked.

Wyatt shrugged. "If he doesn't get deployed before then."

"Hank?" Dax asked.

"My brother. He and Wyatt team rope," Molly explained. "We've got rodeo in our blood."

The closer we got to the stage, the louder the music was. People were grouped together, laughing and talking. Hundreds of strands of white Christmas lights ran back and forth over the crowded dance area. From little boys in boots to old men holding carved canes wearing straw hats, it was clear that you didn't outgrow being a cowboy. At least not in Black Falls, Texas.

Dax was almost floating with happiness when Molly took his hand and led him onto the dance floor. *Poor Dax.* I could just hear their conversation. *I don't know anything about rodeo or western dancing or—*

"Dance?" Wyatt asked me.

I shook my head. "To *this?*"

"Um…" He paused, his smile way too charming. "That's what I had in mind."

A couple passed us. The guy was twisting the girl this way and that, arms and hair flying as they spun together.

"I'm not qualified for that," I said. "Wow."

The couple did some fancy extra twists as the music came to an end, making my mouth fall open and Wyatt laugh.

When the music started back up, it was much slower. "How about this?" He held out his hands to me.

My stomach tightened, reminding me why I should say no. My heart was racing, reinforcing the whole "say no" thing.

"I can teach you," he added.

I couldn't help but pick up on his tension. He was nervous. I could see how fast his heart was beating from the pulse in his neck. I opened my mouth, the "no" ready and waiting to jump out…but somehow I ended up taking his hands and following him onto the packed-dirt dance floor. His hand, rough and warm, made my hand tingle…and my arm…and my shoulder.

A shiver ran down my back, leaving goose-bumps over every inch of my skin. *Get a grip.* By the time we were on the dirt dance floor, I was one raw nerve, tingling and nervous and feeling like a complete idiot for caving to the hunky cowboy with the thumping heart.

His arm went around me, his hand resting on the back

of my shoulder. His other hand still held mine, which was sort of nice since I had no clue what I was doing. A quick glance around the dance floor told me I was supposed to place my other arm along his, resting my other hand on his shoulder. Some women had their arm rigid, others elevated, some drooped. I draped.

"Two big steps," he said, moving us forward, "then three little steps. That's it."

"*That* I can do." I tried to sound playful but the smile he shot my way made that a bit challenging.

Dancing was easy. He led, carefully, his hand steering me through any near collisions as more dancers joined us. We moved a little closer together, it was getting really crowded, when I heard him singing. It was soft...but he was definitely singing. A low, rumbling sound that had me leaning closer.

I smiled up at him. He smiled back, his lips barely moving. "You're singing," I said.

He frowned. "I am?"

I nodded, shooting him a disbelieving smile. "Yep." He pressed his lips shut. "I wasn't complaining," I murmured.

"You weren't?"

"I...No."

He smiled then, spinning me around. He pulled me a little closer, edging around an older couple who swayed in place. Closer still when we moved between two couples. So close that I could feel his heartbeat, thumping like crazy—like mine, against my chest.

His voice was right beside my ear, his breath brushing across my ear. I lost my step, tripping on his boot.

"Sorry," I mumbled.

His hand squeezed mine, but he just kept singing.

I could rest my head on his shoulder if I wanted to. His shoulder was right there. All I had to do was let my head fall a few inches forward...

His hand traveled lower, resting on the back of my waist. His fingers were spread wide, his thumb resting beneath my bra strap.

His heart rate picked up, pumping against his chest and mine. He spun us around, fast, without missing a step. I laughed a little, unable to resist smiling up at him. His gaze was so…I was feeling so…

What was wrong with me? It was hot. It was dark, and I was still sweating. I was tripping through an unknown dance on a crowded floor. People everywhere. Music that, frankly, made me cringe. But I couldn't think of a place I'd rather be.

"Last dance, folks," a voice said through the overhead speakers. "Time to rodeo." An impressive whoop rose up from the crowd.

"I've gotta go get things set up," Wyatt said, still holding me close.

"Oh, okay." I didn't sound like me.

He gaze was intense, like he was studying…me. My eyes, my forehead, my cheeks, my chin, my mouth… I felt my cheeks going hot again.

"I like dancing with you, Allie." His voice was low, rough.

I opened my mouth, but nothing came out. He sighed, one hand slowly sliding from my back while the other still held mine.

"Kiss her or come on, Wyatt."

Wyatt stepped back then, shaking his head. "Comin', Hank." He nodded at me, once. "See you later, Allie."

"Be careful," I said, hearing the strain in my voice. "Or is it good luck?"

He nodded, his smile returning full force.

"You sure you don't want to kiss her?" Hank asked. "Can't hurt."

"It might," Wyatt said. "You don't know Allie."

"I'm Hank." Hank was massive. Broad and thick, he radiated don't-get-on-my-bad-side. But he had a great smile.

"Hey. I'm Allie." I shook his hand.

"Molly's my sister. Is your brother Dax?" he asked, scowling at me.

"Yeah, so please don't hurt him."

Hank arched a thick brown eyebrow at me. "Not making any promises."

"Come on," Wyatt said.

They were like boys on Christmas morning, excited and pumped-up, as they made their way through the crowd to the pens and fences in the distance.

"Your dad wanted you, huh?" Levi stood behind me. *Awesome.* "You know what you're getting into?" Levi's voice was low.

"What?" I asked.

Levi leaned closer, like he had some big, important secret to tell me. "Wyatt."

For some reason it pissed me off. "Levi…" I stepped back, crossing my arms in an attempt not to blow a gasket. "I'm going to the bonfire with you. I danced with Wyatt. That's it."

Levi's eyebrows shot up.

"I don't plan on getting into anything with either one of you," I said, arching my brows right back at him. "Okay?"

He smiled. "Sure. Doesn't mean I'm going to stop trying to make you my girlfriend."

I laughed, surprised.

"Allie!" Dax was on the other side of the dance floor, waving me over.

"Meet me over by the kettle corn after, okay?" Levi said, walking away.

"Sure," I replied, heading towards Dax.

"You dance with Levi?" Dax asked. I shot him a look. "Just kidding. It was Wyatt, right?" I continued to glare at him. "Yeah, that's what I thought."

We didn't say much as we climbed up the wooden bleachers surrounding the arena. It was packed, but Mom had saved enough room for Dax and me to squeeze in.

I'd been to the Dallas Rodeo a few times. Beer, sweat, manure, and leather were all scents I expected on the fairgrounds. I wasn't disappointed. But there was another scent in the air. I glanced at Dax, wedged right beside me. "Are you wearing cologne?" I asked.

Red crept up his neck to color his face. I giggled.

He smiled at me. "I haven't heard you laugh like that in a long time, Al."

I shook my head, brushing off what he said. But he was right. I hadn't felt like this—happy—in a long time...because I had no right to be happy. So why was I?

I frowned as the announcer started talking. I didn't hear a word he said until Dax nudged me in the side. Everyone was standing as Molly rode into the arena. She held a flagpole, the Stars and Stripes flying proudly. I was impressed with her balance. I don't think she was even holding the reins of her horse.

The announcer continued: "Father God, tonight we're here to admire the sportsmanship You've given these fine young men and women. We acknowledge that, through You, we live in the greatest country in the world. Where freedom is part of our daily life. Where faith and family come first. Where neighbors still look out for one another."

I was torn. This was kind of embarrassing. But it was also kind of cool. I glanced around me. Men, young and old, had their hats in their hands and their hands over their hearts. I heard a few amens.

"And today, the Fourth of July, we thank You for America's forefathers," the announcer went on. "We also ask You to watch over those men and women fighting, even as we speak, to protect this great country. We ask that You protect them and the cowboys and cowgirls participating tonight in this wonderful Fourth of July rodeo."

I thought of Wyatt. Bulldogging. I wasn't sure I could watch.

A young woman started singing the "Star-Spangled Banner" into a microphone. Everyone in the stands joined in. It wasn't a hushed kind of thing, either. People weren't pretending or stumbling over the words. No, they were belting them out loudly. Proudly.

As the song came to an end, a roar of applause rose up and Molly pressed her knees hard into her horse's sides. They flew out of the arena, flag flying. Dax let out a long, slow breath.

"You okay?" I asked him. He just looked at me. I shook my head.

"We want to thank tonight's sponsors..." The announcer began listing off names of local and state businesses.

I patted Dax on the knee and shifted, turning my attention to the arena below. First up, bronc riding. It wasn't pretty. I winced, a lot, and ended up people-watching instead. There were plenty of people to watch. There were a lot of tourists, which was kind of weird.

I started to see the difference between the locals and those trying to blend in. Eventually I narrowed it down to four groups: Natives, meaning they'd been born and would die here. Transplants, like us. In-betweens, here to watch but weren't real tourists or out to make friends, probably from San Antonio or Austin. Tourists, complete with the big cameras and grocery-store-bought straw cowboy hats.

"Glad that's over," Mom said to me. "I worry about those horses."

I laughed. "Only you would say that."

"Well, it's true."

"Let's give those boys a round of applause," the announcer's voice enthused. "Well, Cowboy Sam, what's the matter?"

Cowboy Sam was a heavy-set rodeo clown who was meant to entertain the crowd while the next event was set up. So far, he'd only added to the are-you-serious nature of this whole experience.

"Next up, team roping. We have some great teams here today, from as far away as Germany, Australia, and Brazil. That's right, folks, right here in Black Falls, Texas."

I looked at Dax. Dax looked at me. "They have rodeos in Germany?" I asked.

"You learn something new every day." He shrugged.

It didn't matter. This was Wyatt's event.

Wyatt.

I scooched forward on my seat, my hands pressed between my legs. The wind picked up, lifting my hair and cooling my neck. I felt the tension in the air as two riders rode up, right behind metal gates. A cow was herded into a chute between them. A buzzer sounded and the cow bolted out, the two riders quick on its heels.

The first cowboy threw his lasso, hooking the cow's horns. The other rider was close, his lasso twirling in the air. Once he saw the rope was secure on the cow's head, he let his lasso fly, catching the cow's back legs. The cow stumbled to a stop, showing it was caught by both ropes, and the cowboys let go of their leads, letting them fall to the dirt. Freed, the cow ran to the other end of the arena, the ropes falling off as he went, while the two cowboys followed, their eyes glued to the scoreboard.

"That was fast," I murmured.

"Not really, sugar," the man behind me said.

I turned around. The man was brown, his skin wrinkled like leather. His hands were gnarled around the longneck beer bottle in his hands.

"I wouldn't really know what a fast time was," I admitted, smiling.

The man tipped his hat at me. "Well, sugar, I can help you with that."

I nodded. "Thank you." Dax rolled his eyes, but he leaned back to listen too. We were both clueless.

"Now, the boys need to make sure they didn't break a barrier," the old man said. "Once the header gets the steer, the heeler needs to be fast."

I glanced at Dax, who was grinning. *Keep smiling, smart-ass.* "You lost me," I said. "I'm assuming the header is the one that—"

"Next up, Gabe Garza and Jorge Mendoza, from Houston, Texas," the announcer interrupted our lesson.

"Watch." The old man leaned forward, between Dax and me. The buzzer sounded and the cow shot out. The first rider threw his rope at the cow's horns. "Header," the old man said. When the other rider looped the cow's back leg, he said, "Heeler. But he didn't get both legs."

"What does that mean?" I asked.

"That's bad, sugar." The old man smiled, sipping his beer. "Penalty points."

I nodded.

"Next up, some locals, Wyatt Holcomb and Hank Pendleton," the announcer said. "Word is these boys are thinking about heading to Regionals before Hank is deployed."

The crowd went crazy.

SASHA SUMMERS

7 CHAPTER SEVEN

I stared at Wyatt, watched his every move. He had a length of rope in his mouth, his lasso in one hand, and more rope in the other. His knees gripped his horse, but nothing else. He was rigid, his entire body poised for movement.

It was so fast I didn't really see what happened. "Now that was a good run," the old man said, sitting back. "Damn good run."

All I saw was Wyatt, his smile when his score was posted.

"Best score so far," Dax said. "Where's that whistle now?"

I started to, but my dad beat me to it. All the same, Wyatt turned and found me.

I didn't think his smile could get any bigger, but I was wrong. He looked so damn gorgeous as he tipped his hat at me. Why did *his* public display of affection have the opposite effect of Levi's?

"Stop smiling at him," Dax warned. "If you don't like him, don't lead him on."

That's when I realized I was smiling right back at Wyatt, a huge, stupid grin that had no place on my face.

"Shit," I murmured.

"Shit is right." Dax frowned at me.

I frowned at my brother. "I didn't mean…I'm not…I don't want…" I stood up. "I'm going to get something to drink." I paused then. "What's next?" If Molly was coming up, I wouldn't leave Dax—even if he was being a dipshit.

"Kids' calf scramble," the old man said, openly watching Dax and me with interest. "You won't miss nothin' special while you go hunt down your cowboy."

"He's not—" I shook my head, realizing that my parents were watching as well. "I'll be right back."

"Will you get me a water?" my mom asked.

"And some kettle corn," Dax added.

"Oh, and a funnel cake?" Mom said.

I sighed. "Sure, fine, great. Be right back."

It took me ten minutes to get out of the stands and down to the vendors' tents that lined the gravel road along the side of the arena. The wait lines were ridiculous but at least I had some time to myself.

Trying to scale back to our seats carrying two water bottles, a bag of kettle corn, and a plate with funnel cake wasn't easy. It was a joint effort; half of the people sitting in the stands between me and my destination helped me get there.

"Next time, you're up," I said to Dax as I shoved the massive bag of kettle corn at him.

He laughed. "Where's your lemonade?"

"Bite me," I mumbled.

The old man laughed.

"Allie," my mother reprimanded, laughing. "Thanks for the goodies, honey."

I nodded, handing her the funnel cake and water bottle.

"You just missed twenty-five or so kids running around trying to pull a red ribbon off a calf's tail," Dax said before shoving a handful of kettle corn into his mouth.

"Why would they do that?"

"Twenty bucks," the old man said, taking some of the

kettle corn Dax offered.

"This is Bubba," Dax said. "He knows Dad."

"When he was your age," Bubba said.

I risked a quick glance at my father.

"You haven't changed," Dad said to Bubba.

"You sure as hell have," Bubba replied, laughing.

I stared, but Mom and Dad were laughing too. "O...kay..." I said, sitting down and opening my water bottle.

Dax frowned. "I thought that was for me."

"I couldn't carry an open cup and all this crap. So, no, the water is mine." I held the bottle away from him. "Go ahead, pout, I'm not sharing."

Dax shook his head. "Fine."

"Wyatt's up next," Mom said, leaning close to me.

"What?" I asked. "They started steer wrestling?" My heart slammed into my ribcage. "You could have told me," I snapped at Dax.

"Why?" He gave me a look. "I thought you didn't like him."

I heard Bubba snort, and shot the old man a glare too.

"Wyatt Holcomb's up again," the announcer said. "This Black Falls, Texas boy has been attracting some attention in both steer wrestling and team roping."

"When does he *sleep?*" my mom asked.

I shook my head. "Isn't he too young for this?" I asked, wanting to stop this before it started.

"He's eighteen," Dax explained. *Wonderful.*

"Need any lessons on this, sugar?" Bubba asked.

I felt sick when the steer was locked into the shoot.

"His horns have been tipped," Bubba said. They were still long enough to put big nasty holes in a body.

"He has to get the steer to the ground?" Dax asked.

"Yep," Bubba said. "Clear run will have the steer on his side or back, all four feet in the air."

How a cow could suddenly look like a man-eating monster, I'm not sure—but it did. Gone was the docile, sloe-eyed animal I saw in basically every field in Black Falls. In its place stood an animal capable of seriously injuring Wyatt. My chest felt very heavy. My stomach twisted and churned.

"Allie? You okay?" my mother asked.

The chute opened and the steer shot out. Its two-foot horns looked anything but safe. And then Wyatt was flying out of the shoot, leaning far to the right on his horse. I pressed my hands between my knees again, panic rising up. Wyatt was off the horse, one arm draped around the neck of the steer while his hands gripped the animal's horns. One firm twist and they came to a stop, the steer on his side. Wyatt was up before the steer was.

"He made that look easy," Bubba said.

The moment Wyatt looked at me, I looked away. I had to. I had to stare at my hands, my lap, the water bottle I'd all but crushed between my knees. Anything but him.

"Allie?" my mom whispered. I turned. "Are you okay?" I nodded. "You sure?" she said, putting her hand over my knee. I nodded again. "You want to go?" she asked, so softly I knew no one else could hear her. "I didn't think about how stressful this might be."

"The needless endangering of human life for sport, you mean?" I asked, keeping my tone as light as possible.

She smiled, her blue eyes twinkling. "Exactly."

She was giving me an out. We could leave. I wouldn't have to deal with Wyatt or Levi...or Wyatt...or the way I felt around Wyatt.

"Barrel racing is next," Dax said.

And just like that I knew I couldn't bail on him. "I'm good," I said. "It's not like...what happened...had anything to do with this."

Her eyes widened. Probably because I never brought up what happened, *ever*.

"No...I suppose not," she agreed. I could tell she was working through things to say. "Funnel cake?"

I blinked at her then burst out laughing.

With Wyatt's events over and Molly placing second, things got a lot less stressful. Bull riding was beyond me. The fact that there was an ambulance standing by said it all. But, as Bubba pointed out, there was an ambulance standing by at football games too. When I tried to argue that a single player didn't carry around a knife or weigh a couple thousand pounds, he just stared at me.

Then it was over. "Not too late," Dad said to Dax and me. "Nothing stupid or risky."

Dax nodded. "Yes, sir."

"They'll be fine," my mom assured him. "You have your phones?" Dax nodded.

"If Levi or Wyatt drink—"

"Dad," Dax cut him off. "Wyatt doesn't drink. But, yes, we'd call you for a ride."

My dad's expression was hard. He opened his mouth, then shut it, looking at Dax, then me.

I stared at the wide leather cuff I wore around my wrist, pretending one of the pieces of turquoise was loose just so I didn't have to acknowledge him.

"Have a good time." Dad's voice was rough.

I followed Dax to the far side of the arena. Levi was there, with Austin and Dylan and a bunch of other people I didn't know. Molly was there, all smiles for Dax. She was sitting with a group of blinged-out cowgirls.

"Ready?" Levi asked, smiling at me.

Why couldn't I be more like Lindie? Levi was cute. He had a decent sense of humor. He was clearly into me. But I was *so* not into him. I nodded anyway.

"Let's go." He tilted his head in a this-way movement. I followed him. "What'd you think?" he asked.

I shrugged. "It was interesting." He laughed. I glanced back. Molly and Dax were following, walking close together. I hurried to catch up to Levi, giving them some privacy.

"Your brother's into Molly?" Levi asked.

"Looks like it," I agreed.

"She's kind of…well, she…" He shrugged.

"She's what?" I asked, worried.

He lowered his voice. "She's kind of…a tease."

"What do you mean?" I didn't like where this was going.

"She smiles and dolls herself up but she doesn't date," he said.

Meaning she'd probably turned him and all of his friends down. I liked her even more. "Looks like she's into Dax," I said.

He nodded. "I guess."

Levi drove a four-door Blazer, old and so jacked-up he had added two steps to get inside. I used the handle he'd welded to the front and pulled myself up and into the front passenger seat. It was surprisingly clean on the inside, smelling like cleaner and a splash of cologne. When he turned the key, the engine roared to life.

I had no idea where we were going or what was going to happen, but Molly chattered away in the backseat.

"You should be happy," Dax said to her.

"I am, Dax," she replied. "I'm happy that's over and we can enjoy tonight."

I smiled out the window of the car, imagining the grin on my brother's face.

"What did *y'all* do to celebrate wins?" Levi asked.

I shrugged. "Party. Drink 'til you threw up. Sneak in so you didn't get grounded." I watched him closely, waiting for his reaction.

He turned, looking at me. "Hell, yeah," he said, eager.

"Not anymore," Dax said from the backseat.

"Aw, man," Levi argued, slowing down as we crossed a big empty field and parked. "Why not?"

"Because I killed my best friend." I got the words out with no inflection or emotion.

"Allie…" Dax sounded like he was choking.

I opened the door, searching for the handle and steps in the dark. I lowered myself to the ground and walked to the tower of logs in the middle of a clearing surrounded by a ring of big flat rocks.

More trucks were arriving. By the time Levi had the cooler from the back of his Blazer, Austin and Dylan and a handful of others were already setting up around the fire.

Dax walked by me, but he didn't look at me. I knew I'd pissed him off. I didn't know why I'd said what I said. But there was no way I could take it back. I didn't want to take it back. It was true. It was my fault Lindie was dead. But none of these people knew anything about it. None of them knew Lindie. And they never would. Because of me.

I wanted to get out of there. I didn't want to have anything to with these people, their rodeos and bonfires. This wasn't my life. And they would never be my friends. Not like Lindie.

Sadness and guilt clawed their way up, strangling all the other emotions I'd made room for. I don't know how I'd let myself get there, at a party, surrounded by people wanting to have fun, to chill out. I shouldn't be there. I had no right to be there. I didn't want to be there. I wanted to go home.

Home. There was no going *home*.

"Hey." Wyatt's voice was soft.

I turned, staring at him. They'd started the fire, but it was too dark to make out his expression. Not that his expression mattered right now. "Can you get me out of here?" I asked.

He looked at the fire, then at me. "Are you sure?" I nodded. "Want me to take you home?" he asked.

"I don't care where we go, Wyatt, as long as we *go*." My voice shook.

He nodded. "Let's go, then." We headed to his truck.

"Allie?" Molly came running up. "What's up?"

"Wyatt's going to take me home," I said.

"Oh…okay. I'll get Dax."

"No." I put my hand on her arm. "You guys stay and have fun, okay?"

She hesitated. I couldn't see her face clearly, but I could imagine it. She probably thought I was mental. I was acting like it.

"Tell Dax to text me and I'll come get y'all," Wyatt offered.

"Okay," Molly said. "Well…night." She walked back to the blazing fire, to Dax. She whispered something in his ear and he looked in our direction. But instead of looking mad, he smiled.

"Let me move some stuff to the back," Wyatt said when we reached his truck.

"It's fine." I opened the front driver door and slid onto the bench seat. *Stuff* was piled up, taking up more than half of the seat. So basically I'd be in his lap…but I didn't care.

He looked into the truck at me, the muscle in his jaw jumping, before he climbed in beside me. He started the truck and reached for the stick shift. That's where things got interesting.

My legs were on either side of the stick shift, since there wasn't room to put them anywhere else. When he put his hand on the stick shift, his elbow brushed against the front of my skin-tight shirt. For the first time in my life I felt like my boobs were enormous, too big to ignore. Lindie'd given me crap about how I didn't use boobs to their advantage. I could have any guy I wanted, if I let them *accidentally* brush up against me—to show them I was interested. I'd called her a slut and laughed her off.

Thing is, I knew Wyatt would never *accidentally* rub up against me. Honestly, I was the one that jumped into his truck, pressing myself up against him, making him rub and brush against me…so he could *drive*. He didn't have a choice. But I was reacting, a lot, to his *driving*.

He smelled crazy good. The muscle in his thigh moved, pressing against my thigh. When he shifted into second gear, it took everything I had not to turn into his side, to bury my face against his neck. Because he was right there, warm and solid and…touching me without touching me.

96

He shifted into high gear and lifted his hand but there was no place to put it. We were too close for him to keep it on the gear shift handle, or his arm would remain between my boobs. If he tried to rest his arm, it would be draped along my thigh, or awkwardly across his own lap. If he put his hand on the steering wheel, his elbow would be bouncing off of my chest at every turn or bump.

"Here." I moved closer, under his arm, forcing him to drape his arm around my shoulders. But his arm lay along the back of the seat, not my shoulders. Which irritated me. I forced myself to sit ramrod straight, as far from him as I could. Which wasn't much.

We turned, and I slid against his side, his arm wrapping around my shoulder to support me. I didn't hesitate. I melted—against him, into him. My head fell to his shoulder and my arm rested along his thigh. Even though I knew better.

He smelled even better up close. I turned my head, my nose brushing the front of his white button-down shirt. His hand rubbed up and down my arm, the slight tremor in his touch doing something strange to me. What would he do if I turned in to him? If I…if I kissed his neck?

Heat rolled through my body, startling me, exciting me… I closed my eyes, trying to make sense of my feelings. Letting myself feel these incredible feelings.

The truck was slowing down, but I didn't open my eyes. I didn't want to open them and be *there*—the place that was supposed to be home but wasn't. His arm moved, shifting gears again. His arm slid over me, another shockwave of intense heat. He shifted again, and the truck stopped, but I still didn't move.

Every single inch of me was focused on his arm, draped across my thighs now…his hand resting on the outside of my thigh. His fingers brushed along the seam of my jeans. Without the roar of the engine and the whistle of the AC, the chirp of crickets and Wyatt's out-of-control heartbeat filled the confined space of the truck cabin.

"We're here," Wyatt said, his voice soft.

I was trying to breathe normally, even though I was on total sensory overload. Being here was good—or I might just ask him to keep on driving. I opened my eyes. No sign of the old farmhouse. I blinked. "Where's *here?*"

"Come on," he said as he opened the truck door. I followed him. "Watch your step." His voice was low, almost a whisper.

"Okay," I whispered back.

Thank God he had a flashlight. It was dark. Dark-dark. Like I couldn't see the ground in front of me dark. I took his hand when he reached back for me. It made things easier.

Then we stopped. "What?" I asked, still whispering. He flashed the beam of light in front of us.

We stood on a ledge, suspended a good fifty feet above…something. I couldn't tell, it was black. I took a step closer, but his hand tightened around mine. He pulled me back, beside him, and turned off the flashlight.

"Look up," he said, his deep voice echoing.

I did. "Holy shit!" I whispered.

He laughed. I smiled—which was okay since he couldn't see me.

Millions and millions of stars. "Who knew?" I asked, awestruck.

His hand moved, his fingers sliding between mine so our hands were threaded together. I shivered.

"I come out here when I need to be reminded that there are things bigger than me," he said.

I tried to pull my hand from his. "You brought me out here to, what, talk *at* me?"

"No." His hand tightened on mine. "I brought you here to scream."

I relaxed. "Oh." *God, Wyatt…*He squeezed my hand once. "Like you're going to chase me through the woods and chop me up scary-movie scream?"

He laughed. "No."

No. When did I become such a dork? Crickets.

"What do you think?" he asked.

What *did* I think? "You're here," I argued. "I…It's too weird."

"Why?"

"Because."

"You don't have to, Allie. It helps me sometimes, is all." His thumb was moving slowly back and forth across the back of my hand.

I liked it. "It really helps?"

"Me." His voice was soft.

Crickets.

What did I have to lose? Maybe it *would* help. If it didn't, I was standing by an incredibly hot guy. I could always wrap my arms around Wyatt and…

Bad idea. Very bad idea.

"Here." He stooped in the dark, then stood, taking my hand in his. "Throw this. It'll help you get started."

"A rock?" I asked, feeling the solid, cool weight of it in my hands.

"Take a deep breath, throw it, let it all out."

"O-kay…" I had my doubts, but I sucked in a deep breath until my chest ached, threw the damn rock, and let it out. I screamed, yelled, long and broken. And when the air was gone I did it again…and again. Even when my throat was hurting and it was hard to breathe, I kept going.

When I knew I couldn't do it anymore, Wyatt pulled me into his arms and held me, tight, against his chest. I clung to him, wrapping my arms around his waist. His hands brushed tears from my cheeks. My tears. On my cheeks.

"Sorry, Allie." He sounded so sad. I shook my head against his chest. "Whatever happened, whatever hurt you, I'm sorry."

I'd been standing there, kind of limp, in his arms. His words, the anguish in his voice, reached me. Deep down, I heard him.

A piercing whistle split the night, ending with a resounding, familiar pop. I looked up in time to see the shower of bright red sparks overhead.

"Looks like it's time for the fireworks." Wyatt didn't move, and neither did I.

We stood there, wrapped together, in the middle of nowhere, watching the sky explode over and over. White, yellow, green. Shapes, colors, patterns.

And beneath my cheek Wyatt's heartbeat was steady, calm.

When the final fireworks—a crescendo of color— finished I knew we'd leave. I mean, we couldn't stay out here all night...even if I kind of wanted to...which was weird.

He led us back to the truck. It was hard to argue when he hadn't said a word. But there was no way I'd tell him that, right now, all I wanted was to stay here, with him, wrapped up in his arms, in his truck or under the stars.

He pulled the door open and I slid across the truck's bench seat. Once he was beside me I moved, curling into him—my arms around his waist, my face buried against his neck.

He froze, the muscles along his side and back tightening beneath my touch. But then he relaxed, sliding his arm around my waist and pressing me against him—no space between us. Just the way I wanted it. All I knew was that there was something powerful in his touch, his scent. That with him next to me, I felt like things were going to be okay. A dangerous, silly, illusion...but I was too drained to worry about it right now. Instead, I let my fingers run down his side, along his rigid muscles. I listened to his breathing, the way it hitched when I turned my nose into his chest.

By the time we drove down the gravel drive toward home, I was terrified all over again. I couldn't do this. I couldn't let him in. I couldn't care. Because then I'd have to worry about losing him...

My parents were sitting on the front porch swing when we got there. I didn't bother looking at either of them as I made my way up onto the porch, Wyatt behind me.

"Have fun?" Mom asked.

I shrugged. "Bonfires aren't really my thing."

"Fireworks were nice," Dad said. I assumed he was talking to Wyatt.

"Yes, sir," Wyatt agreed. "They pulled out all the stops."

"Perfect view from right here," Mom said, patting Dad on the knee as she said it.

I leaned against the porch railing, staring into the sky overhead. There were still millions of stars up there...so why didn't they look as magical now as they had then?

Wyatt joined me but he didn't touch me. I glanced at him, but he was staring up at the sky too.

I heard Mom yawn. "I'm turning in. It was a long hot day for me."

"Night, Dr. Cooper," Wyatt said.

"Congratulations on tonight, Wyatt," she said. "What happens next?"

"I'm not sure yet. All-around offers some big college scholarships...but I'm not thinking of going pro." He smiled. "If I can't get the money, I'll follow Hank to the Marines after graduation. Then college."

"Sounds like you have a plan," Dad said. "Any degree ideas?"

"I'd like to do what Dr. Cooper does." Wyatt smiled. "Large animal, preferably. Hook up with one of the rodeo circuits, maybe. Or have a clinic somewhere close to home."

"Wyatt," My mother moved closer to him. "Hurry up. I'd *love* a partner."

He laughed. "Yes, ma'am."

"Night," she said as she went inside.

"Why Marines?" Dad asked.

And though it irritated me that he asked, I wanted to

know the answer too. Steers and rodeos and Marines, too? Was he an adrenaline junkie?

"Some friends of mine are Marines. Money's not bad, sir." He shrugged. "I'm a good student, but I know better than to expect a lot of money in academic scholarships. I work, but I have bills so I'm not putting much back."

My father nodded, but didn't say anything as he headed to the front door.

He had bills? Really?

"I'll be over in the morning, sir," Wyatt said.

"I'll be here, son. You get some rest." He paused. "When will Dax be home?" I knew he was talking to me, even though he was looking at the porch swing.

"Soon," I managed.

He nodded. "Night."

We listened to the creak of the stairs as he made his way up to his room. He and Mom were at the other end of the hall from me, lots of squeaky floorboards between us—just the way I liked it.

Leaving me and Wyatt alone.

8 CHAPTER EIGHT

"You good?" Wyatt asked me.

I nodded. "Throat's going to be sore tomorrow." He smiled. "But I'm good."

"I'll go get Dax," he murmured, his gaze falling to my lips.

Just like that I was hot and bothered and confused all over again. *You should kiss me. Right now.*

Wait. No… I didn't want to get involved with him. No matter how amazingly awesome he was—and he *was*, I knew that now. He deserved better.

When he took a step, I took a step back. I couldn't lead him on. I'd been sending him, and myself, mixed signals all night. No more. "Okay…I'll text him. So he knows you're coming."

"Nah. I'll get there soon enough." Wyatt moved closer, leaning on the porch railing in front of me.

Close enough to touch, if I wanted to. And I wanted to, I really wanted to. I sat on the swing, sitting on my hands.

"What are your plans? After high school?" he asked, surprising me.

"I…I *wanted* to be a physical therapist. Sports medicine," I said.

"Wanted?" he asked.

I shrugged. "Things aren't as clear cut as they used to be."

He nodded. "Shit happens."

I laughed then, completely surprised. He laughed too. We stared at each other, awareness growing.

My words ran together: "You'll need to clear out some of the stuff in your truck if you're getting Molly too."

He smiled, nodding, his eyes steady on my face...driving me crazy.

I stood. "I'll help." Anything to distract me.

We moved his saddle, ropes, and three large bags of who-knows-what into the truck bed. Why I felt the need to watch him, the way he moved, was beyond me. But I did.

"Thanks," he said, standing in front of me, his hand resting on the hood of his truck.

"Sorry I didn't help you with it before." My gaze got tangled up in his.

He moved closer. "I'm not." He leaned forward but didn't touch me.

Oh God... I felt myself stiffen and pressed my eyes shut. I wanted this. *Finally...*

I...I couldn't handle this. *Oh, Wyatt.*

He didn't touch me, but I felt his warmth, knew he was close, knew something was coming. I was terrified... I was thrilled...

His lips were soft, brushing my forehead, lingering just long enough for his breath to lift my hair.

"Night, Allie," he spoke against my skin, never touching me.

It was only after he climbed into his truck that I could really breathe again.

***

Dad was in town for the next five days. He seemed to be everywhere I was, which was seriously irritating since I didn't want to see him.

My days fell into a routine: Running before the sun was

high enough to cast a shadow. Home. Shower. Clinic with Mom. Since she hadn't hired any office help, I'd volunteered. It kept me away from the house, Dad, and Wyatt.

Wyatt acted like nothing had happened. Like nothing had changed. He still smiled at me. And when I did catch him looking at me, he seemed to be waiting for something...

Which was what I wanted, right? Not for him to look at me that way, no, but for him to be *normal*—not to act like there was...something between us. Because there wasn't. Couldn't be.

I couldn't do it. Not to Wyatt.

"Allie?" my mother asked. "Did Mrs. Floyd leave her phone number?"

I nodded, opening the patient information forms I'd been inputting since our new computers arrived. I wrote the number on a sticky note and handed it to Mom.

"Thanks. Once I give her a quick call, we can head home," she said over her shoulder, heading into the back.

Dax arrived, looking sweaty and dirty. "Hey."

"You look gross," I said.

"You look great yourself," he countered.

"What are you so happy about?"

"Got a truck."

I stared at him. "What?"

"I. Bought. A. Truck."

I continued to stare at him. "How the hell can you afford a truck?"

He shrugged. "I've been working for Dad."

"So *he* bought you a truck." I wasn't mad—just surprised. "That's nice."

He smiled. "I thought so. I was going to drive Mom home. Can you drive her car?"

Dad had been pretty clear: no telephones (except for emergencies), no computers (unless it was for school), and no vehicles (no exceptions). I crossed my arms over my chest. "Dad said yes to this idea?" He nodded. I frowned. I wasn't allowed to drive. That was one of the...consequences.

"Call him," Dax said.

I stuck out my tongue at my brother. "You're hilarious."

"Hey, Dax," Mom said. "Okay. Prissy is doing well and everyone's settled in for the evening. Let's go home." Her phone rang. "It's your dad. Hold on." She answered. "Hey, Hon. Yes...Yes...Oh...Sure. See you soon...I love you too."

Dax and I exchanged looks.

I love you too... I guess things really were better between them. I wanted to be happy for them, for Mom. But I was...was what? Was I *jealous?*

"Here you are, Allie." She smiled, handing me her keys.

I took the keys and set them on the counter. "I'll turn everything off and be right behind you." They both nodded and left.

I shut down the computer, poked around the office straightening brochures, and emptied the trash, then flipped off the lights. I was locking the door when I saw Levi.

"Hey, Allie." He pulled his massive Blazer into the parking lot. What was it with big vehicles, anyway? Lindie would say the bigger the car, the smaller his— "How're you doing?" he asked.

Code for: You still crazy? "I'm fine. How are you?" I asked.

"I'm great. Any plans for this weekend?" he asked, leaning out of his truck window.

"Well, I—"

"A bunch of us are going to float down the Medina, before it gets too shallow and all." He waited.

"I'm not sure. I might be working."

"You don't think you can get your boss to give you the day off?" He bobbed his eyebrows up and down playfully.

I unlocked Mom's car and opened the door. "You're trying to get me into a bathing suit, aren't you?"

"Hell, yeah." He nodded. "I mean, I want to go out with you. But the bathing suit is all good too, not gonna lie."

I smiled. "I'll let you know."

"You better." He winked, then revved his engine, peeling out of the parking lot.

"What a tool," I murmured as I climbed into the car.

I sat there, double checking the mirrors and adjusting my seatbelt, before I ever started the engine. Once I'd pulled out of the parking lot I was Super Citizen, following all the signs and lights, going the exact speed limit. I wasn't exactly nervous—I loved driving and feeling free and independent—but I wasn't exactly used to it anymore.

By the time I pulled onto the gravel road I'd relaxed enough to turn on the music, blasting it a little. Dad and Wyatt were up on the scaffold. Dax was doing something on the ground, and Mom was nowhere to be seen.

"Looks great," I said as I got out, admiring their work.

Wyatt wiped his face on a bandana, giving me time to run inside before I had to make eye contact with him. Avoiding eye contact was key with us. Once I was lost in his sweet honey gaze, I was done for.

"Allie," my mom called me from the kitchen when I came in. "I wanted to ask you something."

I leaned against the counter. "Shoot."

"Your father and I...well, Saturday is our twentieth wedding anniversary." She paused.

"Oh, shit, Mom. I totally forgot."

"You don't need to apologize for anything. A wedding anniversary is really for the couple. Anyway, I was wondering if you felt comfortable enough being here, you and Dax, while your Dad and I went into San Antonio for an overnight? Maybe even the weekend?"

I blinked. "Did... Have you..." I swallowed. "Dad's good with this?"

Her smile stiffened a little. She knew what I was asking. *Does Dad trust me?*

She nodded. "He is."

"We'll be fine." I smiled, playing with her keys. "So…" I shook my head.

"What?" she asked.

"You and Dad…" I shrugged, uncomfortable. "You guys seem to be…doing well."

She nodded, her cheeks coloring. "I know your father and I have had some ups and downs, but—"

That's putting it mildly.

"We're in a good place," she finished.

"Well…good. Go, enjoy San Antonio. Dax and I won't burn the place down. He'll probably be trailing after Molly the whole time and I'll…I'll paint my room." I'd been meaning to do it since we moved in.

Her brows rose. "Really? That sounds like a great idea. Make a list of what you want and Dad can make sure it's all here before we leave."

I nodded. "Okay." I had no idea what I would do—but it might be okay. Distracting, at the very least. Distracting from… "Mom?" She looked at me. "I know this might sound mean, but… Well, is there a way Wyatt can have the weekend off?" I asked. "I feel bad about him being here all the time and—"

"He and Hank have some rodeo or something this weekend. He'll be leaving in the morning. I know how you feel, he's such a hard worker."

Wyatt would be gone all weekend? I hadn't gone forty-eight hours without Wyatt since we'd moved here.

"Good," I said. "Good," I repeated, trying to sound like I meant it.

She opened the refrigerator, poked through it, then frowned. "I'm too tired to cook tonight."

"I'll do it," I offered. "I'll make…something."

She stared at me. "Are you sure?"

I sighed. "I *can* cook, ya know. Which is good since you

guys are leaving us alone for the weekend, remember?"
She frowned. "Mom, I'm messing with you. Go…take a
shower or relax…or something."

Once she'd left the room, I stared around the kitchen.
Grandma used to make the best fried chicken in the
known universe. We'd been certain to make notes so I'd
remember her tricks—with the warning that they were all
"secret family recipes kept in our family." When she'd said
it, it was like it was *our* secret. And since she was magic in
the kitchen, I'd felt special that she'd entrusted me with
something so important. *Important to a ten-year-old.* I pulled
the secret notebook from the cupboard—not exactly
hidden—and flipped through the pages.

Grandma had been one of those people who made
everything seem effortless. Kind of like Wyatt…

I scanned my big-lettered, loopy notes mixed with
Grandma's perfect script. Fried chicken sounded like a
good possibility. I opened the fridge to make sure we had
everything and got to work.

I cleaned some ears of corn and put them in the large
pot to boil then started pounding out the chicken. "Soak it
in buttermilk for at least thirty minutes," Grandma always
said. Yes. We actually had buttermilk. Go figure.

After the chicken was pounded and skinned, I covered
it in a baking dish and placed it back in the refrigerator. I
turned on the radio, making do with the only station we
could get—country. Thirty minutes to kill…

I made ice tea. And mashed potatoes. Snapped beans.
Then fried the chicken until it was golden brown.
Grandma would be proud. We had some fresh peaches left
so I attempted to put some sort of peach cobbler together,
but the crust was a little too doughy. I hoped I could cover
it with ice cream.

I'd just finished setting the table when I heard someone
clear their throat. Mom. Dad. Dax. Wyatt. They all stood
in the kitchen doorway, wearing various expressions. Mom
was amused. Dad looked surprised—which wasn't

surprising. Dax was impressed. Wyatt was…didn't matter.

"Hungry?" I asked. "I kind of went overboard."

"It looks wonderful." Mom waved everyone in. "Need help with anything?"

I looked around the apocalyptic mess that was the kitchen counter and frowned. "No. It's all taken care of. And I will clean *all* of this up." There was cobbler dough on the floor. And flour.

"Looks great, Al." Dax sat, eyeing the table.

"Thanks," I said, washing my hands before pulling off the apron I'd used. It was covered too, with egg and flour and who knows what else.

"Sit, Wyatt, Allie made plenty," Dad said to Wyatt, who was still standing in the doorway—where I was trying not to notice him.

"I didn't know you were such a cook," Mom said.

"I didn't either." I shrugged. "I was standing at the window and I thought of Grandma. I remembered how she made her fried chicken. I remembered how many hours I'd spent in here helping her…" I shrugged again.

"She made you a little apron," my dad said. I looked at him. "It was red, like the one she wore," he added.

I nodded. "I remember."

His hazel eyes held mine. Dad… *Sometimes I wish I could be that little girl you adored again. And sometimes I wish you would love me now.*

I looked at my empty plate. An awkward silence fell.

"Pass the chicken," Dax said. "And the potatoes. And the corn. Where are the rolls?" I stared at him. Dax burst out laughing. "Kidding. You've got something right…there." He pointed to his eyebrow.

I threw a napkin at him, then wiped at my forehead. I held my breath as everyone took the first bite. It was one thing to make food that *looked* good, another thing for it to actually *taste* good. My food looked okay, nothing photo-worthy, that was for sure. But I had high hopes for the taste.

"Mmm." Wyatt nodded as he chewed.

"Wow." Dax took another bite.

"*I'm* never cooking fried chicken again," my mother said, patting my arm.

"Agreed," my dad said, not looking up from his plate.

It wasn't much. One little word, no inflection or double entendre, just one word of approval. I smiled, my stress easing a little. Things had been more bearable since my screaming session. I glanced at Wyatt, but he was fully invested in eating everything on his plate.

I hadn't caused any upheaval. I'd been behaving, contributing. I hadn't crashed the car. I'd made dinner. Mom and Dad were trusting us.

"I hate to eat and run," Wyatt said as he finished, "but Hank's going to be at my place with the trailer soon."

"Want some food for the road?" Mom asked.

I jumped up. "I'll get it."

"You don't have to—"

I cut Wyatt off and pulled out plastic containers. "It's no bother."

"Okay. That'd be…nice," Wyatt said.

"Where are you headed?" Dad asked.

"El Paso. There's a team roping qualifier."

No steer wrestling?

"No steer wrestling?" my mother echoed my question.

"No, ma'am." He smiled.

I felt an extra bounce in my step. No tackling two-thousand-pound animals with pointy horns.

"A group of us are riding up, ropers and barrel racers mostly."

Barrel racing? Girls? I slapped the potatoes into the container. He was riding with girls. And parents? Hopefully. I knew Hank had just graduated but that didn't make him an adult.

"You be careful," my mother said, standing and opening the refrigerator.

Why did I care if he was going with girls? He wasn't my

boyfriend. He could go hook up with anyone he wanted to. Like I could go float down the river with Levi if I wanted to. I didn't. But I could.

"Allie, did you make cobbler too?"

I popped the lid on the container a little harder than necessary. "Yep."

"Do we get some?" Dax asked.

"Sure." I put the plastic containers in a bag. "Help yourself." I turned, offering the bag to Wyatt without looking at him. Then I began washing dishes. Anything to distract myself from—

"Allie?" Wyatt cleared his throat. I looked at him. So did everyone in the kitchen. "Thanks for dinner."

His brown eyes were so intense, so gorgeous, so hopeful… I nodded.

"Thanks for feeding us," Wyatt said to my mother, holding up the bag. "And thank you for giving me a few days off. I'll make it up when—"

"Wyatt," Dad stopped him, "go have some *fun*."

I frowned at him. Really, Dad? Wait. He *should* have fun…

Wyatt saw the look on my face and turned, walking from the kitchen. "Bye." He looked back, a small smile on his face. I tried not to smile back. Tried—and failed.

His answering smile was huge.

I turned back to the dishes, scrubbing with a vengeance.

***

Twenty-four hours later I was standing in my room, surrounded by sheets of newspapers and rolls of tape.

With a hug from my mom and a look from my dad, the parents were off. Dax disappeared within an hour, yelling "Text me if you need me" over his shoulder. I'd been given my phone for the weekend, but now that I had it I couldn't think of a single person to call. I had twenty-eight messages from people back home, people I missed…but I didn't want to talk to any of them.

Three hours later, my room was a very pretty pale lavender. It was soothing. My ex-counselor would approve.

I went for a run, dodging two scorpions and one snake. Wyatt had said the lack of rain would make everything come out, looking for water. Needless to say, I cut my run short after the snake sighting. It wasn't even close, but it still freaked me out. And coming home to an empty house didn't help.

I spent another six hours painting the trim in my bedroom a bright white. At some point Dax stumbled in and went to bed. It was four in the morning when I finished. I took a shower and went to sleep on the couch downstairs since my room smelled like paint fumes.

I spent the next day sorting boxes. I had way too much stuff. I didn't need half of it. When the back of Mom's car was full, I headed into town to the local charity donation center. Once that was done, I stopped in at the clinic.

Mom texted to tell me they'd be back late tomorrow. I told her to have fun. I hoped they were having fun. I kind of liked the fact that they acted like they were married to each other now—like they more than tolerated each other.

I spent an hour chatting with the very cool weekend vet tech. I knew she had things under control but I was lonely. I ended up spending a few hours entering data, helped clean out a few cages, and bottle-fed an adorable litter of orphaned puppies.

It was getting late when I drove back to the house. Dax's truck was gone. The house was dark. And the clouds were flashing. Thunder rolled in the distance.

I took a few slow deep breaths. "I can do this." I ran from the car to the house, even though there was no sign of rain or lightning.

I turned on the TV, finding the news. "We're in for a long night of pretty powerful storms. If you don't have to go out, don't. We have a high risk of hail, so find covered parking. Get your flashlights and your candles ready."

I glanced out at Mom's car, then the old barn. No cover there. The sky rumbled. "Screw you," I shouted back. The thunder was louder now.

Just thunder. I spent a few hours flipping channels, tried to read a book…but the whole distracting myself thing wasn't working out too well. Anger took over. I don't know why I was angry. I just was. I threw the front door open and walked onto the porch.

"I'm not afraid!" I said it out loud. The thunder argued, rumbling loudly overhead. Followed by a lightning strike that cut across the sky. "Okay, I might be a *little* afraid," I said, sitting on the porch swing.

The rain poured in sheets, fast and thick. I sat on my hands, trying to get a grip on my terror. I couldn't let every storm send me over the edge.

Headlights came bouncing down the drive. Dax. No…Wyatt. He parked, then ran through the rain, up the steps onto the porch. I was frozen.

He shook his head, wiping the rain from his face, before he saw me. "Hey," he said.

"Hey."

"So…"

I looked at him.

"Sitting in the dark's cool," he said, sitting beside me on the swing.

I laughed, a tight, strange sound. Thunder shook the house and I squealed, pressing my lips together.

"Let it out," Wyatt said. "It's all good. Not like I haven't heard you scream before."

I looked at him, really looked at him. He had dark smudges under his eyes and needed a shave. "Good trip?" I asked. He shrugged. "Just get back?" He nodded. "You should get some sleep."

"Wanted to make sure you were okay." His voice was gravelly. "Parents still gone?"

"Yeah. You drove here from El Paso?"

"Ended up taking two cars—girls had too much stuff.

So, yeah, I drove. Straight through."

"And came here?"

He nodded.

I blew out a deep breath and stood up, looking down at him. He looked up at me, waiting. "I don't want to fall for you," I murmured.

"I know," he said.

I held my hand out to him. He looked at my hand, took it, and pushed himself to his feet. I pulled him inside after me, tossing pillows aside on the couch and pushing him down on it.

I let go of his hand and pulled the foot stool around. I tugged off his boots, tossing them over my shoulder, and propped his feet up. He smiled at me. "Thank you."

"Grandma said there was nothing Grandpa liked more than taking off his boots at the end of the day. She said it was the same way a woman—" I stopped.

"What?"

I shook my head.

He laughed. "Go on."

"The same way a woman felt about taking off her bra at the end of the day."

He kept laughing. "I can just hear her saying that, too."

I sat beside him. "You knew her?"

He nodded. "*Everyone* in Black Falls knew Maureen Cooper, Allie. She talked about you and Dax a lot."

I sighed. "I wish we'd made time to see her more often. I know we were busy, that there didn't seem to be time, but we should have *made* time, you know?"

"Yeah."

The house shook again, a crack of lightning ending all electricity. "That's your cue." I said.

I heard him yawn. "My cue?"

"Go to sleep," I murmured.

I felt his hand and took it, letting him pull me against him on the couch. I didn't resist. If anything I burrowed in a little…getting way too comfortable.

"You're okay?" he asked, yawning.

"I'm okay," I assured him, putting my hand over his heart. *I'm great—now.*

I knew Lindie was laughing right now.

And I was in serious trouble.

9 CHAPTER NINE

"Hungry?" Wyatt's voice was soft against my forehead.

"No." I sighed. "Sleeping here." I thought he kissed me, on the tip of my nose. "Am I dreaming?" I asked.

I heard him laugh. "Nope."

I opened my eyes. I was still on the sofa, under the blanket we'd shared. It was dark and raining, but the lights were back on. "What time is it?"

"About two in the morning," he said.

"Do you need to let your dad know you're here?"

His face tightened for a split second. "He's working right now."

"Oh." I pushed off the couch. "He works nights?"

"No." He shook his head. "He's on the road, trucking. He's home maybe once a month."

I froze just inside the kitchen. Wyatt was alone? His dad left him? I didn't know what the deal was with his mom, but she wasn't around, I knew that much.

"So no fried eggs?" he asked.

I shook my head. "Thanks, though." I looked out the window over the kitchen sink. The rain continued to pour, but the thunder and lightning had all but disappeared. "How did it go?" I asked him. "In El Paso?"

He shrugged. "Girls did well. Hank and I are on the fence."

"Meaning…?"

"We need to decide if we want to spend the money on entry fees or forget about Regionals."

I sat at the table. "What about the scholarships you were talking about?" I asked. "Any school in particular?"

"Texas A&M." He grinned. "No surprise there, right? They have a rodeo team, a real good one."

It made sense. He was a cowboy. He wanted to be a vet. Their vet school was the best in the state. Mom had graduated from there, met Dad there…

"It's a great school." I'd applied—because Mom and Dad made me—and because they had exactly the program I wanted. If Dad hadn't wanted me to go there, A&M would have beaten SMU for my top choice.

He brought his plate to the table and sat.

I jumped up and got out a glass. "Milk? Juice?"

"Dr. Pepper?" he asked.

I pulled out a can, filled a glass with ice, and set both on the table in front of him.

"Need to keep my options open," he said, taking a long drink.

"Options meaning scholarships or military?" He nodded. "I'd think rodeo's the safer route."

He arched an eyebrow at me. "Maybe. But it's tough on the body. And expensive."

"I guess…" I shrugged. Fine. I'd tried. If he wanted to keep risking his neck, that was his choice.

He finished eating and sat back in the chair, watching me—curious. His gaze never wavered from mine. His eyes were so dark. Intense. Staring. Searching.

I felt my cheeks warm. "Dax come home?" My voice was husky.

Wyatt's gaze drifted to my mouth. "Don't know."

I swallowed. Why wasn't I getting creeped out that he was looking at me like…that? Oh, right, because he wasn't a perv just trying to get into my pants. No, not Wyatt. He knew it was storming and I'd freak out, so he came straight here from driving all night to make sure I was okay. So he could sit here and stare at me until I was one throbbing tingling...

I took a deep breath. It didn't really help. My chest felt heavy. My throat was tight. I knew I was breathing a little faster than I should be, but I couldn't help it.

The muscle in his jaw clenched. His gaze wandered to my neck. He closed his eyes.

"I'll go check." I stood. "You...staying?" I asked, almost choking on the word.

He opened his eyes, a slight smile on his face. "Probably shouldn't."

God, he's such a nice *guy.* "You sure? It's...raining...and late." *And you'd be going home to an empty house, too.* "Just wait a minute."

I ran up the stairs and to Dax's room. Empty. I wasn't going to freak out or overreact. He was fine. I pulled out my phone, texting as I went back downstairs. *Where the hell are you?*

No response.

Still not freaking. I texted again: *Dax!?!*

"He's not here. And he's not answering my texts," I said to Wyatt as soon as I came back into the kitchen. I frowned, crossing my arms over my chest.

Wyatt pulled out his phone.

"You have a phone?" I asked.

"Never use it," he explained. "Emergencies only."

I nodded, taking his empty plate and rinsing it out in the sink.

"He's at Molly's place. Her parents made him stay over. Their drive washes out whenever it flash floods like this."

"He texted all that?" I asked. Dax was the world's slowest texter—he normally resorted to one-letter responses or bizarro shorthand.

"No, Molly did."

"Oh… It's nice how everyone looks out for everyone else," I said.

"I guess."

"She knows you're here…now?"

He nodded. "She doesn't gossip, if you're worried."

"Okay." I wasn't worried, not really. Not about Molly or Dax or anyone learning that Wyatt was here. I was worried that I was alone, with no fear of interruption or conscience, with a guy I was seriously interested in. A guy that made me understand why girls got so weird when they liked a boy.

So, fine, okay, I like him… Shit.

I loaded the plate into the dishwasher and turned. Wyatt was sitting there, eyes closed, jaw locked, hands clenching his empty glass. If he hadn't been so tense, I'd have thought he was asleep.

"Wyatt?"

"I don't feel right leaving you here alone." His voice had an edge to it.

I paused, trying to think of the right words. "I'm not your problem."

He smiled, his brows going up. "You're nobody's *problem.*"

"My parents would argue with that, but that's not what I meant and you know—"

He stood up suddenly. "You're not my *problem.*" He crossed to me. "But…Allie, I want you to be."

I really like the sound of that. Which hurt. *I'm the last thing you need.*

As hard as it was to breathe, I managed to argue. "No, you really don't." I sidestepped him, needing distance to keep fighting. "I'm one of those damaged goods on the quick-sale table at the grocery store. Pretty packaging makes you curious, interested, but then you get it home and open it up and realize you wasted your time and money on trash." I walked out of the kitchen as I spoke. More distance.

His hand caught my arm. "Jesus, Allie, that's harsh."

I very carefully pulled my arm out of his hold. "Sometimes the truth is. My best friend taught me that."

He stood there. "Lindie?"

I glanced at him. "Dax talks a lot."

"I asked him."

I let myself look at him then. "You could have asked me."

"You'd have told me?"

I shrugged. "What did Dax tell you?"

"You were in a car crash. Lindie and another boy were killed. You survived."

"That's it?" I asked. "When you say it like that, it doesn't sound like such a big deal."

"But it was," he said.

I fixed the couch, putting things back together to give myself something to do.

"You think it was your fault?" he asked.

All the air went out of my lungs, so I sat, hard, on the edge of the couch. He sat beside me, his gaze unrelenting. "I *know* it was my fault."

He shook his head. His brows creased and he started to say something so I cut him off.

"It's easier this way." I shrugged, my throat constricting. "I can't lose anyone else, Wyatt. I *can't* do it."

His hand cupped my cheek. "Oh, Allie—" His voice broke. "Losing people...*sucks*." His voice was hard and fierce, his forehead resting against mine. "But not having anyone to lose—being alone—is worse."

There was pain in his voice. Anguish, real and raw. He was alone. All alone. His dad was gone. His mother was God only knew where. And, somehow, the first thing he thought of when the storm started was me—being here for me.

My heart twisted. He was offering me everything I wanted but didn't deserve.

His other hand came up, cradling my face, tilting my

face to his. His breath was warm on my cheek, my lips.

"Wyatt... I can't, Wyatt." I felt the tears welling up in my eyes and yanked out of his hold. I stood up, gasping for air, trying to break the connection that we had. "I'm going to bed. You can stay. Or you can go home. I'm f-fine. I am."

I ran up the stairs to my room, and didn't look back.

***

He was sound asleep on the couch when I snuck from the house for my morning run. It was wet and the ground was slick, but I wasn't going to let it stop me. I needed to run.

I went down twice in the clay-like mud sucking at my running shoes, but got back up and kept going. The last time I fell, I hit hard, landing on a bed of rocks. A few rocks shifted, rolling under my chin.

The white-hot needle of pain was instantaneous, catching me by surprise. My neck was on fire. Then my cheek. I reached up, pressing my hand over my neck, then my cheek. A scorpion fell onto my hand, stinging my hand and wrist before I managed to fling it to the ground.

I stood up quickly. "Shit!" I slipped but kept going, too terrified I'd find that nasty little rat-bastard again. And, seriously, I was starting to hurt.

By the time I got back to the house I wasn't feeling very well. The stings were throbbing. My head felt like it was being squeezed. I sat on the front porch steps, gasping for air. I tugged off my shoes and shirt, hoping air would make me feel cooler or at least less constricted. Didn't work. My tongue was feeling thick.

"Shit." I stood, leaning against the porch railing to get my bearings. The door seemed very far away... I started walking, getting heavier and hotter and more breathless with each step.

Wyatt's truck was still here. I pushed open the door. "Wyatt," I wheezed. "Wyatt!"

Wyatt popped up from the couch, bleary-eyed. "Allie?"

I slid down the door frame. "Scorpion. Think I'm allergic."

He jumped over the back of the couch, picked me up, and headed toward his truck.

"Shoes? Sh-sh-shirt?" My tongue was swelling.

"Don't need 'em," he said, opening the door while balancing me.

"Need…" I shook my head. "Benadryl."

"I'll get it." He ran back inside and came back—with Benadryl and boots but no shirt.

Five minutes later we were on the road to the nearest emergency clinic…ten miles to go.

"You sure you took two of them?" Wyatt asked for the fourth time.

I nodded, my breathing loud in the cab.

"How do you feel? What can I do?" he asked.

I listed into him, shivering a little. He pulled me close, making me warmer in an instant.

My phone rang but I let Wyatt answer. "Dax? Wyatt. Call your folks. Allie got stung by a scorpion…a few times. Allergic…headed to the ER… Molly can tell you."

I must have fallen asleep against his shoulder. Next thing I knew I was waking up in a hospital bed feeling fine. Well, almost fine. I definitely felt like I'd been stung by a scorpion on the neck, cheek, and arm.

"Hey," I said to Dax and Wyatt.

Wyatt had his hands covering his face. When I spoke, he looked up. He was so freaking happy and reassured, I smiled, forcing my attention to Dax, who was watching the two of us with a self-satisfied grin.

"You just *have* to be the center of attention," he said.

"Screw you," I said, and sucked in a deep breath. "I can breathe."

Wyatt's voice was amused. "That's a good thing."

"A definite improvement. Nothing like seeing your sister passed out, put on oxygen, and getting some big-ass shot to liven things up."

I smiled. "I try."

"Folks are on the way," Dax said. "Heads up."

"Great." I frowned.

"Allie, it'll be okay," Dax assured me.

"Says the golden child," I replied, without bite.

"They'll be relieved." Wyatt's voice was troubled.

"Maybe," I mumbled.

"Allie…" Dax shook his head. "Come on."

I held up my hand. "Okay, that was a low blow, but—"

"I know they're hard on you," Dax admitted. "Dad's hard on you."

It took everything I had not to cry. I wanted to cry. I nodded, but decided changing the subject might be the best thing to do at this point. "So how long have we been here?" I asked.

"Half an hour maybe." Wyatt shrugged. "We walked in, they gave you a shot, you started breathing. Once you were breathing, everyone calmed down. I know I did." He stood up, pacing the room.

"I stopped breathing?" I asked.

"Yeah. Almost. You were pretty grey…" His voice was rough.

"Man." Dax stood up. "Thank you. Seriously. You saved her life."

Wyatt's eyes fixed on my feet, his face hard, the muscle in his jaw flexing and unflexing. I remembered his face, the unfiltered fear, when he'd picked me up. I thought he'd talked to me, saying my name over and over, on the way here, but that was a little foggy. I thought he might have said a few things a boy had never said to me before, but there was no way I could be sure of it. I knew he cared about me, he'd told me as much. He cared about me and he'd cared for me—over and over again.

"Yes. Thank you," I said, aware that my voice was soft and wobbly and not caring in the least.

"Allie…" Wyatt shook his head, running a hand over his face. He paused, then reached out and held my toes

124

through the sheet. He was warm, but his fingers were shaking.

"Be right back." Dax all but ran out of the partitioned room.

"Wyatt?" I wanted to reach out to him. I wanted him to hold me close. His eyes bore into mine, haunted and exhausted and so damn gorgeous. What could I say to make him feel better? To thank him. "I'm sorry—"

He shook his head. "Uh-uh. You don't get to own a scorpion bite. Or an allergic reaction. This could have happened to anyone, so you can't blame yourself. Got it?"

How did he know? "But—"

"But nothing. I've lived here my whole life, been stung more times that I can remember. Hell yes, it hurt more than a fire ant, but I didn't stop breathing." The last few words were so anguished I held my hand out.

"I'm breathing," I murmured.

He took my hand, holding it in both of his. His warm brown gaze never left my face.

"Because of you."

He didn't say anything, but his face...his eyes...his posture said a lot. He was holding back, everything about him was rigid—on edge. The crease on his forehead deepened, killing me. Finally, he reached down, to touch me, but stopped.

My heart lodged itself in my throat. I don't know what I wanted, but not this—not Wyatt all stressed out and tense and worried. "Wyatt..."

He blinked, releasing my hand and stepping back. He looked...uncertain, guilty. *Dammit.* He...he was amazing.

"The doc is talking to your parents on the phone now. I think you'll be going home soon," he said.

"And you can get some sleep. And find some clothes," I said, trying to tease, to ease the tension hanging between us.

"I don't look good?" he asked, staring down at the blue hospital scrub top.

"Um…" I shrugged. *You'd look good in anything.* "Not the way I'm used to seeing you, I guess." *I prefer you all virile cowboy, shirtless and a little bit sweaty.*

Dax came in, eyeing the two of us. He sighed and handed me a cup. "Drink this."

"What is it?"

"Just water," he said with a laugh. "You're supposed to be drinking lots of water."

I emptied the cup, loving the cold all the way down. "Oh, thank you." I finished, handing him the cup.

"More?" he asked.

"Allie?" My mother was crying as she joined us behind the fabric partition in the ER.

"Mom, I'm okay," I assured her, even as she wrapped me in a tight embrace and sobbed. "I'm not a fan of scorpions, but I'm fine."

She laughed. "We'll have pest control come out."

"I was out running. I don't think it's economical to have all…how many acres is it, Dad?" I asked.

"A lot," my father answered.

"Right. It happens. Wyatt said he's been tagged lots of times."

"Too many to count," Wyatt agreed.

"They're everywhere, June," Dad said to my mother. "Now we know she's allergic, we can be prepared if she gets stung again."

My mother's grip relaxed a little. "I'm so sorry we weren't here."

"Mom." I pulled back. "Chill. You and Dad should do…what married people do. Being here wouldn't have changed what happened."

She smiled, touching my cheek. "When did you get so smart?"

"She got it from me," Dax answered. "It's been a slow learning process, let me tell you."

I ignored my brother. "Wyatt's the hero. He got me here."

I saw his face turn red, then a pale white, staring hard at the floor.

"Sounds like a rough time." My father looked at Wyatt. "You okay, son?"

It didn't bother me when Dad called him "son." I'm not sure why. Maybe it was because I knew Wyatt was on his own. Or that it was obvious Dad truly liked Wyatt. Or that I cared for Wyatt. A lot. Too much. But I wanted him to have...affection. And attention. He deserved it.

"Not gonna lie, sir." Wyatt smiled a little. "It shook me up."

My mom stood up, hugging Wyatt tightly. He hugged her back. I saw the way his hands fisted against her back, saw the way he hid his face against her shoulder. And felt my heart swell.

I love you, Wyatt.

Oh God. I do. I love him. Dammit. I love you.

"Can we get out of here?" Dax asked. "I know Wyatt's not a fan of hospitals either."

Wyatt straightened, looking a little less anguished, but my mom hooked her arm with his as she spoke. "Yes. Allie needs to eat something. Peggy's?"

Dad nodded. "Sounds good."

"Sorry I'm not up for cooking right now," I said, sitting up and swinging my legs out of the bed. Wyatt's grin made my pulse pick up. Without thinking, I smiled right back.

I love you.

This could be a problem.

"Need help?" my dad asked, turning to me.

Wait. He was looking at me. Really looking at me— making actual eye contact.

"I'm...I'm good," I managed. "Thanks."

He smiled a little, and nodded. "You're tough stuff, kid."

I've had to be.

I tried to muster up attitude and anger, but I was too tired. I was just happy to be here, breathing, with my family. And Wyatt…who was, really, part of the family at this point. To me, he was definitely someone special.

"I don't have shoes." I noticed my feet were bare, mud still covering my ankles.

"I have some flip-flops in the car," Mom said.

I nodded. "Give me a sec to clean up a little."

Mom coerced a few towels out of one of the orderlies and I spent a good ten minutes scrubbing as much mud off of my legs and neck and face as possible. It had dried but it stuck like glue, grey and tacky.

"This is really gross."

Mom handed me a bag. "My workout clothes. They'll be too big for you, but at least they're clean and dry."

"Thanks." I tossed the towel in the sink and opened the bag. "I'm still all crunchy."

Once I was dressed, Mom leaned closer. "Hurt?" she asked, eyeing the bites on my neck and cheek.

I nodded. "They each have a heartbeat. And they feel hot."

She winced. "Food. Then bed."

"I'm fine," I argued. "I actually feel pretty good."

"Because you're pumped up on epinephrine. I'm kind of expecting you to crash and feel sick within an hour."

"Great." I sighed, shoving my dirty clothes into the bag. "Can't wait." She laughed, holding the door open for me.

Dad was on his phone when we came out. So was Dax. Wyatt was leaning against the wall, his eyes closed. And my heart picked up.

"Mom," I whispered softly, "Wyatt needs sleep. He drove in late last night—"

"Drove in where?" She tried to act casual but I knew what she was asking.

"To our place. It was storming. Dax was stuck at Molly's house so Wyatt came straight over because—"

"Because he knows you're not a fan of storms?"

I nodded. "He's exhausted."

She paused, whispering, "He won't go. Your dad already tried. But I don't feel good about him driving."

He won't go? Because of me. I was so…confused.

She spoke up. "Dax, will you drive Wyatt and Allie to the house? Dad and I will pick up some food and follow you."

"I'm fine, Dr. Cooper—"

"Wyatt, please do this for me. I don't want your falling asleep at the wheel on my conscience, please. Once you have some food in your belly and a nice, long nap, Dax can bring you back here for your truck."

"Unless we're interrupting your plans?" I asked Dax, thinking of Molly.

"Cut me some slack, Al. I did get here in time to see you, blue and unresponsive. I kind of want to hang out, you know, watch you breathe and stuff for a while. Okay?"

I smiled. "Okay."

We were walking out of the hospital when Levi showed up. He jumped out of his truck, looking sincerely worried. "Allie, honey, you okay?"

"How did you know?" I asked.

"My aunt's a nurse here. She knows I'm sweet on you." Levi winked. "But don't tell on her, she'd get fired for telling me."

"Oh?" I paused. "I won't." We kept walking to Dax's blue truck. It wasn't jacked up, with huge tires or fancy metal grillwork—it was just a truck, like Wyatt's.

"Ouch," Levi said, inspecting my stings.

"You could say that." I grimaced.

Levi opened the passenger door for me. "What do you need?"

"I'm taking her home," Dax said.

"I can drive you," Levi offered.

"She's covered. I'm already sort of going that way, man." Dax tried not to sound impatient.

"Okay." Levi nodded. "If you didn't *want* to go tubing on the river, all you had to do was say no. You didn't have to go and get yourself stung."

I had to laugh. "You're hilarious." He smiled.

"It's sweet of you to come check on her, Levi," Mom said. "We need to get her home. Come on, Allie." I nodded, climbing into the truck and sliding to the middle.

"Yes, ma'am. Some R and R is just what she needs," Levi said. "If I can help, let me know. And Mr. Cooper, sir, I'd be glad to lend a hand at your place."

My dad looked surprised. I knew he wouldn't turn him down; there was still a lot to get done. "I'd appreciate that, Levi. If you're free Tuesday, I can put you to work."

Tuesday? Wasn't today Sunday? My head felt fuzzy.

"I'll be there." Levi started to close the door, but Wyatt caught it.

"Hold up," Wyatt said.

"Your truck break down?" Levi asked, a definite edge to his tone.

"Nope," Wyatt said, sliding onto the bench seat beside me.

For the first time, I glanced at Wyatt. It was hard to miss the tension. Levi's jaw bulged while Wyatt's nostrils flared. Great.

Dax started the truck. "See you later," he said.

Wyatt pulled the door shut, making the frown on Levi's face turn ugly.

"Looks like Tuesday will be interesting," Dax groaned.

I smacked him on the shoulder. "You okay?" I asked Wyatt.

Wyatt's smile was tired, drained, but at least he was still smiling. "You're asking *me*?" He nodded. "I'm good."

"You're so full of shit," Dax murmured.

Wyatt laughed. I sighed, resting my head on the back of the seat. "Are *you* okay?" Wyatt asked.

I turned my head, still resting it on the back of the seat. Heavy-lidded brown eyes were waiting for me. Seriously, I could look at him all day. A heavy stubble covered his jaw. I saw the muscle tighten there, clench, and looked up into his bloodshot eyes. He was watching me…and he looked so freaking gorgeous I didn't bother pretending I wasn't admiring him. He pressed his eyes closed, taking a deep breath.

"Comfortable?" Dax asked me.

I nodded, but didn't look away from Wyatt. When he opened his eyes, I arched a brow. He shook his head, a small smile pulling at the corners of his mouth. I smiled back.

Dax took the corner hard, sliding me into Wyatt—who caught me, his arm steadying me against him. *Perfect.*

"Deer," Dax murmured.

Whatever. Possible, but not likely. All that mattered was I ended up exactly where I wanted to be, burrowed into Wyatt's side.

He held me close for a minute, relaxing his hold enough to slide his hand up my back, under my hair. I shivered. His hand rested lightly on the back of my neck, warm, intimate, tingle-inducing. He pressed my head to his chest, slouching against the seat enough that we were both comfortable. I was, at least.

I lay there, watching the scrub top he wore beat in time to his heartbeat. His breathing slowed, his hand sliding down to rest at the base of my spine. I was strangely relaxed but totally aware of his every twitch.

The drive home was nice, but not long enough. Not nearly long enough.

10 CHAPTER TEN

"We're here," Dax announced unnecessarily.

I sat up and Wyatt opened the truck door. He held it open, standing back for me. I climbed out after him, walking between the two of them up the steps and into the house.

"Recliner," Dax commanded. "I'll get you some water. Chill."

Wyatt handed me the remote control.

"Whoa, whoa, whoa." Dax shook his head. "You can't just hand over the power like that. I know she's wounded and all, but she might put on some chick-flick or something."

I laughed, turning on the TV, and searching until I found a soccer game. Dax sighed. "Could be worse," I said. Dax rolled his eyes and headed for the kitchen while Wyatt stood there. "Sit." I pointed at the couch. "Before you fall."

He flopped onto the couch, listing to the side. I really wished I was there on the couch with him. My hand fisted around the remote. Yes, I'd used him as a human pillow on the way home, but that didn't mean anything...as long as I didn't act like it meant anything. I mean, I'd have flopped on Dax if he hadn't been driving, right? Sure.

So treat Wyatt like Dax... I swallowed. Was I really going to try to convince myself that Wyatt was anything like Dax? That the feelings I had for my brother were anything like what I had for Wyatt? I mean, I guess they sort of were. I loved them both.

I glanced at him, and he looked at me. "You okay?" he asked. I nodded. His gaze turned heavy and intense. "Allie..." He sat forward. "I'm sorry—"

Mom and Dad arrived just then, breaking the tension in the room and dragging Wyatt into the kitchen with them. While everyone ate in the kitchen, I was banished to the recliner—giving me plenty of time to wonder what the hell Wyatt was sorry for. I was the one who kept throwing herself at him before telling him I wasn't interested.

Mom tucked a blanket over my lap. "You might get a chill."

"A chill?" I shook my head, my argument only half-hearted. "It's like a hundred and three degrees!"

"Outside, yes," she countered. "So hush. Eat."

I sighed, but smiled. "Yes, ma'am."

I was feeling rotten, both physically and emotionally, and the burger held about as much interest as taking a chemistry test. I hated chemistry.

Mom was right. I was going to crash soon, I could feel it. I was feeling all sorts of new things today and not all of it was good. Scorpions, bad. Falling in love...not so sure. But now that I knew how I felt, I sort of needed to decide what to do about it. *If* I was going to do anything about it. *I guess I could keep pretending I don't feel anything for him. I could try to ignore him.*

I felt sick.

"You look a little green around the gills," Dad commented as he sat on the couch. I grunted in response.

"Need anything?" Mom asked.

"Water?"

Wyatt came out of the kitchen carrying a tall glass of ice

water. He put the glass on the marble-top table beside the recliner.

I smiled at him. "Thanks."

He nodded, his gaze traveling over my face. He sucked in a deep breath. "Well, I've got to get home. Hank'll be there with the trailer soon."

"Dax and I will come." Dad stood. "Then we'll go get your truck."

"Take care of yourself," he murmured softly to me.

"O-okay…I will," I promised, tongue-tied and flustered like an idiot.

He smiled at me, a small smile, looking sweet and concerned and…I took a deep breath and stared at the remote in my hands. When I looked back, he was gone.

***

Wyatt didn't come over on Monday. I spent most of the day with my parents hovering over me. If they weren't doing it, Molly and Dax were.

The perk to Molly and Dax—Molly had a lot to teach me. I knew rodeo was a big part of Wyatt's life. I also knew that I knew next to nothing about it. But Molly was…from his world, so I'd soak up every little thing she wanted to share. I tried to be discreet about it, flipping channels until—surprise!—I found a rodeo event on one of the sports channels.

Three hours later my head and heart hurt. Wyatt was shooting for all-around champion and big scholarship bucks. If I thought steer wrestling was hard to watch, I didn't know how I was going to make it when he was bull riding.

"Wyatt's really good," Molly said for the hundredth time.

I guess my reactions to grown men being thrown twenty feet in the air, stomped on, or hobbling out of the arena weren't so discreet after all. "He…he does *this?*" I asked as the TV showed an especially horrific slow-motion shot of a cowboy getting tossed by the bull's horns into the wall.

"Since he was fourteen," Molly said.

"Fourteen?" Dax asked, letting out a low whistle. "And I thought football was tough."

"You played football?" she asked, turning to Dax.

"No." He shook his head. "I'm not a jock."

I watched the huge smile on her face. "I'm glad."

I turned my attention back to the TV since *my brother was going in for a kiss...*

It was official. This was definitely a parallel universe. My brother was making out while I was sitting in a recliner under a nappy-ass felt blanket, with red welts on my neck and face, getting all hot and bothered over a cowboy. I sighed.

I went to bed early, the big dose of Benadryl helping me sleep the night through.

I woke up to one of my favorite sounds in the world.

Thump.

I lay there, smiling at the ceiling.

Thump.

My heart was going three times as fast.

Thump.

I rolled over, peering out the window.

Thump.

Dax. Dad. Levi...*Doesn't matter.*

Thump.

Wyatt. His shirt was still on...but I didn't mind. I sighed in contentment.

I took a shower—the red was almost completely gone from the stings—and made my way downstairs. Mom had left me a note, giving me the day off from the clinic. I should have been happy, but instead I felt like I was letting her down. Of course, she had staff now; she wasn't alone, and the place was starting to come together.

"How are you this morning?" Dax asked, leaning in the back door.

"Okay," I said, filling a plastic glass with water. "What's

on the schedule for today?"

He shook his head. "You're holding down the couch."

"I'm *fine*," I argued.

"Dad said you're not to do anything. Mom tried to tell him you could go in with her, but he vetoed it."

I frowned out the window at my father. "Why?"

"Um, maybe because you almost died—*again*—on Sunday?" He realized he'd made a mistake as soon as he'd said it. I saw it on his face, the way his smile dimmed and he shook his head as he said, "Dammit, Allie, I'm sorry."

I knew he was sorry. It was a slip. Exactly what I needed.

There is something seriously wrong with me.

It had been four months and I was moving on. Four months since my best friend died and my life went to hell. *Four months makes everything okay?* No. No. Everything was *not* okay. I shook my head, my hands fisting at my sides, my chest heavy. *God, I'm a horrible, selfish, shallow person.* I was...falling in love. I swallowed, hard.

And Lindie was stuck in a box under a couple of feet of dirt.

"Allie?" Dax walked inside, letting the screen door slam behind him. "Don't shut down."

I shot him a look. "I'm going for a run."

"You should rest," he argued, frowning.

"Why? I'm fine."

"You're not—"

"Shut *up*, will you?" I snapped.

He did, for a moment. "Allie..." I saw him flounder. "Can you...can you wait a minute? I kind of need...some advice..."

I sighed. "Advice? From me? Please."

He frowned. "Will you just listen for a minute? Or are you too invested in transforming into your angry self-absorbed witch alter ego—"

I couldn't help it, my mouth fell open. "Dax..."

"It's Molly. I need help with Molly."

137

That took some of the sting out of his words. I knew how crazy he was over her and, judging from his red cheeks and how uncomfortable he looked, maybe he wasn't just trying to distract me from losing it—again. "I'm listening."

"Well..." He cleared his throat, glancing out the back door. "I...We...I keep messing things up."

"Things?" Did I really want to know? *No sex talks, please, no sex talks.*

"I...I keep..." He paused, closing his eyes. "I'm freezing up, when I want to...kiss her." He sounded so frustrated I couldn't help but smile.

Relief. Kiss. Fine. Crisis averted. "But...I saw you, the other day. You totally went in for the kiss."

"And ended up planting one on her cheek." He groaned. "Her *cheek*."

I smiled, trying not to laugh. "Why?"

He looked at me like I had two heads. "I have no idea. *Obviously.* That's why I'm asking you."

Dax had no idea that my romantic explorations were just as limited as his. It wasn't for lack of opportunities, just lack of interest. Maybe it was because I'd known all the guys since we were in diapers practically, or that most of the boys I knew were interested in conquests, not me.

Lindie had said I was too picky. Maybe so. But my focus had always been on the game and competition. Some girls might lump boys into their competitive arena, but to me, boys, dating, and relationships meant distractions.

"You *want* to kiss her?" I clarified. "I mean, you're not having second thoughts?"

"No second thoughts." He frowned. "She's all I think about. Kissing her would be...nice."

I didn't know what to say. I knew I needed to say something. He was really upset. "So you want me to tell you what, exactly?" I asked.

"How to, I don't know, follow through." He shrugged. "I get close to her and panic. I feel all weird when she's

138

around, you know? And then I worry I'm not going to be a good enough kisser or my breath isn't fresh enough or I'll smother her or—"

I couldn't help it, I was laughing. He frowned. "Dax, come on." I shook my head. "She likes you. She clearly wants to be kissed. It's like I told her about roping. Get out of your head and do it."

"I think this is a little different."

"I don't."

"That's your advice?" His brows rose. "Do it? We're not talking about a shoe commercial here."

I was laughing too hard to argue.

"Seriously? Allie, come on. There has to be a...a move." He shifted from one foot to the other, then back again. "Or something."

"No moves here," I finally managed. I didn't really know why I said, "Why not talk to Wyatt?"

Dax glanced out the screen door.

"I guess. I mean, maybe not. He doesn't strike me as the kiss and tell sort," I continued.

Dax shot a wicked grin my way. "You tell me."

I threw a kitchen towel at him. "We haven't—"

"I know."

That stopped me cold. "What do you mean, you know?" Had Wyatt been talking to Dax? About *me*? Was this a good thing? Or did it bother me? Maybe a little... But more than anything I wanted to know what he'd said.

"The way you are around each other—crazy, tense, and nervous. Him looking at you...you looking at him...neither one of you seeing the other one doing the looking. One of you better make a move soon or—" He stopped, shrugging.

I glanced out the window at Wyatt, who was still doggedly hammering a fence post into the ground. "Or what?"

"I don't know. I can only speak for him. He'll explode, maybe." I shot Dax a glare. "Would it be so bad?" he asked, pouring himself a glass of water.

"To explode?" I asked.

"No, smart ass, to admit you *like* Wyatt."

I paused. "I guess…I feel…" I swallowed. *Yes, it would be that bad because*— "I think about Lindie, you know?"

Dax didn't move. I'm not sure he was breathing.

"Having this conversation… Checking out Wyatt…*boys*," I tried to correct myself. "She—"

"Would be laughing her ass off right now." Dax set his cup down on the counter.

I smiled at him. He was right. "I know."

"She'd give *me* shit for asking you about kissing. And *you* shit for falling for a cowboy."

"I have not—"

"Spare me, Al." He leaned against the counter.

"Whatever."

"I can't say I know how you feel, losing Lindie, okay? I don't want to know, honestly. But she was part of the family since you started kindergarten together, so give me a little credit for knowing her, okay? And missing her, too."

I looked at him, not saying a thing. I couldn't say a thing, my throat was too tight.

He took a deep breath. "She was anti-wallowing. All about defeating the opposition and strategies and overcoming obstacles. I'm not just talking about her take on soccer, you know?"

I *was* wallowing. I didn't want to admit it, but I was. He was right. She'd totally be kicking my ass right now. I sighed.

"Don't sigh at me," he snapped. "You know where I'm going with this."

He didn't get that I wasn't sighing at him, but I nodded. I did know where he was going with this.

"So stop it," he finished.

"Stop it?" I was too startled to snap back.

He shrugged. "Stop…stop being angry."

"And *I* give bad advice?" I shook my head. "Talk about an anti-climactic ending." I snorted. "I'm going for a run."

"Dad wants you to rest."

"Good for him." I managed to snap that time. Somehow knowing Dad wanted me to rest only made me want to run more.

"You are so...so...*Dammit.*"

I smiled at him, waiting. Dax rarely blew his cool.

He shook his head. "Why bother? Right? You're going to do whatever you want. You always do." He opened his mouth, then closed it, then opened it again. "In one year we'll be gone. *One* year. I'd consider it a personal favor if you tried, just a little, to make it suck less."

He left the kitchen, a garbled sound of frustration hanging in the air.

Suck less. Not be nice or behave. Just suck *less*...

Was that too much to ask? Really? Dax was the only person I had left. My parents had me firmly boxed in the ticking-time-bomb category. I didn't have any friends anymore, except for Lindie's mom, Mrs. Duncan—and I knew that wasn't exactly a healthy relationship. But I couldn't be mean to her, I couldn't shut her out. I'd killed her only child. I kind of owed it to her to be there for her.

And Wyatt? No way I'd let Wyatt in. What was the point? I'd only screw it up. He didn't deserve someone like me—a flake determined to get out of here graduation day. We'd all be leaving then. But Dax...he was my brother forever. Was he really asking too much?

You're such a bitch. I could hear Lindie teasing. She always called me a bitch. And I called her a "ho." We were such screw-ups. I sighed, slamming my cup on the counter.

Being a bitch isn't fun or funny anymore.

"Morning." Levi was all smiles, peeking into the kitchen. "Thought I saw your pretty little head in the window."

I tried for a smile and almost made it. "Hi."

"How are you feeling?"

"Better, thanks."

"Good enough to go tubing this weekend?"

"Still determined to get me into a bikini?"

"Bikini, huh?" His grin grew. "Hell yes."

I laughed. "I don't know. My dad's in watchdog mode right now, so…" I didn't finish.

"Of course he is," Levi agreed, coming into the kitchen. "You're his baby girl."

He was red and sweaty. And cute. So why didn't I get all worked up over him? *Because he's not Wyatt.* I blew out a slow breath. "Want some water?" I asked, turning back to the sink to refill my cup.

It was sweltering hot out there. I could see the heat rolling off the metal hood of the broken-down tractor. I saw Wyatt straighten, pull off his shirt. The water spilled over the rim of the cup and ran up my arm. Yep, it was *so* hot.

"That'd be great," Levi said, interrupting my inspection.

I pulled a large plastic cup from the stack on the counter, loaded it with ice, and filled the cup to the brim with cold water. He took it, smiling, and finished it off.

"More?" I asked.

"Nah." He winked. "I'm good. Thanks."

"You think…" I glanced out the window at Wyatt and Dad and Dax. "I'll bring out some more drinks."

He nodded, wiping his face on a blue bandana. "That'd be great, Allie. I'll talk to your dad about going tubing. Water's still high enough right now."

"You can try," I said. "Good luck."

"Sounds like a challenge, honey." He winked again. "You just watch."

"Okay. Let's go." I held the door open for him and walked onto the back porch.

He watched me. "Hold up." Several seconds later he emerged with a large glass of ice water. He headed straight to my father, glass in hand. I didn't hear much of what was said.

I saw Wyatt, a little further off, working hard. Dad stopped digging and took the drink, talking to Levi. I saw Dax look my way, then at Wyatt—still working. When all was said and done, Levi gave me a thumbs-up before he picked up his shovel and went back to work.

It was hard to miss the scowl Dax sent my way, turning a meaningful stare at Wyatt. I shrugged. How the hell was I supposed to know Dad would *let* me go tubing with Levi? Didn't make much sense to me, but not much was making sense these days.

"Allie," Dad called out. "Can you get some water for Dax and Wyatt?"

I glanced at Wyatt, but he hadn't stopped working. I nodded and went inside, pulling out two of my gallon sports bottles and filling them with ice and water. I'm not sure why I felt a little anxious as I walked across the front yard—tossing Dax his bottle—to Wyatt. But I did. Big-time nerves.

The muscles in his back strained, his arms flexed, his shoulders rippled... He was mixing something in a ten-gallon bucket, completely clueless that I was standing six feet away.

"Hey," I said, offering the water.

He kept stirring.

"Wyatt?"

Nothing.

I stepped closer and heard the music then. He had earbuds in, listening to angry music—loud angry music. "*Wyatt?*" I said a little louder, touching his arm.

He looked up, his shadowed brown eyes widening. He pulled one of the earbuds out, taking the water jug I held out. "Thanks," he murmured, focusing on the water jug.

"Need help?"

He looked into the bucket, then in the hole. "I've got it."

I nodded. *So, he's avoiding me… Can't blame him.* His amazing brown eyes looked everywhere—the bucket, the shovel, the water jug—but not at me.

"You okay?" I asked.

His smile was fast, but it wasn't a real smile. *Still not looking at me.* "Yeah."

"You sure?" I stepped in front of him, daring him to look at me. *Talk to me…*

"Want to get these posts set." His tone was hard as he brushed by me to put the water jug in a small patch of shade.

"Oh. Okay," I murmured, stepping back. "Hint taken. Leaving now."

"Allie…" he all but groaned. His knuckles were white, his grip on the shovel handle tight. Everything about him, sweat, muscles, tan skin, intense eyes, and crooked smile, made my heart thump like crazy.

Maybe this was better? "All good. You've got work to do."

He reached out, but didn't touch me. His gaze landed on my face for a second, no more. He let out a deep sigh, and his shoulders drooped, like he was deflating. "I'm sorry."

I couldn't take it. "What's *wrong?*"

He stared at me, pulled off his hat, and wiped his forehead with the back of his arm. He didn't say anything, no matter how much I wanted him to. The longer he looked at me, the harder it was to stay quiet. There was something in his eyes, some need or fear or…

"Why does something have to be wrong?" he asked, tearing his gaze from mine. He picked up the water bottle and took a long drink.

I shrugged. "You seem…I don't know…"

He shook his head. "How are *you?*" His attention wandered along my neck, my cheek.

It was like he touched me. I breathed, "Fine. Good. Better."

"I'm glad." His voice was rough.

"Staying for dinner?" I asked.

"Can't."

"Oh." *Why not? Say something. Anything.* I couldn't make him talk to me.

"I got to get back to it, before the concrete sets up." He grabbed the bucket handle, lifting it easily.

"Sure."

He put his earbud back in and went back to work. And I stood there, like an idiot, waiting...for what?

I started back for the house but didn't make it very far before I turned back. Wyatt had his back to me, all his energy focused on the task at hand. He was keeping me out. Why wouldn't he? I'd made it perfectly clear I wasn't interested. I might not have acted like it, but I'd told him "we" weren't going to happen.

Maybe he's just accepting what I told him?

I waited, hoping he'd turn around, hoping he'd look at me. Instead, I felt three pairs of eyes—all not Wyatt's— watching me. Dax looked concerned. Dad thoughtful. And Levi...he was pissed.

I gave them a small wave. "I think I'm going to lie down."

"Good idea," my dad said.

11 CHAPTER ELEVEN

Wyatt was there every day, working, like normal. But everything was different. He brought his lunch and ate outside. He was still super polite to my parents, just distant. Every night my mother tried to convince Wyatt to stay for dinner. Every night he smiled, thanked her, and went home. I hated it.

Levi didn't show up to help out again. That, I didn't hate.

By the end of the week, the pasture was secure and ready for cows. Dad and Wyatt were going to buy calves early Saturday at some big sale...meaning Wyatt wouldn't be going to the river with us. No matter how hard I tried, I couldn't think of a way out of Saturday.

I was awake before my alarm went off but lay there, staring at the ceiling. I knew I needed to do this, to get out of the house and away from Wyatt before I made the huge mistake of telling him or showing him how crazy I was over him.

I'd get over it and he'd never know and life would go on. If there's one thing I'd learned it was that life always goes on.

Dax was up—and whistling—at his end of the hall. Of

course he was happy. Molly would be there, smiling at him, staring at him with her huge brown I-love-you eyes. I rolled over, punching my pillow.

The bounce of headlights and the telltale rumble of Dad's truck drew my attention. I peered outside, into the still dark sky. I narrowed my gaze. The headlights were sort of blinding, enough to make out Dad...and Wyatt. They were checking the trailer, the tires, making sure everything was good before they hit the road.

They talked for a minute or two, and Dad went into the barn they'd started rebuilding. Wyatt stood there, hands on his hips, staring at the hood of the truck.

Not awake yet? He rubbed a hand over his face. I smiled as he yawned.

I sat up, moving forward to the edge of the bed. I'd missed him, being close to him, talking to him, looking at him. *I can't love you, Wyatt.*

He turned, looking up at my window.

But I do.

Could he see me? Did I want him to see me? I stood up, hugging myself.

I saw him straighten, knew he'd seen me.

"Wyatt..." My voice trembled, I heard it. "Dammit."

"Al?" *Awesome. And Dax heard it too.* When had he come in? What did it matter? "Go," he said, motioning down to Dad and Wyatt and the truck.

"I can't," I murmured, frozen in place.

"You *can.*" Dax sounded so confident. "He...he needs you."

"He does not—"

"Seriously, Allie." He wasn't joking. "Go."

I saw my dad come back from the barn and knew they were going to leave. I had no idea what Dax was talking about, or if he was just trying to manipulate my newfound weakness. But it didn't matter. *If* Wyatt needed me...

I didn't stop to think about it. I ran down the stairs and out the screen door. Dad and Wyatt stopped talking to

148

stare at me. "Need anything?" I asked, breathless.

From the corner of my eye, I saw my father frown. I *was* standing there in a tight tank top and boxer shorts... I hadn't really thought through this whole running outside before I'd even brushed my hair and put on decent clothes.

"N-no." Poor Dad. He had no clue what was happening.

"You're sure?" I asked, stalling.

"Your mom says you're going to the river."

I nodded at my dad. Wyatt headed to the passenger door of the truck. *He can't leave.*

"Be care—"

"I'll be careful," I finished his sentence quickly. "Dad..." I looked at my father, hesitated, then whispered, "Can I...can I have a minute with Wyatt, alone?"

I kind of felt sorry for him then. His frown faded, his eyebrows rose, and his expression... He nodded, hesitating for a moment before walking into the house. "Getting some...soda," he called out as he headed inside. *Subtle.*

Wyatt had walked to the end of the trailer, so I followed. He stood there, hands on his hips, staring at the pink-kissed horizon, doing nothing.

My heart was thumping as my thoughts came spilling into the quiet morning. "Are you...are you hiding from me?"

He turned, his wide eyes sweeping me from head to toe. "Um...no." I saw him swallow.

"That sounded like a question." I tried to sound calm—like it was an everyday thing to stand outside barefoot in my PJs talking to the guy I—

"Nope," he said.

"Are you *sure?*" I pushed. I don't know why.

His cheeks puffed up and he blew out a long, slow breath.

"So...you're...going to buy cows?" I asked. *Talk about smooth.*

"Yep," he responded, a small smile on his tired face.

"I'm going tubing."

"Levi's excited."

I frowned. He waited, his jaw locking. "Wyatt?" I cleared my throat. "You...you know how I said—" I swallowed. Why was my throat so tight? His eyes fell to the ground at his feet. "How I said I couldn't...th-that I'm a selfish bitch?"

His shoulders were shaking. He was laughing. "Yep."

I relaxed a little. "How I said I don't want to...to date anyone? I think..." I tried again. "Things have changed." I paused. "I just...I guess I'm worried."

He looked at me then, concerned. "About?" He crossed his arms over his chest, uncrossed them, and put his hands on his hips. "Everything okay?"

I laughed, an awkward, strained laugh. "No...God, Wyatt..." I shook my head. "This is so hard to say."

His expression hardened, like he was bracing himself for something.

"We need to hit the road," my dad interrupted. "Now."

I jumped, glancing at my father. "But—"

"Yes, sir." Wyatt nodded. He waited until my father had moved before he said anything. "It's fine, Allie. You don't owe me any explanation. Levi's a lucky guy."

I felt my mouth fall open. "*What?*"

He smiled, a really heartbreaking, sad smile. "I just want you to be happy." And he walked away.

***

"You've got such a pretty tan," Molly said. "I just burn, freckle, and peel."

"I'd normally have white shins." My head rested on the bouncy surface of the inner tube I'd inhabited for the last gazillion hours—however long we'd been floating. I turned my head to look at her, the black rubber hot against my cheek. "Soccer tan."

She laughed, her cat-eyed sunglasses slipping down her pink nose. "You going to play on our team?"

"I don't—"

"Yes, she will," Dax spoke up. "Dad's put his foot down."

I sighed, closing my eyes under the beating sun.

"I'm glad," Molly said. "Just hope you won't be too disappointed. The Bobcats—"

"Is that our mascot?" I asked. "Huh."

"Yes, ma'am." Molly laughed. "The Black Falls Bobcats. Girls' teams are always Lady Cats."

"You're a Lady Cat." Dax pushed my inner tube, separating me from the two of them and bouncing a group of teens I didn't know were coming with us. I was fine with it though; it kept Levi occupied—until my inner tube bounced off of his.

"Hey there, gorgeous." Levi hooked his arm through my inner tube, his forearms pressed against my thigh.

I looked at him over the edge of my black-rimmed aviators. "Hey. I didn't know you were here." I smiled.

"Ouch." He laughed. "I noticed you. I've been enjoying the view just fine from over here."

I splashed him, sending a spray of surprisingly cold river water over his head. "How's the view now?" I asked.

"I needed to cool down." He shook his head, his curly dark blond hair scattering drops all over me. "Can't believe your dad let you leave the house like that."

I didn't say anything. My bikini was completely acceptable. It was a little plain, even, according to Lindie. Blue with white polka dots, not cut too low or too high. I didn't need to worry about falling out or having anything ride up. I didn't do embarrassing bathing suits—that was Lindie's department. Her idea of a bathing suit had been fabric triangles and string.

"Blondie's showing off a lot more skin than I am." I pointed to the very loud, very curvy girl who was part of our group. Her name was Amanda or Mandy or Amber or something. Her inner tube was surrounded by guys.

Levi looked at me like I was crazy. "Been there. Done

th—"

I held up a hand, splashing him again. "Do *not* finish that sentence." He laughed. *Seriously? What a tool!* I splashed him again. "You just lost major points with me," I added.

He stopped laughing then. "Well, shit, Allie. What do I need to do to earn them back? I didn't think I had any points to lose."

I sighed. "Levi, I'm not really the relationship type."

He shook his head, spinning his tube so we were face to face. "Bullshit."

"Excuse me?" I tried to spin away, but he held the tube in place.

"You heard me, darlin'." He smiled. "Don't go gettin' your feathers ruffled."

I smiled. I couldn't help it.

"If I was Wyatt Holcomb, trying to get in your pants, I bet you'd be the relationship type real quick."

I stared at him. Was it that obvious? "You're a prick, you know that?" I asked, hearing the telltale waver in my voice.

He shrugged, smiling. I splashed him again. "Thought so." He laughed, wiping water from his eyes.

"What?"

Levi sighed. "You've got the hots for my boy Wyatt."

"So I have to like someone else to *not* like you?" I asked. "You're such a...a...guy."

"Guilty."

"You're an ass because you immediately go...*there*." I sighed. "Wyatt isn't the get-in-your-pants sort of guy." As soon as the words were out of my mouth I *knew* I'd made a mistake.

"He's not? *Wyatt?*" Levi's face turned serious. "He *is* one of my best friends."

My stomach tightened. So my first impression had been right? Wyatt was a player, trying to schmooze the parents just to get in good with me?

Levi was watching me closely. "You sure about that?"

Not really, no… "Yeah, I'm sure," I bluffed, hating the knot in my stomach.

"Huh." Levi smiled, a huge smile. He let himself spin slowly in a circle, making me want to hit him. It was only after he said "You nailed him," that I relaxed. "Well, you didn't yet…"

I splashed him again, relieved *and* irritated.

"Look at you, all quick to defend him."

"I'm not—"

"You are." He winked at me. "Even though he's a big boy…I mean, a *big* boy."

"Oh. My. *God!*" I covered my ears. "Stop." I flipped out of my inner tube, letting the cold water close over my head.

What was it about boys talking about their equipment? Why did they think we'd care? I opened my eyes under the water, amazed at how clear the water was. Clear enough to see Levi's hand reach down into the water. I grabbed it and pulled hard, flipping him out of his inner tube while I popped up and climbed back onto mine.

He came up laughing. "So, did I just lose more points?" he asked.

"*What* points?" I quipped back. "Zero points balance, bucko."

He hung on the side of his inner tube, watching me for a minute. "The thing is, Allie, Wyatt's nice. A good guy that's been through a helluva lot of shit." His lips pressed flat and he shook his head.

"Like…?" I wanted to know.

He smiled at me. "He'll tell you if he wants you to know. Or you'll hear it from my grandmother." He wasn't playing when he added, "Just…seriously, Allie, don't screw him over, okay?"

I felt my eyebrows rise. "Okay."

He nodded. "Cool. Guess I'll have to wait a little longer." He hooked his foot through my inner tube and paddled. Everyone seemed to be paddling together into a group.

I didn't respond to Levi; what was the point? "What's up?" I asked.

"Hook up," Molly squealed. "Rapids coming up."

I glanced ahead. The water was definitely moving faster, with white frothy peaks colliding into one another. The river seemed to disappear, dropping away. "Rapids?"

Levi rolled his eyes, shaking his head. *Okay, so nothing to worry about then.*

I don't know how many of us there were, but there were a lot of us, linking our tubes together as the river picked up speed. I hooked my feet through Dax's tube, ignoring Levi as his arms looped mine, and braced as we hit the thrashing, rolling water.

Levi was a dick. There was definitely something to worry about.

We didn't stay connected for long. I got pulled to the left while they hung to the right. Because on the right side you didn't get smashed into rocks, wedged between two boulders, or stuck in a current you had to fight your way out of. I ended up with a scraped knee and elbow by the time my tube shot over the edge of the small river that fed a large pool—down a four-foot drop.

I lost my tube in the fall, swallowed a lungful of water, and plunged deep beneath the surface. I couldn't reach the bottom to push off, it was too deep. When I broke the surface again Dax was waiting, still sitting in his tube.

"Having fun?" he asked, pushing my tube toward me.

I coughed. "Loads." More coughing. I heard Levi laugh, but decided I needed to chill out before I acknowledged his existence. Instead I hung on to my tube, resting, and stared around me.

The pond, or pool, or mini-lake, or whatever it was, was big. Another finger of river picked up on the other side, I could see it. The whole pond was encircled, like it was part of a rock bowl. Gnarled trees, cactus, and plants grew out of the crevices but there was only a small patch of shore. It was more mud than sand, though the kids splashing in it didn't seem to mind. Other than that, people sat or tanned on one of the long, flat rocks that stuck out into the pond here and there.

On the far side, a black rock wall rose up and a huge waterfall streamed into the almost-black depths of the pond. We'd come from a small fall, a trickle by comparison. No way anyone could go over the big falls, it was way too high. It was all familiar...unchanged.

"Black Falls," Molly said. I stared up at the falls.

"Grandma brought us here to swim," Dax said. "Over there, in that shallow area." He pointed to the muddy area full of kids.

"I remember biting flies." My skin itched just thinking about it. Levi started laughing again. I ignored him, climbing back onto my inner tube. *Asshole.* "Dad took us fishing here too, right?" I asked, vague memories surfacing. "A few times."

Molly nodded. "Fishing's pretty good."

"You fish too?" Dax asked.

Molly laughed. "Of course." *She probably hunts, too.*

I wasn't going to touch that. Dax wasn't wearing his P.E.T.A shirts anymore, but I suspected their relationship might take a turn for the worse in the end. They were too different.

Levi paddled over to me, hooking his foot under my inner tube, but I continued to ignore him. A shrill whistle echoed off the cavern walls.

Dax spun. "Well, Dad's here."

"Shit," I heard Levi mutter and I turned toward him. He was frowning in the direction of the falls, so I looked up to see...Dad and Wyatt. Watching us.

Dad sat with his legs hanging off the edge of the rock ledge they were using. He was smiling, his favorite cap on his head, his favorite fishing rod in his hand, and an insulated jug in reach. His beaten-up tackle box was open at his side, a bucket—probably bait—sitting between him and Wyatt.

I risked glancing Wyatt's way...because I *had* to, even though I really shouldn't. He was looking at me. Staring at me. I didn't like the way my heart lodged itself in my throat. Or that my sun-warmed skin felt hot.

Dax and Molly began paddling our linked tubes in their direction. All I did was sit there, trying not to look into those intense eyes. Instead I stared at his broad, golden, shirtless shoulders. Oh hell. I swallowed, forcing my eyes back to the water, and away from his tan...strong...hotness.

"We shouldn't get too close," I murmured. "The fish."

And Wyatt. Can't get too close to him.

"I think Dad's piercing whistle took care of that," Dax said dismissively.

"We're packing up," Dad called, stretching as he stood. "Your mom needs me to go by the store to get stuff for lasagna tonight."

Mom's lasagna. Cool... Why can't I look away?

"I give." Levi sighed before pushing off my inner tube. "Don't break his heart."

I shot him a frown before glancing at Wyatt. Wyatt, who was trying *not* to look at me, I could tell. He was busy securing the hook on the pole so the line wouldn't get loose or tangled, but his gaze kept wandering to me.

Why me?

While Levi and Dax and Molly paddled their way to the ledge, I bobbed, hoping to drown the butterflies, nerves, goose bumps, and every other sort of Wyatt-induced reaction in the cold water.

Dax waved me over. "Come on, Allie."

"Your truck here?" Dad asked Levi.

"Yes, sir. Dallas parked it before he had to go in to work," Levi said, picking up Dad's tackle box and following him up the narrow path along the canyon wall. I saw Levi say something to Wyatt, saw Wyatt stiffen.

"Hasn't changed much," Dad said over his shoulder.

"Catch anything?" Dax asked, following Molly.

Their voices grew softer as they climbed the hill to their waiting trucks, but I wasn't listening anyway. Wyatt stood there, watching me. Waiting.

"Coming out?" he asked.

I shook my head. "I don't think so."

He smiled. "Why not? Don't like your mom's cooking?"

I frowned at him. Not a playful frown; I wasn't playing. I was honestly confused and I wanted him to know it. He'd put a wall between the two of us. Told me to date Levi. Okay, maybe I'd put up the first wall. But his had been way higher—and thicker—and now he was smiling at me *like that*.

It wasn't fair.

He must have picked up on my mood because his outrageous smile dimmed a little. He knelt on the rock, reaching out his hand. "They'll leave us behind."

If I didn't take his hand, he couldn't reach me and I was my own little floating island, safe. So I didn't take it. I stared past him, at the bluff overhead. "I think they already did."

He glanced over his shoulder, then back at me. "I'll take you home."

I didn't say a thing. I closed my eyes and rested my head. My inner tube kept turning in lazy circles. It turned six times before I heard a splash.

His hand grabbed my ankle, tugging me into the water and flipping the inner tube. I screamed as I went under.

His hands grasped my upper arms and pulled me to the surface. We came up inside the inner tube, pressed together. He swam us closer to the wall, where he could stand on his tiptoes and...hold me.

My heart was going crazy. And even if I hadn't been coughing up water, I knew breathing would be a challenge.

In the cold water, it was hard to miss how warm he was—or that he didn't have a shirt on. My bikini top was soaked through, the heat of his chest almost scalding my wet skin. Yes, the water was cold, but it was the look in his eyes and the flare of anticipation that had me covered in goose bumps. *Hell.*

I'd never been so close to a guy before, never felt like this… I didn't even know what I was feeling, but it was seriously intense.

He was breathing hard too, his gaze glued to my mouth. His arms slipped around my waist, his eyes closing briefly as my chest pressed fully against his. The feel of his arms, his strength, his skin…Yeah, breathing wasn't getting any easier.

His heart thumped like crazy, I could feel it. My hands were shaking as I pressed them against his chest, smooth and slick. "This is a bad idea," I whispered, when I could talk.

His gaze shifted to mine. "Probably."

I shivered as his hand smoothed a lock of my hair from my lower lip.

"Allie…" His voice was rough.

I shivered again. *Kiss me.* My hand slipped along his arm. *Don't kiss me.* His hand pressed along my cheek. *Shit.*

"You bringing her home?" Dax called down, not bothering to be discreet. "After you're done…doing whatever you're…doing."

It took a moment for me to process Dax's words. Even then, I was a little caught up in Wyatt to think of a smart-ass comeback. To *think* at all.

Throwing my arms around his neck would be bad. Pressing myself even closer to his holy-*hell* hardness would be *very* bad. But I really wanted to. So I pushed off his amazing chest and slipped out of his hold. I dove beneath the water, putting some space between us. When I came up, I headed straight to the wall without looking at Wyatt. If I hurried, I might catch Dad—and run away. And I *was* running away. I had to.

I attempted to climb out of the water but it was

covered in a lovely slimy moss. When I would have slipped back into the water, Wyatt steadied me…making my stomach hot and heavy. He lifted me up and onto the rock ledge and I scrambled out of his hold.

He tossed the inner tube up before swinging himself onto the ledge beside me. I tried to ignore the trail of water that ran down his throat, down his chest. He didn't move or say a thing. But when my gaze met his, it was impossible to ignore him. I moved, heading up the path.

He was right behind me. I could hear my heartbeat racing in my ears, loud and heavy.

When we reached the top, the others were gone. Just Wyatt's truck and me, in the twilight. Wet, half-naked, and alone. "Shit," I whispered, spinning around.

Why did he have to look at me like that? His nostrils flared, his jaw locked. He walked past me to his truck, tossing the inner tube into the truck bed.

I knew I should say or do something.

He opened his truck door, leaning across the seat for something—all rippling muscles. And I felt…everything felt constricted and tight and hot and heavy. Even though I had no experience with guys—had never seriously thought about being with a guy—I knew what I wanted…and I wanted him to touch me. I wanted him to kiss me. I wanted him. And it scared the crap out of me.

If there was one thing Lindie's string of relationships had taught me, it was that sex made things harder.

Why am I thinking about sex? I am. I'm thinking about sex. My cheeks burned.

He turned around, holding the shirt he'd had on that morning. His eyes wandered over me, toes to head. It was quick, but I saw his jaw go rigid again. "Here." He walked back to me, shaking out the shirt and offering it to me. "It's dry. A little dusty, though."

I took it, my fingers brushing over his. It was like he was radiating some yummy heat.

"Guess it didn't work out with Levi?" he asked.

"Levi?" So he wasn't having a freakish reaction to me? *I'm thinking about sex and he's wanting a relationship status update?* I tore my gaze from his and slipped his shirt on, snapping up the front. It hung down to my knees, the sleeves falling over my hands. I rolled back the soft sleeves, rubbing my cheek against the fabric. It smelled like him.

"He left. So…" His voice was low.

"Friends only. And even *that's* going to be a challenge for me."

Wyatt laughed then, chasing some of the tension away. "Yeah, Levi, he's…well…"

"Not my type." I was smiling too—his smile was contagious.

"This morning…" He put his hands on his hips and looked at his truck. "You said things had changed." He looked at me then, confusion lining his face.

I swallowed the knot in my throat. "It…things have."

He ran a hand over his face. "Allie, I'm in knots here. I almost kissed you, knowing Levi wants you. I don't want to be that kind of guy."

I can honestly say I was speechless. *In knots… Good knots or bad knots? What does knots mean exactly?* "Why?" *Why am I asking him why?* Was I asking about the knots or the kissing or what kind of guy he was or what exactly?

He frowned. "I didn't…couldn't think." He shrugged, his gaze traveling over me. "You make things…mixed up."

Don't screw with his head.

"I don't mean to," I murmured.

He was still frowning at me, almost angrily. "No Levi?" His voice was hard.

I shook my head, fiddling with the hem of his shirt. *I don't want to screw with his head. I just want to be with him.* I did. I wanted to be with him.

I looked him in the eye and said, "This morning, I was talking about you and me." And then I held my breath.

12 CHAPTER TWELVE

His eyes went round, his nostrils flared, his jaw locked—every muscle in his gorgeous body tensed for five seconds. His hands lifted, landing on my shoulders and running down my arms to take my hands in his.

"I'm a mess," I whispered. "You know that."

He shook his head. "You're strong."

"You think so?"

"Yes." His hands tightened around mine. "And loyal."

"Are you...will you kiss me now?" I asked.

"I know it's not a good idea," he said, his voice low, husky, making the hair on the back of my neck stand up.

"Because?" I needed him to explain why I shouldn't launch myself at him.

"Allie..." His hand tucked my damp hair behind my ear. "You're...skittish. I don't want to scare you off."

"You think kissing me would scare me off?" I asked, completely confused.

He didn't say anything for a minute, looking tense yet thoughtful all at once. "I think once we start, it's gonna be hard to stop."

Every hair on my body was on end then, every inch of my body hot. For a moment I thought my heart would literally thump its way out of my chest. "O-okay," I breathed.

He led me to the truck, opening the driver door and standing back so I could slide in first.

"I'm still a little wet," I said.

He smiled down at me. "I don't mind."

I slid across the bench seat. There was plenty of room this time, but I still sat right in the middle, one leg on either side of the gear shift. He got in, looked at me, at my legs, and let out a long, slow breath.

"I can move over," I offered.

"No," he whispered tightly as he started the truck, the engine roaring to life. His arm rested along my thigh, his hand resting on my knee once he'd changed gears. Every time he shifted, I felt another jolt of heavy-hot tingles. His fingers brushed my knee, and I shivered.

"Cold?" he asked.

"A little," I lied.

He lifted his arm. "Come here." His voice was rough again. I loved the way it sounded.

I burrowed into his side, resting my head on his chest. It didn't seem weird to be so tangled up in him, just good and right.

"You have fun?" he asked.

"Today?"

"Yeah."

"Guess so."

His fingers slid through my hair. His heart was beating crazy fast. "What?"

I shook my head. "Next time we'll go when you can come too."

His arm tightened around me. I liked it, a lot. We drove like that the rest of the way home. It was only when he had to shift gears that I moved, and once that was done, his arm was warm and secure around me again.

I was kind of bummed when we pulled onto the gravel drive. "Staying?" I asked as he parked.

He looked at me, smiling. "I can't. Rodeo in Kerrville tonight. Gonna be tough enough to get everything ready and get there on time. Not that I'm complaining."

"No. Sure. Of course. Is there...can I do anything?" Like there was anything I could do.

"Will you come tonight to the rodeo?" His brown eyes watched, waited.

"I think I can squeeze it into my busy schedule," I teased, smiling.

His gaze fell to my lips and he gripped the steering wheel with both hands.

"Wyatt? You okay?" I asked, placing my hand on his leg.

He blew out a slow breath. "I'm wishing I'd kissed you when I had the chance."

I was warm and tingly all over. "What's wrong with right now?"

He nodded to the front porch, where Dax stood...and Mom. Dax was watching us with a huge smile on his face. But Mom looked anxious—distracted. Something was up.

Wyatt opened the truck door and slid out, holding out his hand to help me down.

"Want your shirt?" I asked, reaching up to unsnap it.

He shook his head, the muscle in his jaw bulging as his attention focused on my hands. "Keep it. I'll get it later."

Huh. Who knew I could do this to a guy? Guess it was a good thing Mom was here, since I was definitely rethinking the whole launching myself at him thing.

"Not staying for dinner?" Mom called from the porch.

"No, ma'am. But thank you for the offer."

I was impressed with how together he sounded. Not at all the rough-voiced, nostrils-flaring guy that—I suspected—wanted to rip his shirt off of me.

Whoa. Getting way ahead of things here... Then again, the shirt did snap. All sorts of images ran through my mind. And for the first time in my life I wanted to know what it would be like to...to be with a guy. No, not *a guy*. Wyatt.

"It's a standing invitation, Wyatt," Mom answered. "You're missing out on my lasagna."

"You *are* missing out," Dax agreed. "She rocks the lasagna."

"Sorry, Dr. Cooper. Rodeo tonight."

Mom looked at me, then Dax. "You kids going?"

I sighed. *Subtle, Mom.* Like we didn't all hear the slight inflection on the word *kids*. Guess Wyatt and I weren't being too subtle either.

"Are we?" Dax asked me.

"Molly going?" I returned, knowing that would be the deciding factor for him.

"Don't think so." Dax looked pathetic. "I'll take you tonight, if you want."

Wyatt nodded, glancing at me. "Probably a good idea." The words were for me only. "I'll see you later, then" was loud enough for Mom and Dax to hear.

We stood looking at each other. *Do we just say good-bye?* I mean, nothing had *really* changed, had it? It wasn't like we had defined or labeled what *we* were exactly.

"Be safe," I said, my hands twisting in the hem of his shirt.

He nodded, a small smile on his mouth.

"I'll see you later," I added.

He nodded again.

We still stood there, staring at each other. The screen door slammed. I glanced over to see Mom and Dax were gone—then there was no more space between me and Wyatt. He pulled me against him, fiercely at first, then gently. He pressed a kiss to my temple, his breath caressing my forehead and unleashing new shivers and tingles and...

He let me go, sighed, and climbed into his truck. I wrapped my arms around myself and watched him back down the driveway, loving the smile on his face.

***

"Dad just went off." Dax shrugged, driving onto the right shoulder to let a huge truck pass us on the country road we were travelling. "They haven't fought like that since…"

"Before we moved," I finished for him. "No idea what set it off?"

He edged his truck back onto the road and glanced at me. "Mom got a phone call this morning."

"O-kay. You shooting for cryptic or is it just coming naturally?" I didn't want a lot of build-up or drama.

He laughed. "Ass. You tell me. If Mom got a phone call from someone and Dad stormed out of the house, who do you think it was?"

"What the hell are you talking about?" I made no effort to hide my irritation.

Dax was just as irritated. "Were you really that self-absorbed?"

I punched him on the shoulder. "At least that was past tense."

"You seem to be getting…better." He was reluctant.

"Gosh, thanks." I hoped he was right. I didn't want to be that girl anymore. "I thought it was part of teenager-dom."

"Allie, in your case, it was a full blown episode."

Guilt twisted my gut. "Back to Mom, please."

"You know Todd Dowdy."

"Dr. Todd?" I asked. "From the vet hospital? Taffy Todd?" Dax and I had nicknamed him Taffy Todd because he'd kept a bowl of saltwater taffy on his desk just for us. Dax and I had spent a lot of time at the teaching hospital growing up, our home away from home.

"Yeah, that one." His mouth was pressed flat.

"What about him?"

Dax let out a long, low sigh. "Mom and he…well…they…"

"Are besties?" This wasn't news. Todd had been hilarious, always making Mom laugh.

"You could say that," he ground out.

"Dax, what *about* Mom and Taffy Todd?" As soon as I

said it out loud I got it. And I felt vaguely nauseous. "Mom…a-and Todd?"

"I don't know what happened between them, exactly, okay?"

I couldn't think. "But…how…what do you *know?*"

"We, Dad and I, caught them kissing." He paused. "The night of your accident."

Officially wanting to throw up here. "Oh my God."

"It was…Dad went nuts. He punched Todd in the face, broke his nose."

"Mom?"

"Dad hardly spoke to her. He said you were in the hospital, that Lindie was dead." He paused over the last part, looking at me.

It hurt to hear him say it out loud. But this—Mom and Dad? Had I always been so fricking self-absorbed? A wave of self-loathing washed over me. "I'm a horrible, horrible person. How could I not know?"

"You kind of had a lot going on."

"Dax. Oh my God." I paused, still trying to process everything he'd said. "Poor Dad."

He snorted. "It was a *kiss*. They weren't eating each other's faces, you know? Dad's been kind of MIA for the last two years."

"So you're defending her?" I asked, astounded.

"I'm not defending or blaming either of them, okay? I just know their marriage isn't a rock, it's rocky. I don't know what Todd called about this morning. But when we got home from the river, Dad heard Mom say something on the phone, and took off."

"When did our family get so screwed up?"

Dax was quiet for a while. "I think all families are screwed up. The older you get, the more obvious it is."

I looked at my brother. "Get that from a fortune cookie?"

He laughed. "Nope, I've always been wise and philosophical."

We turned in to the fairgrounds and parked. The sun was dropping and the sky was turning a peachy-pink, with streaks of feather-white clouds. A few stars were beginning to appear, reminding me of that night with Wyatt. The dark, the cliff, the stars…feeling safe and secure and…loved.

We made our way to the gate entrance. "Twenty dollars, honey." The ticket attendant with helmet-hair and bright red lipstick smiled at me. "Aren't you a pretty thing?"

"Thank you."

Dax snorted. "She was talking to me, Allie."

The woman laughed. "You two kids have some fun tonight."

"You do look extra nice," Dax said as we made our way to the stands. "Any reason why?"

I glanced down at my pale yellow strapless sundress. A sundress I'd picked because my back and shoulders were burned pretty badly and I couldn't deal with a bra or anything else rubbing up against me. I was still wearing my boots; lots of girls wore skirts and dresses with boots, so why couldn't I? And some pretty earrings, too. I wanted to look extra nice for Wyatt.

"Allie?" Dax nudged me. "Earth to Allie." I smiled at him. His brows rose. "Uh-huh."

"What, uh-huh?"

"Uh-huh, it's about time."

I nudged him back. "And how are things going in the make-a-move department with Molly?"

He frowned. "Not."

That was interesting. I figured they'd have been having some serious make-out sessions at this point. *Because I'm interested in having some serious make-out sessions.*

"I think there might be someone else," Dax added.

I stopped walking then. "What?"

He shrugged, but kept walking to the bleachers. "I don't want to talk about it tonight. Let's just chill and relax, okay? No Mom. No Dad. No Molly. Deal?"

I swallowed back the questions I had. "Sure."

We headed to the middle section of the bleachers and climbed halfway up. High enough for all the people walking back and forth not to block our view but still low enough that the bugs and bats didn't do regular fly-bys.

The "Star-Spangled Banner" was sung. The announcer did an especially cheesy opening speech about freedom, how blessed we were to live in America, and our troops—and somehow I still ended up teary-eyed.

Mutton bustin' was up. "I'm going to have to dig out the pictures of you doing this," I teased Dax.

He glared at me. "Great."

I laughed, remembering Grandma steering a resistant four-year-old Dax into the dirt-packed arena. I—blond pigtailed princess that I was—got to sit and cheer him on from the stands. Nothing like watching parents put their three-, four-, and five-year-olds on a sheep tearing across a dirt-packed arena for their amusement. Dax had made it almost the length of the arena before the sheep had tossed him off. He face-planted and came up spitting dirt.

"This is just cruel," he muttered now.

"Only for the kids bouncing on the back of the sheep. I think it's hilarious." I kept laughing.

He relaxed after the fourth kid—a genius who rode the sheep backward and made it all the way to the end of the arena—finished. We were all on our feet clapping then.

"Cut the kiddie crap," someone yelled from the end of the stands.

"Sounds like someone's had too much to drink," Dax murmured.

When the kids were done, the rodeo clown entered the ring, wearing baggy pants, a beat-up cowboy hat over his microphone head-set, and suspenders with lots of bandanas tied on. He was making bad jokes and trying to keep the crowd amused. "Anyone here from jolly ol' England?" he asked, with an absolutely horrible accent.

"How about Japan?" He climbed up the arena wall and straddled the fence, searching the crowd.

"Want anything to drink?" Dax asked me.

"Water, please."

"*Please?*" He shook his head. "Remind me to thank Wyatt."

I grinned. "Don't trip and break anything on your way down."

"*There's* my sister." He winked and climbed down the bleachers.

"I think we have a winner," the rodeo clown said to the rodeo announcer.

"Really, Cowboy Jack? Where are they from?" the announcer asked.

"Why, they're all the way from South Africa," Cowboy Jack answered. The family in question was all smiles.

"Cut the shit, Cowboy Jack. Nobody gives a rat's ass if those people are from South Africa," the same slurred voice called out.

Cowboy Jack ignored the heckler, asking the people, "How long is that flight?"

The woman was giggling and nervous. "It took—"

"Who cares? Sit down and shut up," the irate voice continued.

I leaned forward, looking for the obnoxious drunk that was giving poor ol' Cowboy Jack and the South African tourists so much grief.

"What was that again?" Cowboy Jack was good—I had to give him that.

"Twenty-plus hours," the woman said, her enthusiasm somewhat deflated. She kept glancing over Cowboy Jack's shoulder at the heckler.

"You hear that? More than twenty hours just to see our lil ol' rodeo! Well, I'll be." The announcer sounded impressed. "We'll have to get you and your family something special. What do you have for them, Cowboy Jack?"

"A swift kick in the butt back to South Africa?" the heckler continued. I wasn't having any luck seeing him, so I stood—so did half the stands.

The man was leaning against one of the lamp poles that surrounded the arena. His hat was tipped forward over his face, so I couldn't see much of him. He held a longneck beer bottle in one hand, the other shoved into his pocket. He looked relaxed, at ease. Apparently he was completely comfortable being an asshole.

"How about some boots for the whole family?" Cowboy Jack asked the announcer.

"And some hats, too," the rodeo announcer added.

"Give me a break," the heckler yelled.

"How about you give *me* a break, Travis?" Cowboy Jack said to his heckler.

Travis—the obnoxious drunk man—pushed off the pole and threw his bottle over his shoulder, into the arena. Security came running. I think it was security; they were wearing white button-down shirts and white cowboy hats. Travis wasn't impressed. He leaned back against the rail.

"Look, the white-hat brigade to the rescue." Travis laughed. "Am I supposed to be shakin' in my boots?"

One of the men stooped low to talk to Travis.

"Let's get this rodeo started!" the announcer called out. Thumping music blasted—nothing like the twang of a steel guitar and a nasal-voice singer to kick things off cowboy-style. "We don't just have some of the best US roping teams here tonight, we've got some international cowboys too."

Roping. Finally. Wyatt. I sat, ignoring the white-hat brigade stand-off.

"Miss anything?" Dax asked as he sat, handing me my water bottle.

"You did, actually," I replied.

"More child abuse? Wait, let me guess. Animal abuse?"

"Way better. A rowdy drunk. *And* cowboy security."

He looked at me, surprised. "Man, *seriously*? And I

missed it? That sucks."

I laughed, opening my water bottle and taking a long drink.

"Roping's up first?" Dax asked. I nodded.

"First in the chute, a couple of native Montana boys: Cary Green and Lance MacMasters. Points are based on time and any errors the boys make on the way out of the chute. Let's see how they do…"

The gate burst open, the steer shot free, and the team swarmed in. They didn't do so hot. Apparently the heeler broke the boundary before time—whatever that meant. It added fifteen points to their score. I sat back, smiling.

"Next up, all the way from Chile—"

Not Wyatt and Hank. I took another sip of water.

"How's Mrs. D doing?" Dax asked.

I sighed. "Let's add the Duncans to the off-limits topic list for the evening."

He wrapped his arm around my shoulders. "Really?" He gave me a squeeze. "Sounds good to me."

"Da-ax." I felt my guilt rising. "I can't turn my back on her—"

Something was happening. The header had the steer lassoed, but he let go of the rope—almost threw it.

"Ooh, that right there, ladies and gentlemen—a cowboy will put the safety of his horse before the win anytime," the announcer said as the rider leapt from his horse, cutting quickly through the rope that was around the steer's horns. It was tangled between the horse's front legs. "After all, a cowboy is only as good as his horse. The trust they have is what lets them work as a team."

The cowboy stooped, running his hands up the horse's front legs. He patted the horse on the neck and tipped his hat to the crowd.

"Judges will have to decide if they'll qualify for a re-run or not. Next up, Black Falls' best, Wyatt Holcomb and Hank Pendleton."

I sat forward on the edge of the bench but I didn't

have long to wait. Hank was fast, but Wyatt was faster. I knew, after talking to Molly, that the heeler had to be patient. He had to watch for just the right second, when the rope would catch both feet cleanly. And he had to do that as fast as possible.

He has a lot of patience. I smiled.

"Best score tonight, ladies and gents. 16.25 seconds. Let's give them a big hand."

I whistled, standing up and clapping, and I think I might have stomped my foot too—I was *really* proud and happy. Wyatt turned, lifted his hat in my direction, and smiled that holy-hell smile just for me.

Dax laughed when I sat down. "Don't play hard to get or anything."

"Okay, I won't."

He shook his head and nudged me. I nudged him back. *Yep, seriously making a fool out of myself and so not caring.* I watched as Wyatt and Hank rode out of the arena.

"You the Cooper girl?"

I turned. It was the heckler, staring down at me, looking really pissed off.

"You gonna answer?" he snapped.

"No, sir," I spoke calmly, facing the arena, "I don't think I will." I didn't know who he was or what his problem was, but I'd learned ignoring people normally made them go away. I could only hope Drunk Travis would do just that.

He didn't. He stood there staring at me, completely unfazed by the people he was standing in front of.

"Allie?" Dax's voice was soft. I shot him a look.

"That's right. *Allie* Cooper. With the rich parents and fancy big house and college scholarship ideas."

Who is this guy? I glanced at Travis. There was nothing familiar about him. Maybe he was another one of Dad's old friends?

"Hey, buddy, can you move?" someone behind me asked.

172

"Can you shut up?" Travis answered. "*Buddy?*"

"Wanna make me?" the same voice asked.

Dax and I turned to see an overall- and feed-store-cap-wearing giant stand up. He smiled at Travis, crossing his thick arms over his barrel chest. I knew a dare when I saw one. I looked at Travis. *Your move, smartass.*

Travis laughed. "Cool your heels. I'm goin'." He leveled an angry stare at me. "You stay away from my boy. No Holcomb needs a handout."

My boy. Holcomb…

I stared then, too surprised not to. Travis Holcomb's brown eyes narrowed, hostile. I didn't see a sliver of the warmth and tenderness his son's bore. I didn't see *any* of Wyatt in this person. In fact, Travis Holcomb scared me.

I watched him sway as he made his way down the few steps of the bleacher to the ground. He didn't look back, but he did check out a girl not that much older than me before he finished off another bottle of beer.

"*That's* Wyatt's dad?" Dax whispered.

"That dipshit? He's Wyatt Holcomb's daddy, all right." The giant leaned between us, his breath a stomach-turning beer and nacho mix. "Can't imagine Wyatt's too happy 'bout it."

I watched Travis Holcomb swagger to the end of the bleachers and disappear into the sea of cowboy hats. I suddenly understood why Wyatt wasn't all that upset that his dad was gone so often.

"Allie?" Dax nudged me.

I looked at my brother. "Still processing… Kind of…in *shock.*"

The giant laughed. "Sounds about right."

Dax stood and tugged on my arm. "Let's go get some water."

I followed, holding my half-full water bottle against my chest.

When we were walking across the gravel path toward the concession stands, Dax stopped. "Now, you okay?"

"I got the impression he didn't like me." I spoke softly, staring up at the black sky and millions of tiny glittering stars overhead. But there was something cold and twisting in my stomach. Something was...off. "He's the anti-Wyatt, you know? Kinda scary." I tried to tease, but my throat was tight.

"You got that too?"

I shot him a look. "Wyatt's never really talked about him, or his home life."

Dax nodded behind me. "Now's your chance to ask him."

I turned around in time to see Wyatt walking quickly to me—smiling that megawatt smile that made my insides melt, flip, and melt again. I didn't care that I was grinning like an idiot. I could see how happy he was, a little proud even. He should be. I was.

Then his d—his d-dad—*nope, can't do it, can't call him that*—then Travis stepped in his path and Wyatt froze, everything about him changing. It kind of freaked me out to see Wyatt's face so hard, his posture tense, like he was bracing for something bad. Really bad.

But Travis *was* his father. I waited for a high-five, that's-my-boy moment between them. I got the feeling that wasn't going to happen.

"You think 16.25 is gonna cut it at Regionals? Get you to Invitationals?" Travis's tone was a disturbing mix of condescension and challenge—the kind of tone a coach used when he was trying to goad his players into success. The coach that the team hated.

"What an *ass*hole," I whispered, but Dax hushed me.

Wyatt's gaze was fixed on the ground between his boots. He didn't look up, at his father, at me, at anything. "It's not bad."

"*Not bad?*" Travis put his hands on his hips, laughing a short, disbelieving snort. "When did you get so *lazy*, boy?" His words were like hard, fast punches. I could see what he was doing to Wyatt, see the way the boy I loved most in the world withdrew into himself, and it hurt.

Lazy? Does he know his son? Does he know Wyatt works hard every second of every day? I didn't realize I was moving toward them until Dax grabbed my shoulders and held me back.

And then Travis Holcomb did a hundred-and-eighty-degree turnaround from prodding to pity. "You think I like busting my ass every goddamn day so you can come out here and…and not even *try?*"

"A complete and *total* asshole," Dax whispered this time.

"No, sir." Wyatt's voice was low, hoarse—breaking my heart. Didn't his father see how rigid Wyatt's jaw was? How his hands pressed flat against his thighs, shaking? I didn't know what to do. I just knew I wanted to do *something.*

"But I do it, don't I?" Travis continued.

"Yes, sir," Wyatt answered.

I could feel my heartbeat pounding in my head. *God, Wyatt. I…I'm here. And you're not lazy, you're wonderful and sweet and beautiful.* It was stupid to think *at* him, but I didn't know what else to do.

"Yes sir." Travis Holcomb shook his head. "No sir. You best get used to sayin' 'no sir' and 'yes sir,' boy. If you're gonna keep half-assing things here, you'll end up taking orders at the Frosty Palace." He paused. "No matter what that pretty little skirt might tell you."

Wyatt's head popped up, his hands fisting at his sides. And Travis Holcomb smiled, stepping closer to his son.

I felt sick to my stomach. *Am I the pretty little skirt? Am I causing these problems?* I felt really really sick.

Travis's next words were low, taunting. "You even gonna ride tonight?"

I saw Wyatt close his eyes, straighten his shoulders, relax his hands. "Yes, sir."

"*We-ell.* That's good. Real good." Travis clapped his son on the shoulder. "Who you ridin'?"

Wyatt didn't look our way as his dad led him back to

the pens.

"Dax," I blustered, "he...that son of a bitch is Wyatt's *father?*"

"I knew he was a dick, but wow." Dax was just as stunned as I was. "I think we'd better give them space, Allie."

"Obviously," I muttered, staring after the tall, strong figure of Wyatt and the smaller frame of his father.

Dax made some dismissive noise, but I could tell he knew something. I looked at him, waiting. "Molly said Wyatt's dad is trouble," he finally said.

"That would have been news thirty minutes ago. Now, not so much. Nothing else?"

"He's kind of the town drunk. Gets arrested, swears he'll never drink again, gets released and hits the road. Molly said most people try to give him a break."

"Why?" That didn't make much sense to me.

Dax shrugged. "I don't know. Because it's a small town and people in small towns look after each other?" I must have looked a little suspicious because he laughed. "That's all I've got."

"The lazy thing." My throat tightened. "God...I mean...God." I shook my head, anger almost choking me. "Wyatt works harder than anyone I've ever met."

"You're not going to want to hear this, but stay out of it, Allie." He nudged me. "Okay? We don't know the whole story."

I stopped, glaring at him. "Whole story? There's a story that would make *that*," I pointed in the direction Wyatt and his father had gone, *"fine?* Really? I can't think of a single thing that makes any of that okay."

Dax pulled on my arm. "I'm not disagreeing with you."

"Good." I didn't want to argue. The only thing that mattered was telling Wyatt—when we were home—that he was doing a good job. That he was *amazing.*

"Allie, just...don't get in the middle of it," Dax went on.

And once I know he *knows that he's incredible, I'm going to wrap my arms around his neck and kiss him.* That was just what I was going to do. "Fine."

"Fine?" Dax repeated.

I nodded. *"Fine."* Tonight should be about Wyatt, about his successes. Whether or not his father wanted to give him props or not, I would. "We'll enjoy the rest of the rodeo and track down Wyatt when this is over. Deal?"

"Hmm," Dax murmured, not happy about my quick response.

I smiled at him and lined up for a funnel cake and lemonade. Maybe some sugar would chase away the lingering bad taste in my mouth. With a funnel cake in one hand and a huge frozen lemonade in the other, I scaled the bleachers. We'd lost our seats, but that was okay. I'd rather not sit in the same place, in case *Mr.* Holcomb decided to attack again.

We were up high, on the far left, right by the chutes for bull riding—which was up next. The speakers were blaring, making us wince at each other. But we sat, listening to the announcer joke back and forth with Cowboy Jack and two other, less-painted clowns down in the arena for bull reinforcement.

"We're talking points tonight. We have two of the best all-around cowboys here, looking for big winnings. One wants to go to college to be a large animal veterinarian. The other, well, he wants a new truck."

That caused a few laughs.

"First up, David Smith. Let's see if a new truck is in this boy's future. Can we hear it for this Dallas cowboy?"

The crowd clapped, some stomped their booted feet on the metal and wood bleachers, others whistled. The horn blasted, and David Smith and bull—a nasty-looking black thing—erupted from the chute in a cloud of dust.

"Whirlwind likes to spin," the announcer commented as the bull did just that.

It looked like David's ride was going to be fine, until

Whirlwind slammed on the brakes and then took off in the opposite direction. Whirlwind went left, David went right—landing on his knee in a way that couldn't be good. "Ooh!" the announcer called out, with half the crowd.

That was when the clowns kicked into high gear. David was pretty stunned, trying to push himself up in the dirt, while Whirlwind suddenly realized nothing was on his back. The clowns waved and ran in front of the snorting animal, leading it trotting into the exit chute and out of the arena. David stood, shook his head, dusted his hat against his leg, raised an arm to the crowd to let everyone know he was all right, and then made his way to the fence.

"Next up, a real treat, ladies and gents, a real treat. One-time Pro-Rodeo bull rider and helluva nice fellow, Shane Parker." His ride was pretty amazing to watch. He seemed to know what the bull was going to do before it did it. His score was high, a 96. "Good thing he's just here to get the crowd riled up," the announcer said with a chuckle. "Too late to change your mind, Shane. Next up, a young all-around hoping to become a large animal veterinarian. I think we've got some folks from Texas A&M University here tonight to see him. I hear A&M has a pretty good vet school, is that right?"

A group in the bleachers to my right made a lot of noise. I laughed. A&M had one of the best vet schools in the country and everyone knew it.

"Show 'em what you're made of, Wyatt," the announcer went on. "I'm proud to say I've known this young man since he was knee-high to a grasshopper. When he started walking, his first pair of baby shoes was cowboy boots. When he could first sing a song, it was 'Yellow Rose of Texas.' And his first pet? Why, his roping horse, of course. Let's hear it for Black Falls' own Wyatt Holcomb."

One wants to go to college to be a large animal veterinarian. My stomach twisted and my lungs turned heavy. All I could think about was Wyatt. He was bull riding. He was riding a bull. And his dream school was here to watch. *You can do this*. "Shit," I hissed, pressing my hands between my knees.

The horn blew and the chute opened. My ears were roaring, or maybe it was the crowd. I heard the announcer, "…on Rabbit. Why Rabbit? Well…just watch."

How a fifteen-hundred-pound bull could spring up, almost vertical, again and again, was beyond me. But Rabbit did. The bull barely touched down before he was airborne again. And again. And again. All I could see was Wyatt, his right hand buried in rope and his left hand held high. When Rabbit went up, Wyatt leaned back. When Rabbit landed, Wyatt countered forward.

It was the longest eight seconds of my life. I could only imagine how Wyatt felt.

But he made it. He held on, and with style. He lost his glove when he jumped off, but he didn't get tangled up or stepped on or gored. He landed, jumped out of the way of Rabbit, and turned to look at the scoreboard. He didn't seem to be aware of the bull running around him or the clowns doing their best to guide the bull out. When the scores popped up, Wyatt took off his hat and beat it against his thigh.

"Ninety-four points! Let's hear it for Wyatt Holcomb." The announcer went on, "Ninety-four points. Great job, cowboy."

My eyes were glued on him. He seemed…relieved. I jumped up, whistling like mad. He didn't look at me this time. In fact, he turned away, heading out of the arena.

My heart twisted. I started down the bleachers, moving as quickly as I could without stepping on someone's kid, beer, or purse. Once I was on the ground, I hurried to the end. I didn't know where I was going, but I figured I'd find my way.

Behind the announcer's podium were row after row of pens. Some held horses, some calves, some bulls, some sheep. Some were empty. And all along the fences were cowboys. Some had finished their turn, some were waiting, some sat on top of the fence, others leaned on them, just hanging out.

I ignored the "Hey, sugar," from one particularly friendly cowboy and walked on, rounding the corner. For a minute I forgot about everything except Wyatt's smiling face. He was talking to a group of men, very clean-cut, professional. I swallowed. They were wearing collegiate logo shirts—maroon. They laughed, at ease, joking.

Dax came up beside me, but I grabbed his arm. "We can't interrupt."

"That was fast," Dax whispered, nodding toward the college recruiters. "Guess they liked what they saw."

"Of course." I glanced around. "But his dad…"

Dax looked around too. "We're going to have to run interference, aren't we?"

There was no sign of Travis Holcomb, which was a huge relief. "I don't know, Dax."

Dax leaned against one of the fences. "We'll just hang here."

After a few minutes, Wyatt shook hands with the three men. Once the men left, Wyatt went back to collecting his equipment. And I headed his way.

"Wyatt?"

He paused, but didn't turn around. "Hey." His voice was low.

"You were amazing," I gushed. Why wasn't he turning around?

"Thanks." He stuffed the coils of rope in a beaten-up satchel on the ground.

I waited.

"Wanna go get something to eat?" Dax asked.

"Can't. Gotta pack up and get home."

"Okay," I said. Something was wrong.

"Go well with the recruiters?" Dax asked, sending me a questioning look.

"Think so. Having lunch with them tomorrow." He turned around then, but he looked at Dax—not me.

"That's great," I said. "I'm so…so happy for you."

His jaw muscle bulged. "Thanks."

Wyatt! Talk to me. Look at me.

"Need help?" Dax offered.

Wyatt shook his head. "Got it. Thanks, though. I appreciate y'all coming out tonight."

I couldn't take it. I closed the space between us, putting my hands on his arm. I felt the way his arm tensed, saw the way he closed his eyes. "Wyatt?" I whispered.

I heard retreating steps…Dax leaving, probably.

He stared at my hands. "Allie," his voice was a growl, "you need to go home with Dax now."

"You *want* me to go?" I didn't lift my hand, I couldn't. He was trying to push me away, I could tell. Because of his dad?

His lips were pressed flat and he said nothing.

"Okay. I'll go. Just…I just wanted to say…I'm really proud of you. And…well…I–" I mumbled to a stop.

He looked at me then, the pain in his eyes raw and unguarded.

"Wyatt, I'm here. Okay? I want to be here—for you."

His nostrils flared but he leaned closer to me, the rim of his hat touching the top of my head, shielding us. His gaze held mine. "Go home, Allie."

"I'll go." I swallowed, making sure I spoke clearly. "It's just that…I love you."

13 CHAPTER THIRTEEN

He froze, completely surprised. If his breath hadn't hitched, I wouldn't have known he'd heard me. He just stared at me, until I felt like a complete idiot. I stepped back then, lifting my hand from his arm.

It hurt. I hurt. I suspected his life was a lot more complicated than I knew, but I thought...I *hoped*...he cared about me too. Maybe I just wanted him to?

"Night." The word was a garbled mess and I headed back in the direction I'd come.

"Allie," he ground out, taking my hand and pulling me down one of the alleys between empty pens. It was darker, but I held on to him, my heart thumping in my chest.

He stopped and turned, his hands sliding up my bare arms to my shoulders, causing wicked delicious shivers the whole way. His hands, callused and rough, were feather-light along my neck, cupping my cheeks and tilting my head back as he bent low.

His lips were so soft against mine. I hadn't expected that. Or the way his breath mixing with mine made me dizzy. I swayed into him, gripping his dusty shirt tightly. His lips grew firm, a little demanding, and it was perfect. All I wanted was this—and more.

When his lips lingered, the heat between us took over. Pressed against him, his heartbeat bounced with mine. His arms wrapped around me, pulling me closer. His hand pressed against my bare back, hesitant...uncertain.

My hands moved, pressing against his hard chest and sliding up to cup his neck—knocking his hat off—keeping him there.

Why can't I stop shaking? It was okay. He was shaking too.

I parted my lips, sucking in a ragged breath. His lips followed.

He pressed us against the metal pens at my back, keeping us upright and tangled in each other. I didn't think, *couldn't* think. Feeling was everything. Hot and sweet and happy, I ran my fingers through the close-cropped hair at the base of his neck, pulling him in.

The tip of his tongue brushed my lower lip. I made a strange noise, tightening my hold on him, pressing myself flat against him. There was no room between us, none. And it still didn't seem close enough.

One of his hands traveled down my back, resting against the base of my spine, fitting me against him. Holy hell.

"Wyatt?"

His lips closed on my lower lip, tugging. Breathing was no longer possible.

"Wyatt?" It sounded far away.

Wyatt suddenly went rigid, his hands stopped moving, his lips lifted. He pressed his cheek against my forehead, breathing hard.

"Where the hell are you?" We both heard him clearly then. Travis Holcomb.

I held on, desperate. Yes, I wanted to stay wrapped up like this. But I also wanted to...protect him. My hands stroked through his hair, offering him comfort—I hoped. It seemed to work; he relaxed against me, turning his face into my hair, his nose brushing against my ear. His breath against my bare skin made me shiver.

"Wyatt!" Travis sounded impatient, irritated. His voice sounded closer.

"Walk down the end of this alley and go right. You'll end up back by the food stands," Wyatt told me, his voice low. He let go of me all at once, stepping back so fast I almost fell over. He stooped, picking up his hat and dusting it off on his leg. He didn't say anything else before he left, heading back.

I stood there, breathing hard and reeling.

"Where have you been?" I heard Travis bark.

"Checking on something," Wyatt answered.

Travis snorted. "Let's go. I'm starving."

"Travis?" A voice I didn't know. "Hold up."

"Evenin', Clint. See you got your posse with you. What'd I do now?" Travis's insolent drawl sounded amused.

"Meg says you didn't pay for your ticket." I assumed that was Clint talking.

There was a long pause, then a laugh and Travis said, "Are you shittin' me?"

"No, Travis, I'm not." This Clint guy sounded *very* serious.

"I'll pay for it." Wyatt's voice was smooth.

"Like hell you will," Travis interrupted. "I paid that bitch."

"Be careful, Travis. It's not the only complaint we've had tonight. Sheriff's department was called—"

"Complaints?" Travis again.

"Complaints. Giving Cowboy Jack a hard time while he was working—"

"Jack called the sheriff?" Travis asked.

Clint was quick. "No, but about twenty people in the stands did."

Travis snorted.

"And the fight? In the parking lot? Before the show?"

Travis tried to joke it off. "Wasn't much of a *fight*."

185

Clint's tone stayed calm. "Harassing the Cooper girl in the stands?"

"What did you say to her?" Wyatt demanded. I don't know if Travis heard the edge of anger in Wyatt's voice, but I did—even though it was new to me.

"Your old man's in trouble and that's what you're gonna ask me? I told you, boy, that girl's trouble." Travis's voice grew hard, aggressive. "I told her to stay away from you. Like I've told you to stay away from her."

"You need to come with us, Travis." Clint again.

"You gonna make me?"

I heard Clint sigh, heard the sound of boots on gravel. "If that's the way it has to be." Although I couldn't see it, I could just imagine the white-hat brigade closing in on Travis Holcomb.

"Just go with him," Wyatt said calmly.

"You tellin' me what to do, boy? You think you're the man of the house?"

"No, sir. But I—"

The sound that followed made me flinch and move. I ran—not away, but toward it. I'd seen fights in school, knew the sound of a fist hitting flesh. I didn't want to believe that what I knew had happened *had* actually happened.

A big guy—Clint, maybe—had Travis's hands behind his back. It wasn't hard to do, this guy was big and broad—and sober. Two other men stood nearby, looking back and forth between father and son, stunned. It was clear everyone was shocked by what had happened.

Mr. Holcomb wasn't resisting. He was standing rigid, staring at the ground.

And Wyatt? Wyatt was staring up at the sky, breathing hard, his shoulders slumped—trembling. *Wyatt.* I ignored the three men, ignored Travis Holcomb, and went straight to Wyatt's side. My hand found his, holding it tight.

He looked down at me, surprised. And then—he frowned. I knew he'd sent me away to protect me, but I couldn't go. His left eye was swelling, a small cut through the brow. My heart was in my throat, choking me, making it hard to breathe. I wanted to do…say something. Instead, I squeezed his hand.

"You gonna be okay, son?" Clint—not the guy holding Mr. Holcomb—said.

Wyatt nodded, still looking at me. I didn't know how to react. I tried not to frown or cry or freak out over the fact that Wyatt's dad had just punched him in the face.

Clint cleared his throat. "He'll spend the night at the sheriff's."

Wyatt nodded. "I appreciate you looking out for him, Mr. Javorsky."

"You did real good tonight, Wyatt," he added. "You ready, Travis?"

Mr. Holcomb looked at me, a narrow-eyed look that had me moving closer to Wyatt. Then he looked at his son. I could see the regret, frustration…but he didn't say a thing. No apology, no begging for forgiveness, nothing. "Let's go," he answered Mr. Javorsky. We didn't move until Mr. Javorsky and the others had escorted Mr. Holcomb away.

Wyatt went back to packing his bag. I helped, or tried to help. I understood he didn't want to talk about what happened, but it was hard. Nothing I could say or do could undo what had happened. So I held his bag open when he needed it and smiled at him whenever he looked at me. I don't know if it did anything for him, but it calmed me down.

By the time he was packed, his eye was so swollen I doubted he could see much out of it.

"You want some ice for that?" I asked.

He shook his head. "It's fine."

"So you're finished here? Do you have someplace you need to go…something you need to do?" I asked. I didn't especially want to say goodnight, but… "I guess I don't want to crash anything."

"Nope. I'm done." He took my hand, leading me through the maze of pens and cowboys.

"You should get some sleep so you can wow the recruiters tomorrow." I squeezed his hand. "Are you excited?"

He nodded. "I didn't know they were coming. Doc Bergmann, the rodeo announcer, called them."

I remembered the announcer talking about Wyatt. "Perfect timing."

Wyatt nodded. "Scores were good."

"Good? Wyatt, you were…amazing." I tugged on his arm, making him stop. "Seriously."

He smiled awkwardly, pulling me against him with one arm. "Thank you."

I stood on tiptoe and kissed his cheek. I didn't care that we were surrounded by people; it was the right thing to do. His smile told me he felt the same way.

We headed toward the back pasture, toward his truck and trailer. Everyone seemed to know one another, and they all seemed pretty proud of Wyatt. He got slapped on the back, nodded at, and a whole lot of "Atta-boy!" in his direction.

Dax was waiting at Wyatt's truck. "Geez, Allie, did you have to clock him that hard?" he asked, wincing over Wyatt's eye.

Wyatt laughed. "Got hooked with a horn."

I glanced at Wyatt. The lie came quickly, easily. Rodeo was an easy way to cover all sorts of bruises. How many bruises had his father given him? I wanted to pull him close, to hug him, to tell him I loved him… I swallowed.

"Oh." Dax nodded, pushing off Wyatt's hood. "Then I guess you got lucky."

Wyatt nodded. "Hungry?"

Dax shrugged. "I don't want to intrude."

I looked at Wyatt. He was looking at me, his eyes so full of emotion I sucked in a deep breath.

Dax said something like "Yeah, so, this is awkward." I

think. I couldn't really concentrate on anything else but Wyatt. Warm brown eyes searched mine, peering inside of me, making me light-headed.

"Barbecue okay? Good place in town." Wyatt's rough voice made me jump.

Dax laughed. "Okay."

I forced myself to stop looking at Wyatt. "Food sounds good. What about this?" I nodded at the trailer.

"I'll come back after and take it home." Wyatt smiled down at me.

The drive to the restaurant was...different. Maybe it was because I was no longer ignoring the way I felt about Wyatt or the power of those feelings. All of a sudden I *wanted* him to touch me. I *wanted* him to know I cared. Luckily, he was on the same page. If he wasn't holding my hand, his arm was resting on my leg—natural, calming, wonderful.

The restaurant was busy. Young and old, sober and drunk, the bar was crowded and the tables were full. But Levi and his group were there and they waved us over to the tables they had commandeered out on the large patio. We crowded around two large tables pulled together, pushing some of the empty cups and pitchers, baskets half-full of French fries, and ketchup bottles aside.

Levi smiled at Wyatt. "Man of the hour."

"Heard you kicked some bull-ass tonight," Austin said and laughed.

"Made it your bitch," Dylan added. "Bull give you the shiner? Or your girlfriend?"

Boys. Wyatt shrugged but didn't answer. Everyone laughed.

"Some right hook." Levi shook his head. "Shit."

A big-haired woman approached Wyatt, enveloping him in a sweetly perfumed hug and planting a sticky pink lipstick kiss on his cheek. "I'm so proud of you, honey. Your momma would be too."

"Thanks," he murmured.

"What can I get you? Anything you want, my treat."
The older woman kept gushing. "Hell's bells, honey, what
happened to your pretty face?"

"We're taking bets, Miss Sue. Bull? Or Allie here?" Levi
pointed at me and smiled at the woman.

She looked at me, then shook her head. "Bull."

Wyatt winked at the woman. "I'm starving."

"We'll take care of that. What about your girl, here?"
Sue sized me up, her eyes thorough but kind.

"I'd love a drink. And some fries."

Dax leaned over my shoulder. "Brisket sandwich?"

Sue laughed. "Got it. Y'all sit."

We joined the others, squeezing in at the tables. Wyatt
and I shared a chair. He draped his arm along the back of
the chair, his hand resting on my bare shoulder. I shivered
a little, leaning into his side, as his fingers stroked my skin.

No one at the table missed it. Levi started laughing.
Dylan frowned and handed Austin some money.

"Really?" Wyatt shook his head.

"It's been a long summer." Austin was all smiles.

"Is betting on who hooks up a typical summer
activity?" I asked.

"Hooks up?" Levi asked, eyebrows raised.
"Meaning...?"

"Can we *not* go there? She's my sister," Dax groaned.

The three of them laughed.

"Good job tonight, Wyatt." The curvy blond from the
river leaned forward, her boobs resting on the laminate
tabletop. They were kind of hard to miss in the low-cut
thin cotton t-shirt.

I leaned back, thinking about what Levi had said. Or
almost said. *Been there, done that.*

Wyatt nodded. "Thanks, Loretta."

She shot me a smug little smile before leaning back in
her seat.

"Where's Molly?" Austin asked.

"Family night," Dax said, sighing.

"Family night? Is that what you call it?" Dylan laughed.

"Yeah. Family night," Wyatt said. "Hank left right after we rode. He'll be shipping out again soon."

That ended whatever that was.

Sue came out, balancing three baskets piled high with brisket sandwiches and French fries. It was a perfect opportunity for me to sit back and watch the dynamic.

Wyatt seemed to be the voice of reason. Levi, Austin, and Dylan were clearly the unofficial full-of-crap leaders. Loretta had two equally pretty yet intimidating friends with her. There were a handful of other guys, but they were too busy being loud and obnoxious to hold my interest. Besides, Wyatt was looking at me again.

I pretended I didn't know. It wasn't that I was trying to be coy or flirtatious. Honestly, I was afraid I'd climb into his lap and do...do...I didn't know what I'd do. And that scared the shit out of me.

"Not hungry?" he asked softly.

He must have read my thoughts when I looked at him because his jaw muscle bounced and there was the slightest flare to his nostrils. I swallowed and picked up a fry, then hesitated. I didn't want to choke. And there was a pretty good chance that might happen if he kept looking at me like that. He shifted in his chair, turning all of his attention on his sandwich.

"Heard about your dad," Levi said softly to Wyatt. "Sorry, man. You can't catch a break." He looked at me then. "Never mind. You're gonna be fine."

I smiled. "That was pretty sweet, Levi."

"That mean you'll dump him and *hook up* with me?" He made his eyebrows go up and down.

I sighed. "Aaaand you're back."

Wyatt's fingers stroked the back of my arm, covering my entire body in goose bumps.

"Ready for Monday?" Austin asked to nobody and everybody.

"You have to say the M word?" Levi groaned, throwing

a French fry at him.

"Senior year. Can't *totally* suck," one of Loretta's friends offered and shrugged.

"You'd know all about sucking, Kim."

"You wish, Dylan," Kim said without missing a beat, rolling her eyes. I liked her for that.

"As long as I get to can a few freshmen, I'm good." Austin finished off my fries.

"Can?" I asked. "Er...do I want to know?"

"You don't know about canning?" Dylan looked incredulous. "Throwing freshmen into the trash? When it's full?"

"An oldie but goodie," Levi agreed.

"That's hazing," I argued.

"Hazing?" Austin shook his head. "Allie, sweetheart, it's just harmless fun. Part of life."

I pressed my lips shut. I didn't know anything about life here, clearly. For all I knew the guy I was losing my mind over threw kids in trashcans and slept with girls like Loretta to pass the time.

"It doesn't have to be." Wyatt sighed. "And y'all know Principal Diaz will kick your asses out of school if you keep that shit up."

My hero.

Levi crossed his arms over his chest. "Oh, Dad, you're no fun." We all laughed then.

"You done?" Wyatt asked me. "I need to go get the trailer. Pecos will be getting anxious." I nodded, glancing up at him.

"I'm done too, in case you're leaving," Dax teased, making everyone laugh again.

"Let's go." Wyatt stood up, his hand holding mine.

"Y'all be safe tonight," Sue called out.

"Yeah, safe," Levi agreed. "You know, *safe?*"

"Wyatt's always real safe," Loretta said, clearly trying to make a point. I didn't miss it. Dylan, Austin, and Levi snorted.

Wyatt shot Loretta a look, confused and a little pissed—I think. "Thanks for the food, Sue." Without another word to the group, he led the way to his truck.

Being jealous didn't make any sense. I knew that—logically. I knew that Wyatt, looking the way he did, was probably one of the guys all the Black Hills girls would want. It didn't mean I wanted to think about who and what that meant, exactly. Especially since Loretta and I were nothing alike.

Once we were in his truck and his arm slipped around my shoulders, I decided not to go there. Lindie hadn't been the jealous type and she'd kept all her exes as friends. I didn't have any exes, but I knew—no matter what happened between Wyatt and me—I didn't want to lose him. Even as a friend.

Wyatt was singing softly as we drove along the dark road. I turned my head, pressing my ear and cheek against his chest. His voice, his heartbeat, the regular thrum of the tires on the road—I don't remember falling asleep.

I do remember waking up, in bed, Wyatt leaning over me.

It was dark. If it wasn't for the faint green glow of my clock and the pale white of the moon spilling in from my window, I wouldn't have seen Wyatt. But I did.

"Sorry," he whispered.

"For?" I whispered back.

"Didn't mean to wake you."

I was very aware of him, me, my bed…him. "I'm glad you did."

He shook his head. "I need to get home."

I nodded, placing one hand along the side of his face. "Okay."

He sat on the edge of the bed. "Allie…I'm sorry about tonight."

I pulled my hand away and sat up. "You are?" I managed.

He turned on my bedside lamp, revealing how swollen

and purple his eye was. I wanted to touch him again, but I locked my hands together and pressed them against my thighs. He hesitated for a second, then cupped my face in his hands. "Not about this. About us."

My hands covered his, the pressure in my chest easing instantly.

"My dad…" He shook his head. "He's…well, that's just him. And Loretta? I didn't want you to think we've ever… Never." He shrugged.

I smiled. "Oh."

He smiled, a little lopsided considering how swollen the side of his face was.

"Does it hurt?" I asked, running my fingers along his forehead. "Because it looks like it hurts."

He shook his head. His eyes were fixed on my face. "I feel pretty good right now."

"You do?"

He nodded, his eyes never leaving mine. "Remember when you said you were a mess?" He laughed, a hard, bitter sound. "Tonight…well, you see what my life—"

I stopped him. "I'm so sorry, Wyatt." The sadness on his face twisted my heart. "I heard him—he doesn't want us to be together?" My voice broke. "I don't want to make things worse with your father or…well, I don't want to be…trouble."

"You can't make things worse with my dad, Allie."

"Okay." I sighed. "That's not exactly what I was wanting to hear, but I guess it's something." I hadn't meant to say that out loud. *Huh.*

He laughed. Then stopped, remembering he was in my bedroom—at night—alone. "What do you want to hear?" His eyes sparkled, crinkling as he smiled.

I sucked in a slow breath. Considering how warm and tingly and aware I was, I wasn't sure I wanted to hear anything right now.

The tremor in his voice surprised me. "Being with you is the only time everything feels better."

"R-really?"

He nodded. I smiled, a big, goofy smile. His smile was amazing, until he winced and covered his eye.

"I'm sorry." I slipped forward on the bed, lifting his hand to assess his bruise. Raising up on my knees, I tilted his head, angling his face in the light. "Are you sure you shouldn't go to the doctor? The white of your eye's all red. What I can see of it, anyway."

But when I stopped talking I realized he was staring up at me. His hands gripped my waist, hot through the thin cotton of my dress.

I smoothed my hand across his forehead and bent my head to him. I was nervous—freaking out—but it didn't stop me from pressing my lips to his. I was off-center a little, hitting the corner of his mouth. But he turned his head until our lips were fitted together perfectly.

Kissing Wyatt was one crazy, emotional, needy ball of flaming-hot perfection. I didn't want to stop. I loved the way our breaths mingled. The feel of his tongue against mine had me gripping his shoulders. And his hands, slipping up my back, pressing against me—skin on skin.

"I have to go." He broke away from our kiss, but his grip on me tightened.

I nodded, but didn't let go of him.

"I *do*," he said again.

I rested my forehead against his.

"Allie. I don't *want* to go."

"Stay," I whispered, dropping a light kiss against his forehead.

Stay? What did that mean? What was I asking? I knew exactly what would happen. And I knew why he was so determined to go. And I loved him even more for it.

"Al-lie," he groaned. He sounded like he was being tortured.

I sat back, putting some much needed space between us. His arms were still around me, looser now. "I know. I know." I was gasping for air. Which couldn't be sexy.

So now I want to be sexy?

"Gotta get Pecos unloaded." He ran a hand over his short-cropped hair.

His horse? "Wait…is he still at the fairgrounds?"

"No. We already went and picked everything up. You slept right through it."

"Oh." *I must really have been out of it.* "Need any help?"

He smiled. "I got this."

"Okay."

He kissed me, a soft, sweet kiss that had me melting into him. He groaned a little, let go of me, and stood up. "Going now."

"Wyatt?" I followed him to the door. "There's…a squeaky board out there," I cautioned him.

He looked down at me and nodded.

"I…I'm not sure my dad would be cool with my boyfriend sneaking out of my bedroom," I murmured.

He pulled me against him, kissing me once. "Am I your boyfriend? Even though I'm a stupid redneck?"

I winced. "You're not stupid. Or a redneck. You're the real deal: a cowboy. And I really like your kisses."

He kissed me again. "Guess I'll take that as a yes, then."

I stepped back. "You better go take care of Pecos, cowboy. Don't want to make him mad. I need him to take care of you. Since you're my boyfriend now."

He smiled again, that crazy gorgeous smile. "Shit," he bit out, gingerly covering his eye.

"Sorry, sorry."

We stood there, staring at each other. I didn't want him to leave. He didn't want to leave. But we both knew he needed to go. Neither one of us was ready to go *there*. Okay, our bodies were *so* ready. I was beginning to think my body really might explode. But emotionally…I wasn't so sure.

"Night, Allie." His whisper was so soft. His hand turned my doorknob, making me whimper. He stopped.

"No, no, go…" I whispered, hugging myself. He frowned. I smiled. "Go on. Poor Pecos."

"I'll be back first thing in the morning."

I shook my head. "You sleep, Wyatt Holcomb, and then you go show those college boys how much they need you."

He nodded. "After, then. Tomorrow's the last day of summer. I'd like to spend it with you."

God, I was so happy. "Me too."

He opened the door and slipped out, walking softly down the hall, sidestepping the squeaky board, and disappearing around the corner.

I hurried across the room, staring out the window at Wyatt's truck below. As soon as he was in the yard, he turned back. He waved at me. I waved back. I sat there watching until the brake lights of his trailer disappeared into the black night.

14 CHAPTER FOURTEEN

Dad was back in the morning. He and Mom kind of danced around each other. And for the first time, I felt sorry for my father.

Dad was this incredibly fit, incredibly capable, slightly OCD get-it-done guy who also happened to be super good-looking. Lindie said she'd totally sleep with him if he wasn't married to my mom—which creeped me out. But she wasn't the only one of my friends that felt that way, she was just the most vocal about it. That was just Lindie.

I could only imagine how he felt. Mom picking a short, non-masculine, brains over brawn type had to be tough on his ego. *If* she'd actually cheated on him, which was something I had a really hard time believing. Okay, they kissed, but one kiss didn't—

I stopped then.

I *knew* what a kiss could mean, now. I thought about Lindie and figured all the guys she'd kissed hadn't made her feel the way Wyatt made me feel or she wouldn't have gone through so many of them.

I frowned at my mother, watching her pull the last of the French toast from the skillet. One kiss could mean a *lot*.

This was new, hard territory. Mom was the…the bad guy? Well, maybe not the bad guy. But…I'd spent so long being mad at Dad—for everything—that I never stopped to think what his side might be like. After last night, I realized my father might be a little overbearing, a little competitive, and a little opinionated. But he was a good man. There was no question in my mind—now—that he honestly put us first. Uprooting us from our home was a bit extreme, but I guess it made more sense now. It wasn't all about me; it was about him preserving his family.

And he would never, ever, raise a hand to any of us.

"What's the matter?" my mother asked, passing me the plate of French toast.

I shook my head, taking one piece and passing the plate on to Dax. What would happen if I told them I realized how lucky I was to have them for parents? *They'd institutionalize me instantly.* It's just that I was. I was very lucky. And the thought of Mom screwing it all up was…well, it pissed me off.

"Have fun last night?" Mom asked.

"Yeah." Dax nodded. "Faces are starting to get familiar. Met some new people, too."

I poked my toast, wondering if Travis Holcomb was still locked up. I hoped so. Wyatt didn't need him underfoot while he was meeting with the A&M people.

"…wasn't as good as the other one we went to," Dax was saying.

"How did Wyatt do?" Dad asked.

He rocks. I smiled, pouring some syrup on my toast.

"Awesome. High scores all around," Dax offered.

That wasn't enough. *His* dad might not be proud of him, but I knew Mom and Dad would be. "He was amazing. Really. You guys should have been there. Highest scores for bull-riding. Caught the eye of some college recruiters, too," I added.

Dad looked at me. It was quite a speech for me. I couldn't help it—I smiled.

I saw the complete and total surprise on his face. "Oh?"

"He's having lunch with them today before he comes over," Dax finished, looking at me like I'd grown another head.

"We should all think positive thoughts," Mom said. "Cross our fingers."

"He'll do great. He's a sharp kid." Dad piled his plate high. "So..." He cleared his throat and took a sip of orange juice. "You and Wyatt..."

"He's my boyfriend."

They all stared at me then. I took a bite.

Dax burst out laughing. "Um, pass the syrup."

Mom was smiling, albeit a little concerned. And Dad... I waited, watching. His brows went up. "Well."

"Do you know his dad?" I asked. "Travis Holcomb?"

I saw Dad's frown. "Not personally."

"But you've heard of him?"

"People talk in a town this small," Mom admitted. "I have to say, I haven't heard a lot of nice things about the man."

"Because he's an asshole," Dax said before biting into some bacon.

"Dax," Mom chastised.

Dad frowned at him. "Dax, I don't think—"

"No, he really is," I said quickly. "Big time asshole. He was arrested last night."

Mom and Dad froze then. "Why?"

Dax and I looked at each other. "Fighting or stealing or something," I murmured.

"Should have been for child abuse," Dax offered.

Mom and Dad froze again. "He *hit* Wyatt?" Dad asked.

Poor Wyatt. I knew this was the exact thing he didn't want to happen—people talking about him.

Dax nodded. "Black eye and split eyelid. Though I guess it's not exactly child abuse since Wyatt's eighteen."

A black eye so swollen it hurt him to smile. My

stomach clenched. As angry as I was accused of being, I didn't *hate* people. Normally. Travis Holcomb was making me reconsider that.

"Oh my God." Mom sat back. "That poor boy."

"That kid's had more than his share of heartache," Dad murmured. "Doesn't seem fair."

More than his share of heartache? "Just...please don't say anything to him about it," I said. "He...he's proud. He wouldn't want people talking about him or his family."

Dad was watching me closely. "I can respect that."

Mom was still upset. "But—"

"Please, Mom," I begged. "His dad's on the road most of the time anyway."

"So he's alone?" She paused, frowning. "I won't say anything, but...I can't *not* do something now. I don't care if he's eighteen or five, he's a child," she argued. "Davis." She turned to look at Dad. "Maybe you could invite him to stay here? We have extra bedrooms. He's here anyway. He does so much around the place. I just want to make sure he has food and clean clothes and...and people around that care about him, expect him to check in."

I loved my mother so much. She had such a big heart; she always had. She didn't like to see anyone or anything—animals included—hurting...which made the whole cheating on Dad thing that much harder to deal with. My stomach clenched tighter.

"I will," Dad agreed, then looked at me. "As long as you promise me the two of you will...behave."

I smiled, shoving another bite of toast into my mouth. I didn't want to lie to my father, so keeping my mouth full seemed like a wise idea.

The house phone rang. "Mrs. Duncan?" Mom asked.

"Probably. Weekly visit." I didn't want to feel deflated, but I did.

"Done?" Mom asked, reaching for my plate.

"Yes, thank you." That was when I noticed the strange look between my parents. "I can call her back."

My father shook his head and stood. "Go on," he said and slammed out the back door.

We stared after him, but the phone kept ringing so I went into the living room and answered the phone. Whatever was bothering him now would probably still be bothering him later. I pressed the talk button on my phone.

"Allie?"

"Hey, Mrs. D."

"How's my girl? Ready for school tomorrow?" She sounded so happy.

"Um, not really," I admitted. "I'm trying not to think about it, actually."

"But it's senior year. You'll rule the school. I remember all of your plans. Weekend getaways to the coast. Dances. Tournaments. Still planning on taking that Spring Break to Europe? Oh, Allie, you should be beside yourself, counting down until you're free."

Lindie and I had made those plans—mostly because that's what Lindie wanted to do. I was happy to go with her, because she made everything more fun. But trips and dances didn't have the same pull as they did before. And the countdown I'd been keeping? I hadn't bothered with it much recently. I only had this year with Wyatt before everything changed all over again. I'd never thought of a school year as being short before.

Wyatt... I smiled. "You're right." Mrs. D. would have no idea I was gushing because I was thinking about my...my *boyfriend*. "How are things?" I braced myself.

"You know us. Never a dull moment. I'm getting Marcie ready for the next show." Marcie was Mrs. D's pampered pure-bred show Corgi. "Mr. D finally traded in L-Lindie's little Porsche for something pretty—just for me."

I was proud of her. And of Mr. D. I knew it wasn't easy, moving on without Lindie. "Ooh, what does it look like? Send me a picture. Knowing Mr. D, it's got all sorts of bells and whistles."

"It does, indeed." She paused. "Have your parents talked to you?"

I stopped bouncing my leg. "No. I mean…I don't know. What about?"

"Oh, nothing. Nothing at all. So, tell me about what classes you'll be taking? You were in so many advanced classes—will they even have something for you to take?"

I hadn't really considered that. "Guess I'll find out tomorrow."

Mrs. D yammered on for a while. She did a great job of sounding calm and fine. And she was, until our conversation started to wind down. I knew tears were coming, but amazingly she said, "I miss you like crazy and hope to hear from you soon, okay, Allie dear?"

"I miss you too."

"Well, if you need or just want to talk to me, please do. I'll answer the phone as soon as you call."

"I will." I smiled, looking out the front picture window at the oak trees lining the property. They were swaying gently in the breeze—green and lovely. It was a pretty picture altogether. "You have a great week."

"You too, Allie dear." She paused. "Let me know how everything goes, promise?"

"I promise. Bye."

"Bye, Allie."

And I hung up.

Mom was standing in the doorway. "How is she?" She looked anxious, antsy.

"Fine." I sat forward. "Is something going on?" I asked. "With Mrs. D?" Mom shook her head. "Something's up," I pushed.

She shook her head again—once.

"I don't believe you." And it irritated me. I didn't like not knowing what was going on. She smiled then. "So?"

"Your dad and I are talking a few things over."

I flopped back into the seat. "Taffy Todd?" It was out

COWBOYS & KISSES

before I realized what I was saying. I jumped up. "I don't know why I said that."

She stared at me, her blue eyes huge. "No...no... Of course you know. I don't know why I thought you wouldn't. You're so perceptive."

"I shouldn't have—"

"There's nothing to hide. *Nothing*." She sounded so desperate. I wanted to believe her, I did. Swallowing down my questions was harder than I thought. She must have noticed because she sighed and said, "You can ask me anything, Allie. I'll always tell you the truth."

I knew I shouldn't ask, but I had to. I'd lost too much to lose her too. "Okay. Well, Dax said you were kissing."

"He kissed me. I hope Dax saw that I was pushing him away," she added. "Until that night, we were friends and colleagues."

"And now?"

"I haven't spoken to him since I left the college—until he called. That kiss was it. A horrible mistake. It cost me your father's trust and the friendship of a man I'd respected for years." She shook her head, crossing the room to stare out the front window. "I should have slapped him. I-I was just so surprised. I never knew he...I didn't think."

"Have you told Dad that?" I asked.

"I've tried, believe me. I *love* your father. I've loved him since I was...a little older than you are now. Have we had our ups and downs, yes, you know we have. One kiss and..." She shook her head. "Your father's the only man I've loved. And, at the risk of grossing you out, I know he's...the only man that lights me up from the inside. The only man I want to spend my life with."

I knew exactly what she meant. I did.

"Take a walk with me," my dad said, making us both jump.

He was leaning against the doorframe of the kitchen, staring at Mom. I wouldn't exactly say it was a lovey-dovey look. But there was an intensity, and tenderness, in his gaze. I hoped that was a start in the right direction. Mom nodded and followed him out the back door.

I glanced at the clock. Ten-fifteen. Run. I'd go for a run. I didn't want to think about Mom and Dad, school starting, how much I loved Wyatt, or the fact that my life was so…so…so different than I'd ever imagined it would be.

In five minutes I was dressed and running. Once I was done, I pulled out a soccer ball and started working through drills. Dribbling first. Then toe taps.

"Where are your cones?" Dax asked, trying to take the ball from me. *Trying.*

"I don't know," I answered, dancing around him with the ball, tapping it just enough to keep it out of his range.

He pushed me out of the way with his shoulder.

"Look at you!" I laughed. "Who knew you had a shoulder tackle in you."

He shrugged, running with the ball. "It's not like I've been forced to watch you play since we were three or anything."

I ran alongside him, letting him have the ball. "Watching is different from playing. I didn't know you were coordinated."

He stopped then, frowning at me.

I kicked the ball away and ran it down. "Can't take the heat, get outta the kitchen."

He ran after me. "You're mean."

I turned back to him. "I'm sorry." —and he stole the ball from me, laughing.

We played for a while, using rocks and cactus as our goals. When the sun was too high to ignore, we went back inside.

"Shower," I said, running up the stairs.

At two-thirty I was dressed in some blue jean shorts and a lightweight blue tank top. I braided back my hair and dug through my rarely used cosmetics bag for lip gloss.

Dax came in and flopped onto my bed. "What are you wearing tomorrow?"

"Why is everyone talking about tomorrow?" I groaned.

"Because it's happening—soon. You know, like, tomorrow?"

I rolled my eyes. "So what am I wearing? Clothes, I guess."

"Good call." He lay on his stomach.

"So, is everything okay with Molly?" I glanced at him. "Can I ask?"

He didn't say anything.

"Dax?"

He rolled over. "She has a boyfriend."

"What?" Anger, hot and fast, rose up. "Are you sure?" I wanted to punch her in her pretty little face.

"Yeah." His smile was sad.

I sat on the edge of the bed. "Can I talk to her?"

"No. No point," he said, sitting up. "We were never a couple."

"Um, you so *were*. I saw it—everyone saw it."

"Saw what?" His blue eyes were so blue, so disappointed.

I leaned against him. "Come on, Dax. I know she likes you. Everyone knows she likes you."

"She might *like* me, just not enough. And now this Cannon guy is home after a summer of working on his uncle's ranch."

"Cannon?" I asked. "Seriously?" He smiled, a tight smile. "She's dating a guy named after a weapon?"

He shrugged, his smile growing. "They've known each other since they were kids."

I didn't say anything. What could I say? Molly was a tease? Molly picked guys with strange names? Molly wasn't a nice person?

"She said they'd been going through a bad time."

"Well, I guess that makes stringing you along okay," I snapped.

"Allie, she didn't."

"Oh, Dax, come on."

"She's a nice girl."

"Bullshit. Nice girls don't yank amazing guys around. I know this because I'm not a nice girl."

He smiled. "You have your moments. But I'm glad things are good between you and Wyatt."

"Me too," I agreed. "Doesn't make me want to punch Molly any less, though."

"Al-lie," Dax groaned, flopping back onto my bed. "Let me handle this."

I stared down at my brother. My tender-hearted, funny, and obviously crushed brother. I honestly believed Molly cared about him. I'd never admit it to my brother, but I couldn't imagine any guy that could top him as a boyfriend. Except Wyatt, maybe. *Stupid girl.* It took everything I had not to get bitchy—tear Molly apart—but I could tell that wasn't what he needed from me right now. I put my hand on his shoulder and squeezed. "I'm really sorry, Dax."

He nodded. "Me too."

We sat there in silence for a few minutes.

"Back to tomorrow. You ready?" he asked.

I stood and opened my closet. "God, no. Not in the least."

Dax laughed. "Right there with you."

"Allie," Mom called from downstairs. "Dax. Wyatt's here."

It's safe to say that those four words changed everything. I went from feeling edgy and frustrated to…euphoric. My heart felt so full, my chest tight, and I had to move.

"What are you waiting for?" Dax asked, laughing.

I looked at him and shrugged. *What was I waiting for?* My feet barely touched the ground as I ran from the room. How had I not heard his truck? Because I was considering Molly-revenge scenarios? Scenarios I wouldn't think

208

about—for Dax's sake. Honestly, I didn't want that kind of negativity anyway. I was sad for Dax, but if he was *handling it,* me getting in the middle of *it* wouldn't help.

There was only one thing I knew right now: I wanted to be with Wyatt. To make sure he was okay, that his lunch went well, that his dad wasn't around… And he was here, so I could ask him about all of that. *This anticipation is crazy.* I'd only said good-bye to him a few hours ago, even if it felt like days…

It was only when I was on the bottom step that I realized I probably shouldn't run across the room and plant a serious kiss on him. Which was going to be really hard because that was exactly what I wanted to do. I walked casually across the living room floor to the kitchen, practically vibrating with repressed enthusiasm.

He was standing, his back to me, talking to my father. My mother was looking at him, clearly upset. She kept trying not to look at his eye, but I knew she was having a hard time with it. Physical violence wasn't acceptable, ever, no exceptions. My parents believed that, heart and soul.

I walked into the kitchen, not sure how to act. I knew that whatever I wanted to do, I shouldn't do it in front of my parents. "How'd it go?" I asked.

He turned and I winced. The white of his eye was dark red, like all the blood vessels had burst. It was purple and swollen and angry, but the cut through his eyebrow wasn't as bad as I'd thought it was. Or maybe it was just too swollen to see it clearly.

He frowned. "That bad?"

"Painful, maybe." Dax followed me into the kitchen.

Screw it. I slid my arms around his waist. "Makes you look rough and tumble—which is a good thing for a rodeo cowboy."

He hugged me with one arm, hesitantly, and laughed softly.

I looked up at him. "So?" Even with one good eye, I could tell he wanted to kiss me. I couldn't help the smile that spread across my face.

"What did they say?" Mom chimed in.

"Make 'em sweat. Don't tell 'em a thing," Dax teased.

Wyatt shook his head. "It went really well, Dr. Cooper. They want me on their team and are willing to pay for most everything to get me there."

My heart went crazy. No deployment. No worrying about combat or fighting or death or war. A good school, doing what he loved, close by—depending on where I ended up. I was so…so *happy*.

"Congratulations, Wyatt," my father said, shaking Wyatt's hand.

I stepped back, but he grabbed my hand. "Thank you, sir. I know I've been given a chance here. There are a few things I need to figure out, but I will. I'm not going to mess this up." His hand was tight around mine.

A few things to figure out? He's amazing.

"Congrats." Dax shook his hand too. "I'm glad it's gonna happen for you, man."

"Just promise me you'll try not to break anything." My mom—ever the mom.

"Yes, ma'am. Injuries slow you down." He smiled, even though it had to hurt to do so.

"Wyatt…" My father cleared his throat. "I've got something I need a hand with out in the barn, if you have a second?"

I frowned. "Right now?"

"It won't take long," my father said, glancing at our joined hands.

Oh my God. Did he just *smile*? So Dad was good with this? Welcome to a whole new level of weird—as if that was possible at this point.

Wyatt squeezed my hand and followed Dad out the back door.

I felt a little confused. And a lot deflated. Wyatt just got here and I wanted to hear everything about his meeting. I wanted him to stay. I guess I didn't do a good job of hiding my emotions because Dax laughed and Mom hugged me.

"Your father didn't want to talk to Wyatt about *things* in front of everyone. He's a proud young man, something you made clear. So let them talk in private. Hopefully, Wyatt will listen to what your father has to say."

"Cool," Dax said. "I'll go start cleaning out Grandma's old sewing room. It's big and far enough away from the rest of us to give him some privacy."

Mom nodded. "Great idea, Dax."

"What?" I asked. They'd actually talked about this? About Wyatt living here? "Are you guys serious?"

"We agree Wyatt needs a base, some security—a home. I know you're not all that fond of us, but I think we're better than what he has. There's not a single reason for Wyatt not to go to college. Your father and I can help with that, too."

There was no arguing that they'd make sure he stayed on track. They nagged the crap out of Dax and me. But I knew we'd get accepted to the schools we wanted to go to; they'd been making sure of that for the last three years. As long as I didn't screw it up, I'd be able to go anywhere I wanted to. I was headed to SMU after high school graduation—or at least that had been my plan. Lindie and I's plan, anyway. Dax wasn't sure where he wanted to go yet, but he had options. Music was his life. He wanted to play, and teach.

"He might say no," I murmured.

"He probably will try," she agreed. "But your father's not going to take no on this one. And neither will I."

I followed her into the sewing room. It was on the front of the house, downstairs. It would totally work for a bedroom and had a decent closet, but there wasn't a full bathroom downstairs so he'd have to clean up in the bathroom Dax and I shared.

Grandma's old sewing table was way too heavy to lift, but we managed to push it into the far corner. Dax and I carried the few boxes we found into the attic. On my way back down, I located some clean sheets and towels. Mom wiped down the large wooden rocking chair and the old wrought iron bed that Grandma had used when her knees hurt too much to go upstairs. Once that was done, Mom and I made up the bed and Dax swept the floor.

I heard the screen door—it was in serious need of some oil on the hinges—and headed back into the kitchen. Dad was at the sink, alone.

"Did he leave?" I asked. "He was upset, wasn't he? I knew he'd get embarrassed—"

"Allie." He looked at me, his hazel eyes boring into mine. "Wyatt went home to pack. You and Dax go help him with his stuff. I'm going to start getting the barn ready for the horses."

I stood there, staring at him. "Really?"

"He argued, but so did I." He looked at me—a long assessing look—and shook his head.

"What?" I asked.

He shook his head again. "Nothing. Come on. Let's get this done before dinner."

Dax and I made the drive to Wyatt's house in silence. I guess I was still processing everything that was happening. It was all happening so fast.

We bounced along a rutted dirt road and rounded a large bunch of cedar trees to find a mobile home. It was small, old, with visible signs of wear and damage. The front paneling was patched in places and had several black-rimmed stains. A single air conditioning window unit sat in a tiny window on the front of the house, while the other two windows were covered with plywood. The sagging roof was a patchwork of odd shingles and mismatched sheet metal.

A lone wind chime hung off a board that had been nailed to the roof. I stared at it. Something about that chime made the place a tiny bit less...depressing.

The horse barn didn't match. It was a big, traditional-looking wooden building with a hay loft and two massive open doors. It looked like something out of a movie or children's book, without the red paint and smiling animals. It was easy to see where Wyatt spent most of his time—keeping Pecos' home safe and surprisingly neat.

One of the stall doors was open to the pen or paddock or whatever you called the large fenced-in area for animals. Pecos trotted forward, his caramel-colored ears pricking up as Dax pulled up beside Wyatt's truck and parked.

Wyatt came out on the porch, a strange look on his face.

"Hey!" I was all smiles, jumping from the truck and running up the wooden steps—straight into his arms.

He pulled me against him, hugging me tightly.

15 CHAPTER FIFTEEN

I sighed, relaxing into him. "We came to help," I murmured.

"You didn't have to," he answered, his voice against my ear. "Not much to get."

"Then it won't take long," Dax said, brushing by him and into the house.

Where the uncertainty came from, or the case of nerves started, I'm not sure. But I had a hard time looking at him.

He tilted my face towards his, his eyes almost gold in the bright afternoon sun. "You look pretty."

I was smiling so big my face hurt. *He thought I was pretty?* "Mm?" My gaze was fixed on his mouth.

He smiled. "Mm." His voice was husky.

"What's going and what's staying behind?" Dax called from inside.

Wyatt sighed and let go of me, taking my hand to lead me inside. "I wasn't planning on taking much. It's not exactly mine to take."

I don't know what I expected to find inside the shabby trailer, but this was not it. It was old but clean. An old cast-iron woodstove sat in the far corner; two ancient recliners sat on either side. Hummingbird-print curtains fluttered over the boarded-up kitchen window, and little china hummingbird knick-knacks lined the built-in shelving on the far wall. I moved closer, looking at the framed pictures sitting behind the porcelain figures. One was of Wyatt when he was little. God, he was cute. Big hat, big belt-buckle, big grin. I smiled, touching the picture.

Another was Wyatt, his dad, and a woman I knew must be his mother. Then another picture of just her drew me closer. She had Wyatt's smile, the same light-brown hair. Her eyes were pale, more grey than copper, but she had the same warmth, I could tell.

What happened to you? Seeing her now, I wondered how she could have left Wyatt. "She looks like you," I said to him.

Wyatt looked at the picture of his mother, then picked it up and tucked it into his bag.

The last picture was Wyatt's father and mother, at a rodeo. His father was smiling, holding a huge belt-buckle. I frowned. This Travis Holcomb looked nothing like the man I'd met at the rodeo. This man looked normal. Happy.

"Anything else?" Dax asked.

Wyatt's gaze scanned the interior quickly. "That's it." Wyatt handed his bag to Dax then stooped to pick up a large wooden chest sitting just inside the door.

I wanted to poke around, to get a glimpse inside Wyatt's everyday world. But something held me back. He wasn't offering to show us around. If anything, he seemed eager to get out of here.

"Your dad around?" Dax asked the question I didn't have the nerve to ask.

He shook his head. "Left this morning."

"Left?" I asked.

"A delivery. He'll be back next weekend. Maybe." His laugh was short, hard.

That laugh hurt. How long had it been since his father was the man in the picture? How long had Wyatt lived alone? What had happened to his family?

Wyatt locked the door behind us and tucked the key into his pocket, balancing the wooden chest on his broad shoulder. He whistled and Pickett came running, barreling into the truck bed.

"Hey Pickett," I cooed at the dog. Pickett's stubby tail went crazy.

"You know he's a working dog, right?" Wyatt grinned, sliding the chest into the truck bed next to a worn suitcase I hadn't noticed before.

"Who needs love too," I added, rubbing Pickett behind the ears.

Dax laughed, then asked, "What about Pecos?"

"I'll bring Pecos and Daisy over once we get the barn ready for them." I could tell he wasn't happy about it.

"How long will that take?" I asked.

"Depends how much help I get." He smiled down at me, closing the tailgate.

I love that smile. I love him. I covered his hand, still resting on the tailgate. "I'll help," I said.

"Dad's already started," Dax said. "If that's it, I'll head back."

Wyatt nodded, opening his truck door. I slid in, taking my spot in the middle of the seat. When Wyatt slipped in next to me I reached up, put my hands on his shoulders, and leaned forward for a kiss. His breathy laugh brushed across my lips right before his mouth met mine. It was a long, firm kiss.

"Wyatt," I said against his mouth.

"Mm?" he murmured, his lips traveling across my cheek to my ear.

I wanted to talk to him about his father. About his mother. But then his lips latched onto my earlobe and I sort of forgot everything else except how absolutely mind-blowing his lips felt on my ear. *Holy crap.* My hands went from resting to gripping his shirt, tugging him against me. I heard my breath hitch and grow ragged. Pure, unfiltered sensation was taking over. I wanted to pull away. No, no I didn't. I wanted to pull him *closer*.

His hands slipped under the hem of my shirt, pressing against my bare back, sliding up. When his fingers slipped under my bra-strap—between my shoulders—he shivered, then went completely still. Something about that touch, skin on skin, made him stop. He was breathing hard—like me—when his mouth released my earlobe. He pressed his face against my neck, groaning softly. "Sorry." His voice was gruff.

I was gasping. *Don't stop*—which was probably the wrong thing to say at this point. But since I couldn't seem to form actual words yet, it didn't matter. *Don't be sorry.*

When he looked at me, I could tell that I wasn't the only one eaten up by this all-consuming need. He dropped a soft kiss against my mouth, then another.

I wound my arms around his neck. "Don't be sorry," I whispered against his lips, the tip of my tongue brushing against his lower lip. I hadn't planned on doing it, it just happened. And once it had, I knew I was testing both our control. We were moving, lying back on the truck seat, pressed together…

He made a strange noise then sat up, putting space between us. "Damn."

I lay there, panting. "*I'm* sorry." My voice shook. He reached out, not looking at me. He didn't mean to touch the exposed skin of my stomach. But that's exactly where his hand landed—his roughened palm on my soft stomach.

He looked just as surprised, his eyes glued to his hand. He was red-cheeked and breathing hard. I covered his hand with my own, lifting it, pressing it over my heart. I don't know why I did it, but I did.

He sat there, staring into my eyes, so beautiful I wanted to climb into his lap…or stay right here, staring at him staring back at me.

He pulled me up, ran his fingers along my cheek, and

kissed me once before he started the truck. Once we were off, his arm draped—comfortably—around my shoulders.

Pickett barked, so I glanced out the back window, the "I Support Second Base" sticker catching my eye. I giggled.

"What?" Wyatt asked.

"Nothing."

He backed up, shifting the truck into first gear. His arm brushed against my chest, making me laugh again. "You're laughing." I nodded. "About?"

He shifted gears. Another brush.

"Your bumper sticker," I admitted, smiling.

He looked at it. "What about it?"

He shifted gears again and I shot him a meaningful look. "Um, really?"

He looked honestly confused.

"I thought you were kind of a dick when I saw that sticker," I admitted.

"Why?"

"You're advertising you're a boob man." I felt really awkward having this conversation.

He shifted gears again, glancing at my chest. "I didn't know I was."

"Good answer." I smiled, leaning against him. "Why the sticker, then?"

"My mom put it on my truck."

I glanced up at him. "Oh." That was kind of weird.

"I told her no pink, but that made her laugh, so…" He shrugged. "She had stickers on just about every car in town before it was all over." He sounded proud of her. "She went down fighting."

I froze, unable to look away from him. *Pink. I Support Second Base. She went down fighting.* I couldn't move. *Shit. No.* Even my heart seemed to stop—before pain kicked in big time.

I replayed all the snippets of conversation that hadn't made sense. Tragedy. Heartache. Don't know how he's managed to stay so positive.

Oh God no. Wyatt… It's not fair.

He looked at me. "Allie?"

I nodded, blinked.

He checked behind us then pulled the truck off the road, onto the brush-covered shoulder of the country road. The truck bounced a few feet before he put it into park. "Allie?"

I shook my head. *Shit. Say something.*

"What's wrong?" He sounded worried, urgent.

Breathe, Allie. This isn't about you. Be here for him. Give him what he needs. "I'm so sorry, Wyatt." I sounded like I was choking. "I didn't know."

The shift of emotion on his face was intense. Worry. Confusion. Then horrible realization. "Fuck, Allie." His voice was low, almost apologetic. "I thought you knew."

"No, no, I…" I shook my head, wishing my voice wasn't so high. "I… Oh, Wyatt."

He looked through the windshield, his voice soft. "Small town, people talk—all the time. Still, I should have said something."

I couldn't seem to stop shaking my head. "Why would you? It's…how…" I mumbled to a stop. "Sorry. I'm just…God, I'm so *so* sorry."

He looked at me then, the slight sheen of moisture in his copper eyes my undoing.

"Wyatt." I turned to him. "I wish I'd known her. I'd tell her what…what an amazing son she has." My voice broke. "But she knows…I know it." It wasn't enough, even though there was nothing I could say that would ever be enough. "You are the most amazing person I've ever met. You know that?"

He shook his head. "I'm just me."

"Exactly. You are…awesome." Still not enough. He *was* awesome—and so much more. "Everything."

His hand rested against my cheek, his gaze holding mine. "I love you, Allie."

I climbed into his lap, facing him, wrapping my arms around him and hugging him as tight as I could. I pressed my face against his neck, breathing his scent deep. I didn't know if touching me comforted him the way it did me, but I hoped it did.

His arms were like steel bands around my waist. His chest rose and fell, unevenly. His breath blew hot and fast against my neck. I wanted to cry. *For* him.

The last six months had been all about me. If I was being honest, it had been the last three years. How or when I'd let myself believe that I was the center of the fricking universe, I wasn't sure. *I don't deserve him.*

He was dealing with a son-of-a-bitch father *and* the loss of his mother. He was alone and functioning, a kind, positive person. I was surrounded by people who loved me, who were hurting because of me, and I never once thought about them.

I couldn't ease my hold on Wyatt. I didn't want to. He was this remarkable guy-man-cowboy...who loved me. *Me.*

I had it all. Everything. It was time I started appreciating it.

"I love you," I whispered. "I love you so much."

His arms tightened, making it a little hard to breathe. I didn't mind. How long had it been since someone had held him, loved him, and let him know it? I'd stay like this until he ended it, because this was exactly where I wanted—needed—to be.

I'm not going to cry. I'm not going to cry. My eyes were burning.

I don't know how long we ended up staying like that. Being in his arms was my favorite place to be. His hold eased slowly, his hands smoothing over the fabric of my shirt. When he raised his head, I saw the moisture on his cheeks.

I kissed him, a soft kiss, and he shook his head.

"You start kissing me and we'll never get to your folks' place." His gaze traveled over my face, slowly. "We should go."

"Okay." I nodded, slipping from his lap. "Let's go." I sat as close to him as I possibly could, not willing to sever all contact.

He started the truck and pulled back onto the road, driving the short trip to my parents' house. Pickett jumped out of the back of the truck as soon as we stopped, barking.

Wyatt opened his door. "Pickett," he said softly. Pickett stopped barking. I laughed. "You need to learn some manners," Wyatt said to the dog as he slid out of the truck.

"Manners?" I asked, following him.

Wyatt walked around to the back of the truck, Pickett at his heels. "He's a good dog. Just gets worked up sometimes."

I smiled at the two of them. Pickett was watching Wyatt's every move. When Wyatt looked at the dog, the dog sat, ears perked forward, waiting. "He sure loves you." I smiled, following them to the end of the truck.

Wyatt slid his suitcase to the end of the truck bed.

"I'll get it," I offered, lifting the bag.

"Thank you," he said, sliding the wooden trunk forward and hoisting it onto his shoulder.

"Got it?" I asked.

"Need help?" Dad was there.

"No, sir, thanks. Where should I——"

"This way," I said, knowing he'd follow me.

As soon as he put his trunk in the room, he went out to the barn with my father.

"Help with dinner?" Mom asked. I nodded. "Feel up to making the chicken?" I nodded again. "Everything okay?" Her blue eyes watched me closely.

"I'm good, Mom. Really good." I hugged her then, tight. I felt her stiffen and knew I'd surprised her. She hugged me back, enveloping me in her familiar floral scent—her comforting embrace. I pressed a kiss to her soft cheek and stepped back. "I'll set the table first?"

"That would be great." I could tell she was still grappling with my unexpected affection. "Five places."

I smiled. "Yep."

***

"If the whole sports medicine thing doesn't work out, you can open a fried chicken place," Dax said, his mouth full.

"Gosh, thanks." I grimaced. "I would've been fine with you swallowing first."

"Really, Dax." Mom sighed. "That's disgusting."

I glanced at Wyatt, who was smiling as he said, "Main Street doesn't have a chicken place."

I shook my head. "Guess it's good to have a back-up plan."

"What classes are you taking this year?" Dad asked Wyatt.

Wyatt swallowed and took a sip of iced tea before he answered. "Calculus, physics, English, government... Think that's it."

"Physics?" Dax shuddered. "Why?" Wyatt laughed, shrugging.

"Good for you, Wyatt." Mom nodded. "Getting into the vet program is hard. Any advantage you can get is a smart move."

"Yes, ma'am." Wyatt's gaze lingered on my mom.

My chest felt heavy, achy. Mom didn't see how much that slight praise meant to him, but I did. For the second time that day I was reminded how lucky I was. Not only did I have two parents who loved me *and* a dork-brother best friend, I loved a boy who knew what love really was— a boy who was teaching me to love.

"Maybe you can help me with Calculus?" I asked him. "Math is my...weakness."

Dax snorted. "Weakness? It's going to be a lot harder to find a tutor here than it was in Dallas."

"No more chicken for you." I reached across the table toward his plate.

"Hey!" He swatted my hand.

I laughed and sat back.

"Behave," Mom chided us half-heartedly, smiling.

"I *can* help, actually," Wyatt said, grinning. "Math isn't a problem. Writing papers—research papers—different story."

"*I* can help with that." I sat forward, smiling broadly at him.

"I'd like that." His voice was soft. His warm copper gaze traveled over my face, making me sigh.

"What time does school start in the morning?" Dad asked, breaking our moment.

Wyatt turned to my father. "Eight-thirty."

"Not too bad," Dax murmured.

"Don't sound too excited." I forgot, for that split second, that he and Molly weren't...he and Molly. "It'll be good, Dax. We haven't met everyone in the senior class." I paused, looking to Wyatt then. "Have we?"

Wyatt shook his head. "No. Most of 'em, but not all."

"Is Cannon McCracken a senior?" Dax asked.

Wyatt looked at me, then Dax, a frown on his face. "No. He graduated last year."

When Wyatt's gaze returned to me, I shrugged a little. Wyatt's frown remained, but he didn't say anything.

"Who's Cannon?" Mom asked.

"Some...some guy," Dax mumbled. "I'm stuffed." He stood, taking his plate to the sink.

"I know it's early," Dad said and stood, following Dax's lead, "but I don't want you staying up too late. Eleven, no later."

"Work?" Mom asked, her blue eyes following my father.

He nodded at her then winked. "Won't take long." He turned to Wyatt. "You can use any of my tools you need. Just be careful."

"Thank you. Mr. Cooper. Dr. Cooper. I can't thank you enough for taking me in." He stood, shaking my father's hand.

Mom came around the table and hugged him. "I want you to think of this as your home now, too. We're lucky to have you, Wyatt."

"Yes, we are," I whispered softly.

Dax squeezed my shoulder. "Keep looking at him like that and he's going to have a hard time being the good guy."

I frowned. "I didn't mean to be so…insensitive, Dax. I know tomorrow's going to be harder now."

He shrugged. "I'm going out to the barn to work for a while."

After I'd cleaned up the kitchen—I couldn't cook without using almost every pan in the kitchen—I turned off the kitchen light and went outside to check on the boys in the barn.

Mom was sitting in a wicker chair on the side of the wrap-around porch. I was surprised to see Pickett sleeping by her feet. Apparently, Pickett felt at home too. Being happy felt so fricking good.

"Allie," Mom asked, "is Dax okay?"

Less happy now. *Poor Dax.* "Did you talk to him?"

"I *tried*, but he told me being moody was part of being a teenager." She sighed. "He's very good at using humor to get out of difficult conversations."

"I think it's awesome. I wish I could laugh the hard stuff off, instead of turning evil and spewing venom."

Mom stared at me with round blue eyes. She opened her mouth, then closed it.

"He'll be okay." I tried again. "I think…I think he's going through…*something.* But I don't *think* we need to worry."

"Okay." She smiled. "But you'll let me know?"

"If we need to worry? Oh, yeah, definitely. I won't hesitate to call in reinforcements."

"Good." She paused. "Can I… You're… You seem good." I heard the fear in her voice and hated myself all over again.

"Mom," I said, watching her stiffen a little, "I know I've been…well, a bitch. And I know that Lindie…that— somehow—Lindie's death kind of made me being a bitch okay, even though it's *not*. Losing her hurts, a lot, every day, but that's a really lame-ass excuse for treating you guys the way I have." I hugged myself. "And I'm sorry for that. I'm really sorry."

Mom looked like she was carved from stone. She didn't blink. She didn't look like she was breathing.

"Mom?" I took a few steps closer to her.

"Allie…" Her voice broke and she leaned forward, her elbows resting on her knees and her hands over her face.

"I didn't mean to make you cry. I'm just… Today kind of made my self-centeredness glaringly obvious. I'm really…I'm happy you're my mom. That I have you."

Her shoulders were shaking now, so I knelt in front of her—careful not to squish Pickett—and hugged her. Her arms went around me as she sobbed.

The back screen door slammed, followed by a tone I knew all too well. "June? What happened?" Dad's words were so hard, so biting. "Dammit, Allie! Can't we make it one week without drama?"

I pulled away from Mom and stood.

"Davis." Mom stood, her voice thick. "She—"

"Stop defending her, June. She needs to grow up, to know that she's not the only one in the world who's dealing with heartache."

He was right. *You are absolutely right.* "I just wanted—"

"Attention," he snapped. "I know, Allie. You can't seem to help yourself."

Ouch. That stings big time. But he was still right.

Mom tried to stop him. "Listen, Davis, please stop—"

"I don't have the energy for this tonight." He looked at Mom, then me, making no attempt to hide his complete frustration. "Goddammit. I don't know what to say anymore. Doesn't matter, since you stopped listening to me a couple of years ago." He sighed. "We all miss Lindie, we all loved her. But…but you can't keep striking out at people. You can't get even by hurting people. Or bring her back."

I went rigid—I couldn't help it.

And he saw it, his tone softer as he added, "Think about Wyatt, about all that young man has been through. He's an example of making the best of a bad situation."

"I know…"

"You know? Do you *really?*" he interrupted me. "You *know* what it's like to be alone?"

I understood what he was trying to say. And even though I really wanted to shout at him—to beg him to let me finish what I was going to say—I didn't. Instead, I shook my head. I had no idea, not really. I never would. I was surrounded by people who would always be there for me, no matter what. As angry as he was, my father, Dax, and Mom would never *desert* me. Neither would Wyatt. If I could only get the words out—

"I can't believe I'm saying this to you." He ran a hand through his hair. "Go to your room. I don't care what you do there, but I hope you'll take some time to think about your life and the woman you want to be."

The woman I'm trying to be, right now, if you'd just listen to me for a minute.

Looking at him, seeing the hurt on his face—the disappointment—told me now wasn't the time to talk. "Yes, sir," I murmured, almost choking on the words. Old habits die hard. But I *was* trying. I didn't want to be self-absorbed Allie, even if sneers and cut-downs came easier to me than doing what my father said, walking into that house and up the stairs to my room. I closed the door, sliding down it to sit on the floor.

I could hear them yelling at each other. I couldn't hear every word, but my name came up again and again. So did "selfish" and "out of control". I pressed my forehead against my knees, wishing there was something I could do.

Mom and Dad had enough to deal with, without my adding to it. There was no denying the fact that I'd screwed things up. I didn't want to screw things up anymore.

My eyes burned, stinging so bad I sniffed. I would not cry. Not now. What was the point? Instead, I tugged off my clothes, pulled on an oversized sleep t-shirt with David Beckham's face on it, and flopped onto the bed. I closed my eyes, counting backwards from fifty over and over again.

My phone vibrated. At first I ignored it. But it kept vibrating so I reached for it, sliding the lock over and reading the text.

Sweet dreams. I love you.

Wyatt had used his only-for-emergencies phone. To text me.

I smiled, rolled over in bed, and closed my eyes.

16 CHAPTER SIXTEEN

I was nervous as I made my way downstairs the next morning. I paused at the bottom of the stairs, checking my reflection. My favorite FC Dallas t-shirt was tucked into slim-fitting jeans. The ponytail wasn't working—too cheerleader. I slipped the band out and fluffed my hair around my shoulders. A little better, even with bags under my eyes. I glanced toward the kitchen, took a deep breath, and moved.

But there was no reason to get all worked up; Dad wasn't there. I didn't ask why and Mom didn't offer. Wyatt had yet to make an appearance, Dax was fidgeting nervously in his chair, and Mom was making a ton of pancakes—enough to feed the entire town of Black Falls, from the looks of it. Something told me it wasn't first-day-of-school nerves that had Mom on edge. She chattered away, ninety-to-nothing, about supplies and lunches and schedules. "No one has after-school stuff yet, right?" she asked.

I shook my head. "Don't think so."

Dax grunted.

"No, ma'am," Wyatt said as he walked into the kitchen.

"Morning." She smiled at him. "What about football?

Don't they start practicing before school starts?"

"Not playing this year. Between rodeo and work, I had to choose." He nodded his thanks as my mother put a plate in front of him.

"Not many guys would walk away from football," Dax said around a mouthful of pancakes.

"Swallow before talking?" I asked, without bite. "Please."

Wyatt's gaze swept over my face, the warmth in his eyes instantly making the morning better. "I was a defensive lineman—replaceable."

Somehow Wyatt being replaceable, in any way, was just wrong. *No way.* I caught Wyatt's look and shook my head at him. He smiled—so freaking gorgeous, I froze. He shook his head back at me, his cheeks turning an adorable shade of red.

Dax made a big production out of swallowing and clearing his throat. "Better?"

I nodded, barely glancing at him—I was way too caught up in Wyatt.

"You ever play?" Wyatt turned to Dax, breaking the rapidly warming connection between us.

"Um, no." Dax laughed. "Allie's the athlete. I'm the cheering section."

"Reluctant," I added.

Dax nodded. "Reluctant cheering section."

"How long did you play?" Mom asked as she joined us at the table.

"I played freshman and sophomore year. Junior year I started working." He shrugged, without adding anything else. I knew that was probably when his mother had passed away.

"Looks like you made the right choice," Dax commented. "A&M's where Mom and Dad graduated."

It was a good school. No, it wasn't a good school, it was a really *great* school. They had an amazing Sports Management program and a respected Health and

Kinesiology school and a Sports Therapy program—exactly what I wanted. I'd applied but never considered it because it was Dad's school. *Because I'm an ass.*

And now it was Wyatt's school.

"Allie, would you like to take my car?" Mom asked, interrupting my what-the-hell-is-the-matter-with-me moment. "You can drop me off at work and pick me up on your way home."

"I…"

"I don't mind driving, if you want," Wyatt offered, glancing at me. "Least I can do, with y'all puttin' me up and all." He turned to my mother as he finished.

"Wyatt." My mom patted his shoulder. "That's sweet of you to offer. I'll let you work it out amongst yourselves."

Dax snorted. "I think I'll drive myself."

Mom laughed.

I felt Wyatt's knee brush against mine and I shifted, letting my knee rest against his. I saw Wyatt smile as he scooped eggs onto his plate. Touching Wyatt kept my first-day nerves away. So I went out of my way to make sure we were touching. He didn't seem to mind. If anything, he seemed to like it too.

Driving to school, I stayed happily pressed against his side—even though there was plenty of room since Dax insisted on taking his truck. Wyatt tried to ask me about Dad, but I didn't want to talk about any of that this morning. He pressed a kiss to my forehead and let it go.

"I'll take you to get your schedule first thing," Wyatt said as we pulled into the parking lot. Trucks were apparently the vehicle of choice for the high school students, but there were also lots of older family cars, SUVs, and the odd van. Not a single Lexus, Mercedes, Porsche, or Volvo…nothing like my old school

"Okay," I murmured.

He put the truck in park and looked down at me. "Ready?"

I shrugged, my stomach knotting. "Sure."

He nodded, his eyes resting on my lips a second before he kissed me. It was a soft kiss, lips gentle, breath mingling, his hand resting on the side of my neck. His forehead rested against mine and he whispered, "*Now* it's a good morning."

He draped his arm along my shoulders as we walked across the parking lot. I liked it, this open declaration of couple-hood. When we reached the office, he held the door open for me, taking my hand once we walked inside.

"Good morning, Wyatt." A tiny elderly lady with metal-grey hair greeted Wyatt at the counter. "How was your summer? I heard you were whipping Maureen's place into shape."

"Yes, ma'am." Wyatt nodded toward me. "This is Miss Maureen's granddaughter."

Grey eyes peered through metal-framed glasses. She smiled, her face crinkling into a million feathery wrinkles. "Of course you are. The spitting image of Maureen when she was young. I'm Mrs. Jansen, school secretary. And you are…" She flipped through a haphazard stack of papers and files on the corner of her desk. She pulled two files from the stack. "…Allie Cooper. Here's your schedule, honey. Turn it in to your last period teacher and they'll get it back to me. Wyatt, will you be showing her around?"

"I was thinking about it," he teased, squeezing my hand.

"Thought so." She smiled, handing me my schedule. I glanced at it. "Welcome to Black Falls," Mrs. Jensen said as we made our way from the office.

"Looks like we have…" Wyatt took my schedule, reading over it. "…everything together except Health Professions and…athletics."

I couldn't help smiling then. Maybe senior year at Black Falls wasn't going to suck.

We sat at the black-topped science table together. Wyatt was shaking hands, clapping shoulders, and smiling hellos at everyone who came through the door. He introduced me, but there was no way I'd remember them all. Some of them were familiar—having floated down the river with me. But I couldn't match any names with faces.

"Welcome to Physics." Mr. Abernathy was a barrel-chested man with a receding hairline. "I won't lie to you and tell you this is an easy class. It's not. It's physics. But you'll do fine as long as you do the homework."

Physics first period. *Awesome*. Wyatt's knee nudged me under the table, making me smile.

"This is your seating assignment for the year." He put a piece of paper on our lab table. It had a diagram of the tables on it. "Fill this out and get to know your lab partner. You will be doing a lot of team work, so find a smart kid to sit next to."

I laughed, a little startled. Wyatt wrote our names on the paper and passed the sheet to the table behind us. The class was small, maybe fifteen kids. Fifteen faces I didn't know. One face I did. Wyatt winked at me.

After sitting through Physics, World Economics, and College Algebra, we found the cafeteria...and my brother.

"How's day one going?" Levi asked as we sat across the table from them. "You surviving?"

"Loving every minute," I replied, smiling sweetly.

Dax laughed, glancing between me and Wyatt. "How many classes you two have together?"

I grinned. "All of them, so far." Wyatt's arm wrapped around my waist, pulling me close—making my smile grow.

"That's gonna be distracting," Levi murmured, looking back and forth between the two of us.

Wyatt's brown eyes met mine. "Maybe," he said, but he smiled. "I'm good with it."

I felt my cheeks warm and turned my attention to the bag of carrot sticks in my lunchbox. Distracting? Maybe. Bearable? Completely.

So far, so good. My teachers weren't horrible and I had

Wyatt—no complaints. Dax and Levi were in Economics together, cutting up and getting into trouble already. But the teacher was good-natured, so hopefully Dax wouldn't spend half of the year in the principal's office. I couldn't help but wonder if Dax was acting like a tool because Molly was also in that class.

I glanced up and saw Molly, walking into the cafeteria with her tray, looking...conflicted. *What was the deal?* It was clear she had a thing for my brother. She was staring at him as she made her way to our table.

"Hey." Molly's voice was soft, trying for enthusiasm.

Levi slid over, making room for her—beside Dax. *Poor Dax.*

Here I was, practically in Wyatt's lap, smiling from ear to ear and crazy-happy, while Dax had to deal with his feelings for Molly...and Molly's boyfriend. He went from smiling and teasing to tense and silent.

I squeezed Wyatt's thigh, glancing at Dax and Molly with meaning. He sighed, his shrug all but imperceptible.

"How's your first day?" Molly asked Dax.

I peeked at my brother, watching his features go hard. "Fine."

"I'm glad." Molly looked at her food, then at me, then at Wyatt. "How's it going for you, Allie? Coach can't wait to meet you. I had PE this morning and he's been asking all of us about you. Guess he's real excited about this year, with you being here and all."

Shit. Nothing like a coach building you up to put a big fat target on your back. "Oh, great." I couldn't keep the edge from my voice.

Molly frowned and Wyatt glanced at me.

"Don't want to disappoint anyone," I added—hoping to explain that my tone wasn't directed at Molly.

Wyatt smiled. "No worries there."

Molly was watching us, all smiles. "Aw, Wyatt. You're so sweet."

"Like Cannon?" Dax ground out.

Ouch. I saw Molly flinch. I couldn't decide if I was proud of Dax or sad for Molly. Maybe a little of both.

"Dax…" Molly's huge eyes filled with tears. She sniffed, smiling. "Never mind." She shrugged, picked up her tray, and walked away, alone.

"Dax?" I murmured as he crushed his empty soda can in his hand.

He was watching Molly over his shoulder. "What?"

Not touching the Molly thing. "How are classes going?" I asked, hoping to distract him.

Wyatt leaned forward. "You've got Mr. Hastings for Spanish, right?"

Dax nodded, still tense.

"Shit, man." Levi shook his head. "That sucks."

"Take notes. On everything," Wyatt offered. "Seriously."

I knew he was trying to distract Dax. Dax probably knew it too. But it didn't stop me from loving Wyatt all the more for it.

Lunch was followed by World Literature, a Health Professions class, and then girls' athletics. The athletes of Black Falls were…interesting. Half of the girls were uncoordinated and giggly; the other half looked like they'd kick my ass and enjoy doing it.

Coach Garza was a red-faced, angry-looking guy—like he was constantly on the verge of a heart attack. Standard coach. "Allie Cooper." He read the slip from the office. "My soccer star. Glad to have you," he continued. "Work hard, play hard, win. That's the Bobcats motto."

I nodded, feeling the hostile stares of my soccer teammates. We dressed and headed out onto the field.

I left them in the dirt, weaving through them, owning the ball, and driving it into the goal without any resistance from the goalie. I heard the whistles from the stand and spun. Wyatt was sitting there watching, all smiles.

"Cooper! I'm putting you in charge of drills." Coach Garza was staring at me.

"Oh." I glanced at the other girls, to see a mix of reactions. "I'm not—"

"I'm not asking." Coach Garza handed me his whistle and walked off the field, toward Wyatt.

I looked at the whistle, the other girls, and tried not to be upset. I didn't want this. I didn't want responsibility. I just wanted to skate by until graduation. Not exactly the grateful attitude I was supposed to be working on.

"I don't know your names…yet," I said. "I'm Allie."

"We know," one of the giggly girls said. "And you're freakin' amazing."

Another girl snorted. "Bet you can't do it again."

Don't take the bait. Don't do it.

Someone else laughed. "Bet she can."

"Who wants to drill?" I asked.

No one raised their hand. A couple of them crossed their arms over their chests, clearly not excited.

"Great. So, laps then?" I asked.

"Let's drill." The first girl jumped up and down. "Can't wait. Drilling is my life."

A few girls laughed then. I smiled.

I worked on toe-touches with them, one on one. When they seemed to have that down, we worked on passing. I had one girl run down each side of the field, passing the ball back and forth, then setting it up for the shot. It didn't go very well. A few of them knew what they were doing, but most of them acted like they'd never seen a soccer ball before.

When Wyatt and Coach came onto the field, I noticed the visible shift in the other girls' attitudes. Wyatt was hot and I wasn't the only one that noticed it. While they straightened their ponytails and stuck out their chests, I put my hands on my hips and stared him down.

"You're all sweaty," he said as he stopped, inches from me. His eye was healing, which meant both his wonderful brown eyes were focused on me—all red and sweaty and grinning like a fool.

"I do that." I leaned forward. "Want a hug?"

"Why do you think I walked over here?" He cocked an eyebrow at me, pulling me against him. His lips brushed mine as his arms wrapped around me.

"Isn't PDA against school rules?" I teased.

"School ended thirty minutes ago," he said before kissing me again.

One quick glance around told me that everyone was leaving the field. "How are you?" I asked, slipping my arms around his neck.

"Lonely." He smiled. "Your cheeks are all red."

I laughed. "That happens when I'm overheated."

"I like watching you when you play. You're amazing."

"I love the game."

"It shows."

We walked off the field slowly, to his waiting truck. He stopped walking then, pulling me against him. "Got everything you need?"

I was wrapped up in his arms—so yeah, pretty much. But that wasn't what he meant and I knew it. I shook my head. "My backpack's still in my locker."

"Let's go."

I smiled. "You don't have to come."

He pressed a kiss to my forehead before stepping back, taking my hand in his as we headed back toward the school. Walking down the halls of the high school, talking soccer with Wyatt, feeling happy—life had changed so completely.

***

Friday. "Who'd have thought school wouldn't suck?" I asked Pickett as he ran around me, eyeing the stick I held in my hands. I smiled at him.

If I was completely honest with myself, which was still a new concept to me, school had never sucked so little. So my classes might not be the most exciting thing in the world, but the teachers were all decent—so far. Athletics was going to be a challenge, but dealing with competitive, bitchy girls was nothing new to me. I could handle it. I was making friends, sort of.

And I had Wyatt. My smile grew.

Pickett whimpered, running around me in smaller and smaller circles until I was forced to stop walking. I laughed. "Fine, here." I threw the stick and jogged the last few feet to the beaten metal mailbox at the end of the long driveway.

I pulled out the stack of mail as Pickett dropped the stick at my feet. His stubby little tail wiggled and he spun around, bursting with energy. "You're hyperactive, you know that, right?" I asked, bending over to pick up the stick. "Shit," I muttered as the pile of letters slipped from my hold, scattering all over the dusty road. I picked up Pickett's stick, threw it, wiped the dog slobber on my jeans, and picked up all the mail.

A letter from Southern Methodist University caught my eye. It wasn't the only letter I'd received from a university. Kentucky State, University of California, University of North Texas, and Harvard had all replied to my early applications. I'd had two yeses so far—Kentucky State and University of North Texas. It was good to have options.

I swallowed, ignoring Pickett as he circled me. My chances were good with SMU too, I knew that. I'd applied before the accident, when my game was the best it had ever been. The scouts had been impressed when they'd come to see me, tossing around scholarship amounts and generally making it feel like I was in. Which was what I wanted…had wanted. Having Dr. Duncan on the Board of Regents took a lot of the worry out of the whole thing.

I stood in the middle of the long dusty driveway and opened the letter. "Congratulations," I read. "We are pleased to inform you that you've been accepted to…" I wanted to feel excited. I wanted it to feel right. So why didn't it?

I threw the stick for Pickett as we made our way back to the house. SMU wasn't the only college that had sent scouts to watch me play. A lot of them had. Not just Texas schools, schools from all over. But I was a Texas girl at heart. I didn't want to go far. Maybe A&M was far enough… I hadn't heard from them yet.

I took my time, trying to separate my feelings for Wyatt from my plans for the future. *Had* SMU been where I'd wanted to go? Or where Lindy and I had wanted to go? At SMU I'd have to transfer out for my master's degree. I could stay at A&M the full course.

But was I seriously considering A&M? And if I was, was it for Wyatt or because it was the best choice for me?

"What's up?" Dax asked as I came inside.

"Nothing." I set the mail on the table, tucking the letter into the back of my waistband, smoothing my t-shirt over it.

Dax rolled his eyes. "Right." He turned back to his homework.

"Dax." I put my hand over his book. "It's Friday night. Don't you want to do something?"

He shrugged. "Like what?"

"We could go watch the Bobcats' first football game," I suggested with a smile.

Dax's eyes narrowed. "Fine."

Which surprised me. "Fine?"

He smiled. "Yep, let's go."

"Okay." I turned around…and Dax grabbed the letter. "*Dax*," I growled, spinning around and reaching for the letter.

Dax ran into the bathroom and slammed the door, locking it.

I thumped the door. "Dax!"

Silence.

"Dammit, Dax." I thumped the door again.

The door opened. "Congratulations, Allie! This is fantastic!" He grabbed me in a bear hug. "Call Mom. And Dad."

I took the letter back. "I'm not sure."

Dax frowned. "About?"

"I'm not sure about this."

He blinked at me, then frowned. I didn't say a thing. "This is all you've been talking about. Leaving, going home, to SMU."

I shrugged. "There are other schools…"

"Such as?"

I shook my head.

He smiled. "Huh."

"Huh, what?"

"Huh, I never thought a guy would get to you like this." He leaned against the wall.

I sighed. "It's not just Wyatt."

He crossed his arms over his chest, giving me a look.

"Just. I said *just*…" I frowned at him. "It's everything."

"That makes sense. Not."

"I…I don't know what I *want*. SMU was a Lindie-and-me thing, you know?" I sighed. "Everything's different now. I need to figure out what's *me*… What's right for *me*."

He nodded slowly. "Okay." I cocked an eyebrow at him. "But—and don't get pissed at me for asking this—is A&M even a possibility?"

"Yeah. I-I think so. They have the exact program I want, you know? But—" I held up the letter. "These scholarships are kind of hard to argue with."

"Have you heard from A&M yet?"

"No." I refolded the letter and tucked it back into the envelope.

"Then wait," he said. "You going to tell Mom?"

I shrugged.

"Wyatt?"

I shook my head. "No…you're right. I should wait…for now."

He cocked an eyebrow. "Wyatt's coming back Sunday?"

I nodded. Wyatt and Hank had headed to Ft. Worth for a rodeo. As cool as Mom and Dad had been about

Wyatt staying with us, I knew better than to ask if I could go on the road with him. He'd left while I'd been in athletics class.

"So, football?" I asked.

"I guess. I'd *rather* go to a movie."

I laughed. "Way to support your school."

Dax rolled his eyes. "At least it's not Homecoming yet."

I didn't say a thing. Homecoming was a big deal at our old school. Ridiculous mums, huge pep rallies, a week of spirit activities and parties...homecoming court. It made me think of Lindie, of how much she'd wanted to be Homecoming Queen this year.

I imagined Homecoming in Black Falls would be very different from Homecoming in Richland Hills. Sure, Black Falls was crazy over their football team, but I didn't know if it was because the team was good or because there was nothing to do when there wasn't a rodeo to go to. I guessed tonight I'd know the answer to that.

***

Thunder woke me.

I glanced at my clock. Two in the morning. *Awesome.*

Wind howled outside, and a crack of thunder so loud I sat up.

Was Wyatt home—safe and sound? He'd called earlier to let us know he'd be home late—they'd had a flat and then it had started storming. Dad had checked the weather and Mom had tried to convince them to stop for the night, let the weather clear—but he'd promised to be careful.

I hadn't wanted to worry—but that wasn't going to happen, so I'd done some laundry, made a batch of blueberry muffins, then some oatmeal raisin cookies. After I'd cleaned up the kitchen, I swept off the porch, glancing at the driveway a dozen or so times before I decided I needed to get away from the house. Pickett was all too happy to go for a run with me until it was too dark to keep going. I showered, picked out my clothes for tomorrow, packed my lunch box, and poked around, looking for anything to keep me preoccupied.

He'd been gone two days. It felt like weeks.

Apparently my agitation irritated the crap out of Dad. At eleven, he'd told me to go to bed. Pickett had flopped down on the mat at the edge of my bed. "You miss him too?" I'd whispered to the dog. Pickett had stared back at me, his ears pricked forward and his eyes watchful. I'd fallen asleep waiting for the sound of Wyatt's truck.

Thunder rumbled, sounding far too scary-movie for my liking. "Pickett?" I whispered, needing some reassurance.

No head peeked up. I glanced across the room. My bedroom door was open, just enough for Pickett to get out. Was he out in the storm? I frowned.

Or, hopefully, Wyatt was home and Pickett was sound asleep on the floor by Wyatt's bed.

Thunder shook the house, rattling my window. I'd shoved the bed into a corner of the room—nothing like solid walls at your back to help chase away a panic attack. I'd made sure I could still roll over to see Wyatt working in the morning: a win-win situation.

More thunder.

Wyatt. I hoped Wyatt was home.

More rattling glass.

A flash of lightning that had me pulling up my quilt.

"It's a storm. A stupid storm. Nothing to get freaked out over. Nothing at all." I shook my head. Like talking to a storm was going to help? But I wasn't just freaking out over me. If Wyatt wasn't home, was he driving through this? Which was way scarier than sitting here right now. But I didn't know if he was here or if he was out there, on the road, right now.

I flipped on my small bedside lamp, hoping it would chase away my nerves. It flickered, but didn't go out. Watching the light dim and flicker was *so* not helping. I sat in a smaller ball and stared at the light.

This is stupid. He's either here, sleeping right down the hall, or he's not home yet.

I slipped to the edge of the bed, hesitating. The thunder and lightning made my decision easy. Right now, more than anything, I *needed* to know he was safe. I pulled the sheet over my head. *I'm pathetic.*

I jumped up, dragging my sheet with me. In my sock feet, I tiptoed—avoiding the squeaky giveaway floorboard—along the hall and down the stairs. The hall was illuminated with a sudden flash of white and I paused, my heart in my throat. *Deep breath—moving on.* I tugged the sheet up, like a hood, and hurried the rest of the way to Wyatt's room.

I thought about knocking, but a clap of thunder changed my mind. I opened the door and slipped inside, leaning against the closed door to get my bearings. The digital alarm clock on the bedside table cast everything in a pale glow. Pickett was curled up in the corner, snoring. And Wyatt—Wyatt was sleeping on his stomach, shirtless, his sheet draped low around his waist.

I could breathe easier. He was here. He was safe. He *was* wearing something underneath that sheet, wasn't he?

Oh. Good. Lord. Now my heart was thumping for an entirely different reason.

17 CHAPTER SEVENTEEN

I stood there, frozen, staring. Seriously? He should be a model. An underwear model...or something.

He rolled, flipping onto his back and throwing his arm over his face. I held my breath, but the sheet stayed in place.

Now his chest was on display...his beautiful sculpted chest. *Not breathing.* I almost lost my hold on my sheet. How could someone so wonderful be so gorgeous? Lightning lit up the room, jolting me from my staring session, and making me move, quickly, to the edge of his bed. I sat by his feet, the springs on the bed squeaking loudly. *Great.*

"Allie?" He moved, leaning off the side of the bed. A light came on...from under the bed?

"I-I needed to know you were...back safe," I whispered. "Sorry I woke you up." I was lying. I wasn't sorry I'd woken him. If I hadn't woken him, he wouldn't be looking at me, scooting closer to me, making me forget about the storm. It wasn't the first time I'd dreamed about being with Wyatt...in bed...up close and personal...half-naked, even. *But this time I'm not dreaming. He's here. I'm with him.* I smiled at him. "So, hi," I whispered.

"Hi. You okay?" His voice was pitched low. He slid closer, one long leg sliding around me.

"Yeah, sure," I murmured. It was so hard to breathe.

He cocked an eyebrow.

"I always run around the house with the sheet over my head." I tried for humor, but my voice was tight and quavering. "You have a flashlight under the bed?"

"I'm used to power outages." Which made perfect sense. "Miss me?" he asked softly.

"I thought that was sort of obvious."

"I missed you." His arms slipped around me, pulling me against him. Somehow that made it easier to breathe...and harder to think. His scent wrapped around me, like his muscled arms, his lean thigh... I shivered in his arms, overwhelmed. "Just a little rain. Nothing to worry about." His voice was low, soft, wonderful.

I believed him. Fear was quickly being replaced by sensations that were just as powerful, but completely different. My head fell forward, against his bare chest, my cheek against his shoulder. I took a long, deep breath—drawing him into my lungs—and managed to sound almost normal. "How'd you do?"

"Came in second." He yawned, making my head go up and down against his chest.

"That's great." I stared up at him. It was kind of hard not to notice how tired he was. *Dammit.* "I really am sorry I woke you." I was...now.

"You didn't. I've been tossing." His gaze was dark in the dimly lit room, dark black-brown-warm-and-wonderful. His fingers brushed a hair from my eyelashes.

The thunder made me jump, the springs of the bed squeaked, and the flashlight rolled out from under the bed—illuminating us on the bed. Wyatt, all backlit rippling muscles, was mind-blowing.

"Storms bother you, too, huh?" I sounded breathless.

"No." His jaw clenched. "I was worried about you."

"Oh," I managed.

His smile grew, his gorgeous dimples making my stomach hot and heavy. He took my hand in his and pressed it to his lips.

Hot and heavy *and* twisting in an alarming way.

He smile dimmed a little. "I wanted to see you but I didn't want to risk it."

I slipped my arm around his waist. "Risk it?"

"Slipping into your room. At night. Thought your folks might not appreciate that." He sounded worried. "I wanted to…but…"

He was right. Him, in my room, at night—probably not a good thing. He was, after all, the golden boy. I hadn't really thought through what would happen if Dad found me here with him—in his bed in the middle of the night. *Probably not the best idea I've ever had.* But I'd needed to know he was safe. And now, being wrapped up in his arms, in him, I felt too good to leave. Being with Wyatt made me feel loved and wanted…and a little crazy.

For a split second I wished I was wild-and-rebellious Allie again—just long enough to throw myself at Wyatt guilt-free. I didn't want to think about my father right now. I didn't want to think about anything but me and him.

"Things any better with your dad?" he asked.

I shook my head.

"I'm sorry things are so hard, Allie." His voice sounded so sincere.

"You're sorry? For me?" After everything he'd been through? "Wyatt… You're kind of…amazing, you know that?" I looked up at him, loving the sound of his heart under my ear, the shift of his back muscles beneath my hand. "Yeah, my dad and I aren't exactly in a happy place, but it's just the way things are."

"Your dad doesn't seem all that unreasonable." He seemed hesitant. "I don't exactly have the best measuring stick to compare him to, but I like him."

"He's not unreasonable. I like him too," I agreed. "I don't *not* like him, I guess. We're messed up, we don't *get* each other. He wants a loving, smiling daughter. I want a loving, smiling father. Which is kind of hard, since I sort of made hating on him my second favorite hobby—after soccer."

He didn't say anything, but he looked...sad.

"I don't have any excuses, Wyatt. I wish I did. *I* did this."

"Allie..."

"When I was old enough to kick a soccer ball, he made it my thing—*our* thing." I shrugged. "I gave it one hundred and ten percent. I wanted him to be proud of me. My victories were his victories, but so were my losses. It was a lot of pressure. Making State Select Team changed things. My coach, my team...Lindie...made me realize I didn't need to prove myself to him anymore. I played for the team, for me. And the less I listened to Dad, the more frustrated he became."

Wyatt didn't say anything. But the frown on his face said enough.

"I told him I had a coach, I needed a *father*. I wasn't all that nice about it. I know it sounds stupid and selfish now. I do." I swallowed the lump in my throat. "And then after Lindie's accident I went a little...mental."

Wyatt's voice was soft. "Losing her like that...you were upset."

"I was. And him sitting there, not saying anything while I lay in that hospital bed—knowing I'd killed Lindie. I said horrible things to him, told him I knew he'd wished I'd died instead of Lindie." I could still see the shock on his face...the anger...the sadness. "Part of me believes...believed it. Now it's too late for me and him. Just too much *stuff*. I don't want to disappoint you but I don't want to lie to you either. I *am* a mean girl. I am. Or I was. I'm trying not to be now. I really am trying not to be." I sucked in a deep breath. "I-I don't know how to have relationships..." I shook my head.

His hand cupped my cheek. "He's your father. It'll

never be too late to make things right with him."

I leaned into his hand. "I hope you're right."

He smiled. "Don't give up on him."

I nodded.

"Don't give up on yourself," he added. "One thing my mom would say, the past can make you or break you, but which one is up to you."

I nodded, repeating the words softly to myself. "How do you do it?"

"Do what?" he asked.

"Smile. Live. Love."

"She had another expression. Momma was full of them. Fake it 'til you make it." He shrugged, his hand rubbing up and down my arm, his heart thumping steadily beneath my cheek. "I did a lot of faking it until I met you."

It was my turn to frown. "*Me* me? The bitch me?"

He sighed. "You're hurting, Allie. I get it. The anger. My dad's not your dad, but I get hating your father and still wanting his respect—maybe his love. I understand."

"You do?" It was a revelation. He understood. Sort of. "But you have an actual *right* to feel those things. I don't. You didn't do anything wrong. You're this awesome, caring, gentle guy. Lindie's death was *my* fault—"

"You didn't make the car hydroplane."

"No, but I—"

"You weren't driving drunk. In an ice storm." He paused, whispering, "Dumb shit."

"He wouldn't have driven us if I hadn't—"

"Allie." He tilted my face back, our eyes locking. "The eighteen-wheeler? *That* driver lost control on the ice. *His* brakes locked up. He hit your car. It *was* an accident." His fingers slipped through my hair. "I know you said things to Lindie you wish you could take back, that you two fought, but you can't own this."

"How do you know all of this?" I asked, feeling nauseous.

"Dax." He looked at my hand in his. "People."

"*People?*"

"Around town—the little old ladies that sit in Peggy's on Sunday nights... It's not hard to find out anything if you know who to ask. And I know everyone." His smile was uncertain.

"But...why?"

"So I can be here for you. I need to be here for you."

He was so matter-of-fact about it. I sat up, putting some space between us. Not because I was upset with him, but because I was going to cry. And I didn't want to cry. Too many thoughts were racing together, bouncing off one another, making my emotions just as mixed up. I tried to calm myself, to take deep breaths, to count backwards and clear my head.

I don't know how he made things so clear, but he did. One thing I accepted immediately, because it was true. He *needed* to be here for me. I needed to be here for him—I needed *him*.

But Lindie...The crash...*Was* it an accident? I swallowed. But...it *was* my fault, wasn't it? Or...maybe not... The hope he stirred was powerful, and painful too.

"You mad at me?" he asked softly, anxious.

I looked at him over my shoulder. "No. I'm not mad at you. I just...It's just that..." I had to keep swallowing. I didn't want to fall apart on him but I sounded desperate. "I want to believe you."

"About?"

"Lindie. The c-crash." My voice hitched. "*I know* what really happened. If I hadn't made her leave, none of it would have happened."

"You would have left eventually, Allie, right?" He waited for me to nod, then kept going. "Say you two didn't argue and you waited to leave, how would you have gotten home?" he asked, making no move to touch me.

I shrugged. "Lindie probably would have driven us back to her place."

"In the storm, on the ice, at night, after drinking..."

His voice faded away.

He was making sense, but my guilt was strong. I turned toward him. "We *might* have made it home just fine."

"Maybe." He nodded. "Maybe not."

"It doesn't really matter," I argued.

"I know," he agreed, sharing in my sadness.

We were quiet for a while. My mind was racing, turning over everything he'd said. Sitting here, not quite touching him but completely aware of him, I wished there was some way to convey how much he meant to me. I loved him, but that word didn't seem enough…

"I wish I could change what happened, Allie, to make that hurt go away." His voice was rough. "But I'm…I'm glad you're here…with me…now."

My heart responded. The guilt was still there, missing Lindie was still there, but his words stirred a vital warmth deep inside me. "Me too." I couldn't think of one place I wanted to be more, which really freaked me out. "But I don't know how to make this work. You're…you." *You're perfect and I'm me.* "You've been through enough. I'm…I'm…*me*." I turned away, having a hard time getting the words out. "I…I…God, Wyatt, I don't deserve you."

He didn't say anything. The only sound was the rain and thunder and our breathing. When I couldn't take it anymore, I looked at him. He was staring at me, sad, tired…loving. "You're going to have to get over that."

I almost laughed. "What?"

"Thinking like that. You don't deserve me?" He shook his head and reached forward, his hand cupping my cheek—finally touching me. "I love you, Allie. *You* make me happy. I feel like…I'm home with you."

It was still raining. Thunder was still rattling the whole damn house. But nothing compared to the thumping of my heart. I was light-headed, euphoric, and overwhelmed all at once. Everything about this moment was perfect.

He loved me. I might not deserve him, but I knew—without a doubt—that I loved him. I loved him in a way that I didn't understand yet, not really. It was so...complete. And it scared me, to accept what he was offering. His gaze held mine, boring into *me* without wavering.

His eyes held such promise, such faith. I knew, then, there was one thing that scared me more—losing him.

I moved quickly, kneeling between his legs and resting my hands on his bare chest. His skin was warm and smooth beneath me, making me breathless and shaky as I leaned forward to press my lips against his. "Welcome home, Wyatt," I murmured.

It was a soft kiss, lips brushing feather-light. The sweep of air, the mix of our breaths, the stir of longing and love all mixed up. I smiled down at him.

He looked happy...and sort of like he was in pain. His jaw was locked, his nostrils flared, and a dark flush colored his cheeks. It was holy-hell hot, making my stomach quiver and every inch of me tense. Waiting. Hoping. Anticipating. His hands twisted in the sides of my shirt, like he couldn't decide whether to pull me closer or hold me back. And all I could think about was kissing him again, with a little less sweetness and a whole lot of want.

He shook his head. "You make it hard for me to remember whose house I'm in."

He is such a good guy. "You're worried about disappointing my dad? You're thinking about my dad. I'm thinking about yanking off my shirt—" I broke off, stunned that I'd admitted what I was thinking. And I *was* thinking about it. My mind was full of what might happen if...

His hands released my shirt, but his palms brushed along my exposed thighs in the process, making us both jerk with awareness. He sat back, resting his fisted hands on the sheet at his waist.

Was he caught up in this all-consuming yearning? Was he...throbbing? I certainly was. I *so* was. Thinking about being shirtless, here, now, in Wyatt's bed—*with Wyatt*—

was making me feel totally out of control, breathless, hollow, heavy.

He closed his eyes. "Allie…" It was a plea, I knew it. He did feel it. *Thank God.* And the way he said my name did something to me, called to me. It was a new kind of ache, a new kind of pull. He was fighting for control, and…I was ready to let go.

"If it makes it any easier, I feel…*this*, too." I sat back, the space between us humming with pure, unfiltered desire. "Even if I've never felt it…*this*…before."

His eyes opened, the need in his gaze boring into mine. *Keep breathing.* "I know we can't. And we won't. Not tonight. But I want to. With you," I murmured.

He swallowed, the muscle in his jaw twitching and his mouth pressed flat.

Way to lay it all out there. What am I doing? "Was that the wrong thing to say?" I whispered.

"No." The word was pinched.

I reached out, searching for his hand. His fingers wrapped around mine. He hesitated for a second before he drew me against him. Somehow this felt different. Maybe it was because I felt every inch of him pressed up against me. Maybe it was because I wanted more.

A strange little sound came from him, part growl, part laugh. I shivered…the sound amping up the already crazy intensity between us.

"Are you okay?" I asked, turning my face into his chest, brushing my nose over his collar bone, and breathing deep. He shivered this time.

"Not sure," he admitted. "You just told me you wanted us to…well, that you…want me."

My face felt hot. At least he couldn't see my flaming cheeks in the dark. Besides, my face was basically buried in his chest. "Yeah…I guess I did. I do."

There was that little growl again and then he cleared his throat. His hand slid up my back, under my hair, to rest at the base of my neck. "Kinda surprised," he whispered, pulling me closer to him.

"In a good way?" I managed before his lips closed over mine.

I was gripping his shoulders then, pressing myself close as his hand slid up and into my hair, holding me. His other hand pressed against my thigh, his callused fingers stroking my skin, unsteady and amazing.

We fell back onto the bed. I'm not sure which of us made that happen…but once we were there, our hands were searching, our mouths were locked together, and our bodies couldn't seem to be close enough—even though there wasn't much between us.

When he rested between my legs, I felt a flare of nerves. He wasn't naked, neither was I, but there was no mistaking that things were getting carried away. He rocked against me, his back flexing beneath my hands, his arms bracing him over me. I couldn't tell who was breathing harder, me or him. All I could do was *feel*. His skin, his muscles, his breath, the way he pressed against me. It was overwhelming, and wonderful, and desperate—heat raged in my blood.

"Allie," he rasped, his hands cradling my face. "I don't want to rush this."

I heard him, but my body was still on fire. My knees pressed against his hips, my fingers slid through his short hair, pulling his lips back to mine. His kiss was soft, his lips lingering…before he groaned and flopped onto his back beside me.

I wanted to cry. I was gasping for breath, my hands gripping the sheets at my sides. Part of me, a little tiny part buried deep down inside, was relieved. He was right. We didn't need to rush things. Was I ready for *sex* with him, now? I didn't know. Did I *want* to? Yes. More than anything I'd ever wanted. I took a deep breath. *Definitely.*

He slid his arm beneath my head and pulled me against his side. We lay that way for a while, but the pull was too hard. When my hand rested on his chest, his heart picked up. When he turned his nose into my hair, I slid closer to him. The tension was too strong to ignore.

He slipped from the bed, pulling Grandma's old rocking chair to the bedside. He pulled the extra quilt off the wrought-iron footboard and sat in the chair.

"You can't sleep in that," I argued.

He laughed, low and soft. "I can't stay in bed with you."

I couldn't really argue with that. "I'll go back to my room." The storm was still raging, but so was my pulse. *This is ridiculous.*

"Stay," he said, taking my hand in his. "I've slept in rougher spots than this."

"Like?" I said, rolling onto my side to face him.

He yawned. "Horse trailers. I can't always find a motel room floor to sleep on." He rubbed a hand over his face.

I sighed. "That chair is wood. At least you had some hay in a horse trailer."

"And horse shit," he added.

We both laughed.

"Get some sleep, Allie. I'm here," he promised, squeezing my hand.

I squeezed his hand, staring at him until my eyes wouldn't stay open any longer.

***

"Allie?" Someone yelled.

The coo of a dove. Pickett barking.

I opened my eyes, exhausted—disoriented.

I glanced over at Wyatt, still in the rocking chair. He was sound asleep, his chin on his chest, leaning towards the bed. He'd have a crick in his neck this morning.

"Allie!" Again. Not dreaming? Footsteps on the stairs.

I realized what was happening as Wyatt's door opened. My father stood there, his hair on end, his face pale. When he saw me, he froze. A ragged breath escaped, his chest rising and falling so quickly I worried he was having a heart attack.

"Dad?" I sat up, wary. I was in Wyatt's room… Shit.

He walked into the room, his eyes never leaving my face. When he reached the side of the bed, he sat, grabbing me by the shoulders. "You were gone."

My heart was lodged in my throat.

"I went to your room." His voice was gravel, rough and uneven. "You were gone. I thought…I thought you ran away."

I swallowed against the burn in my eyes.

My father—who never cried—had tears in his eyes. "That you left, in a storm."

"I'm here." I forced the words out. "I'm right here."

He shook his head, his hands slipping from my shoulders. "I…I…"

"It's okay, Dad. I'm here. I didn't mean to scare you. I'm so sorry." I meant every word, taking his hand in both of mine. "For everything."

We stayed that way for a while—him looking at me, me holding his hand. I could tell he wanted more, a hug maybe—something. But we'd spent too long keeping our distance for that kind of contact, which was sad. Dad had always given great big bear hugs.

"Your mom's made breakfast," he murmured, pulling back. "Go on and get dressed." For the first time he acknowledged Wyatt. I waited for the tirade, the hostility, but Dad just nodded at him. *Interesting.*

I pulled the blanket around me and slid to the edge of the bed. Following Dad from the room seemed like the right thing to do, so I did, even though I wanted to say something to Wyatt. At the same time, I didn't want to push it. Dad was handling my spending the night in Wyatt's room with remarkable calm. I really wanted to keep it that way.

Dad gave me an awkward one arm hug before he let me go up to my room. Once the door was shut, I stood there, stunned. So many changes… Today was a new beginning, I could tell. It was time for me to get it together, be positive, be thankful. I had everything I could ever want or need.

"Good morning," I said to the posters of Abbie Wambach, Mia Hamm, and Maroon 5 on my walls. I knew I was smiling like an idiot but I didn't care. Even the fact that I had a killer physics test tomorrow and a five-page literature paper due Wednesday that I hadn't yet started couldn't chase away my grin.

I opened my closet and stood back. This week was all about Homecoming. I might be a reluctant Lady Cat, but I felt the need to show school spirit. Our colors were black and silver, so I tugged a black lace-up t-shirt from its hanger. I dressed quickly, tugged on jeans, black canvas flats, and silver hoop earrings. I brushed my hair out, put on a headband then took it out, before heading to the kitchen for breakfast.

Dax was sagging on his elbow—more asleep than awake.

Mom was bustling around. "Morning, Allie."

"Morning." I didn't care that I sounded almost as chipper as she did.

Dad set his paper down and smiled at me. "You look nice."

"Thanks," I answered. "Black Falls colors. Homecoming week, you know. And our team totally doesn't suck."

"Good to know." Dad nodded, sipping his coffee, still smiling.

Dax perked up then, looking from me to Dad with narrowed eyes. "Where am I?"

I laughed, rolling my eyes.

My gaze wandered around the kitchen. No Wyatt. I felt a twinge of guilt for keeping him up so late, but... I smiled as I pulled a bowl from the cabinet.

"Eggs and bacon and biscuits okay?" Mom chattered away. "Scrambled—your favorite."

"Thanks, Mom." I smiled, noticing the flowers on the

table for the first time.

"Seriously," Dax insisted, "I'm confused."

Mom patted me on the shoulder, then leaned over and kissed me on the cheek. "It's important to start the day off right."

"Looks great, June," Dad added.

Dax leaned back in his seat, scrubbed his hand over his face a few times, and shook his head. "Crazy storm last night. Were you guys electrocuted or something?"

Dad laughed, shaking his head. I saw him glance at me. It hurt to think he'd believe I hated him enough to leave in a storm. They all knew how storms wigged me out. That was what had earned me my sleeping pill prescription. I thought he didn't worry over me anymore. *Because I'm stupid. He's my dad. He'll always care and worry about me.* I was lucky.

"It was pretty bad. Everyone sleep okay?" Mom asked, her worried blue eyes turning my way.

I shrugged, careful not to look at Dad as I confessed, "It did wake me up."

"Morning." Wyatt came in, his hair wet and his eyes bright.

"Morning," Mom answered him, pointing to his chair with her spatula. "Lots of breakfast this morning."

"Something weird is going on," Dax whispered loudly. "Everyone's getting along. So…I'm still asleep? This is all a dream?"

Wyatt sat, laughing a little at Dax.

Sitting there, seeing the smiling faces of my family gathered around the kitchen table, *was* almost dreamlike. Dad looked at Wyatt, then at me, before he turned back to his paper and coffee—a small smile on his face. He didn't seem angry, just…relieved.

I glanced at Wyatt. He gave me a look, a slow smile that lit him up from the inside. If he wasn't such a guy's guy, I'd say he was beautiful. But I couldn't—he wouldn't take it as a compliment. He was a cowboy. Were cowboys beautiful?

Screw it. You're beautiful.

"Letter on the counter for you." Dad glanced at me.

I leaned over, grabbing the letter. It was from Texas A&M. I glanced at Dad, at Mom. They were both looking at me, waiting. I sat, terrified.

Mom passed the bowl of scrambled eggs around the table. "When did you get in, Wyatt?"

"Around midnight." Wyatt passed the bowl on. "Hope I didn't wake anyone."

"With that storm going on?" Dad shook his head, glancing at my letter.

"Sleep okay?" Mom asked.

"Rough start, but I slept like a log, ma'am."

She laughed. "Good. Dax is falling asleep at the table. Bacon? Biscuits are almost ready."

"I'm awake now, I *think*. I need food," Dax said.

My hands were shaking as I opened the letter. *Congratulations! We are pleased to inform you...* I dropped the letter onto the table.

"Well?" Dad asked.

Everyone looked at me then. "It's an acceptance letter," I managed.

"From?" Wyatt asked.

"Texas A&M," my dad answered for me.

Mom jumped up and hugged me. "Congrats, honey."

"She tell you she got into SMU too?" Dax asked, shoveling pancakes into his mouth.

My parents exchanged a look. "No," Dad said and sighed. "Guess I know which you're going to pick."

I looked at the letter. "Not so sure. Both have good programs...but only one has the graduate program I need."

"And free rent," Dad added.

I smiled at him. He and Mom had bought a four-bedroom house on a small piece of property which they rented to vet students. He'd made no secret about wanting

Dax and me to use it when we went there—not that either one of us had listened. Until now. "You won't charge me rent?"

"Hell, I might even go to A&M," Dax said between bites.

"I'd like that." Dad looked around the table. "All of you kids, looking out for each other."

"It's your choice, Allie." Mom patted my hand before she passed the bacon to Wyatt.

Wyatt took the plate of bacon, his gaze never leaving my face. "Thanks, Dr. Cooper."

"You can call me June, Wyatt. Dr. Cooper seems so formal. Especially over breakfast."

He looked uncomfortable as he said, "I'll try."

Mom laughed. "You don't *have* to."

Pickett was barking like crazy. He stopped, then started again, whimpering now and then. "Excuse me." Wyatt scooted his chair back and headed to the door. "Pickett," he hissed.

Pickett whimpered and stopped. But as soon as Wyatt opened the door, he was barking like crazy again.

"Better go see what's up," Wyatt explained. "Snake or raccoon or something, probably."

"Be careful," Mom said.

Dad stood, following Wyatt out the door.

Dax was spooning jam onto his first biscuit when Dad came running back into the house. "Call the fire department, June," he said.

Mom reached for the phone as Dax and I ran out the back door.

18 CHAPTER EIGHTEEN

It was already warm outside, the air thick with humidity. The roof still dripped from last night's storm, and the peaceful call of the morning doves' coo was faint, but the billowing black smoke breaking in the distance was the only thing I cared about. It was too far away to be a danger to us—

Then I understood.

My lungs felt like they were empty, drawing up, twisting painfully. *No.* The smoke was coming from the direction of Wyatt's house.

"Wyatt!" My dad's voice was stern.

"I've gotta go." Wyatt's voice was just as firm, his gaze locking with my father's.

Dad frowned but Wyatt was already to his truck.

"Wyatt," I yelled after him but he didn't stop. "Dad…" I turned back. "He could get hurt."

I could see the indecision on my father's face as he said, "Let me get my keys."

"I'll drive," Dax offered, pulling his keys from his pocket.

Panic reared up. Helplessness almost brought me to my knees as Wyatt's truck bounced down the gravel drive, the tail lights fading too quickly.

Dad nodded. "Let's go."

We climbed into Dax's truck, tense and silent. Dax turned the key but nothing happened. He tried it again but nothing happened. No engine noise, no AC blasting us in the face…just a grating click.

"Start, dammit," Dax ground out, turning the key again.

"*Shit*," I bit out.

"Come on." Dad got out of Dax's truck and ran back to the house. My legs felt wobbly as I climbed out of the truck.

Time was ticking away. We were here—Wyatt was there. Alone.

"Allie," Mom called out. "It'll be okay. The fire department is on their way. It's probably nothing to worry about."

I wanted to believe her. But one glance at the column of black smoke didn't offer much comfort. What could I say to make her understand that the only thing that would make this *okay* was following Wyatt, making sure *he* was okay.

Time slowed as I dodged puddles and mud en route to Dad's truck.

"Sorry, Allie," Dax murmured.

"Not your fault," I replied, watching my father run to meet us at the truck. Thank God it started right away.

It took us too long to get there—every bump and twist in the road pushing me closer to the edge. When Dad finally navigated the last bend in the road, I stared in horror.

The fire must have started a long time ago. The house was gone, the remaining walls smoldering red and orange. That was where the billowing smoke was coming from. The once-round hay bales, neatly lined up from the house to the barn, were flaming brightly—carrying the fire from the house to the barn. The side of the barn roared, literally. I could hear it from inside the truck.

Wyatt's truck was there, the driver door closed. Pickett was running frantically back and forth on the truck seat. No Wyatt.

"Where is he?" I asked, pushing Dax out of the truck and jumping out. "Wyatt?"

"Allie!" My father grabbed my arm. "Wait. Wait a minute."

I almost jerked my arm away. I pressed my lips into a hard line, refusing to cry or beg.

"Please." Dad's voice was so frantic that I paused. "Let me look, Allie. Let me look, okay?"

I nodded.

The barn groaned, a horrible creaking, followed by snapping and crackling. The back corner of the roof sagged, making the frame of the barn shift like it was leaning.

"Be careful, Dad," I called, louder than I'd intended. But I couldn't help it.

"Don't worry about me, Allie. You two look for Wyatt...*away* from the fire." Dad headed toward the barn.

Wyatt. I wrapped my arms around myself. "Wyatt?" My voice was soft, choking. I cleared my throat, my eyes scanning the tree line...hoping. "Wyatt!"

"Wyatt!" Dax's voice joined mine. I spun to face my brother, startled and comforted that he was with me.

I saw my father as he circled the barn, his arm up, shielding his face. He was yelling too, but whatever he was saying was lost beneath the roar of the fire. My heart was already thumping its way out of my chest; now it lodged itself in my throat. I knew Dad would be careful, he never did anything haphazard. But I didn't like how close he was to the flames—flames that seemed to leap and jump higher every second.

"*Wyatt!*" I yelled, angrily.

More wood creaking, and the side of the barn shifted, the wall folding in on itself. The whole structure shrugged, the roof sliding forward dangerously.

"Wyatt?" Dax called again. "Wyatt!"

All of Wyatt's neatly organized tools, his rodeo gear—I could see it hung with care on the pegboard walls inside the barn. It was all lost to the black smoke pouring out of the gaping hole, floating up into the murky morning sky and making the air heavy.

I was sobbing.

A lone fire truck arrived then. "Anyone in there?" one fireman asked as he jumped out of the truck, still shrugging into his volunteer fire department coat.

"There might be someone in the barn," Dax said.

"Not certain?" the man asked.

"No sir," Dax answered.

Wyatt, where are you? I wanted to scream it, but I couldn't force the words out.

"Stand back now, you two, hear?" the fireman directed.

"My dad's over there." Dax walked with the fireman, pointing to Dad as he went.

Everything seemed to slow down. I saw the firemen, saw the smoke and flames, heard the fire, but it felt hazy…disjointed—like life was moving frame by frame. The thudding of my heart and rasp of my breath seemed to muffle everything else.

With one huge groan, a deafening roar of the leaping flames, and a sudden burst of black smoke, the barn collapsed. I covered my mouth, holding back the scream. I saw my father, saw him run back, safe. But the barn, and anything inside of it, was lost.

Wyatt…No, please…Wyatt. Fear choked me; panic closed in.

This was a nightmare. It had to be. This wasn't happening. "Wyatt," I croaked. Maybe I was still sleeping? Dreaming? I had to be… I could almost believe it if I didn't taste the sulfur and smoke on the back of my tongue…If smoke wasn't burning my eyes…If I could stop crying…"Dammit! Wyatt!" I cried out, emptying my lungs. "*Wyatt, answer me!*"

"Allie?"

I spun, slipping in the wet grass and landing hard on my butt in the mud. It didn't matter—Wyatt was walking quickly toward me, his soot-smeared face worried.

I jumped up, running at him as fast as I could. "Wyatt." No blood. No limping. No burns—that I could see. Just dirt and grit. He was okay. When he was close enough, I launched myself at him, wrapping my arms around him.

He caught me. I knew he would. "You okay?" His voice was rough.

I was sobbing. Yes, I was okay, I was wonderful. But I never ever wanted to experience this kind of fear again.

He held me close, his arms fierce around my waist. "You hurt?" His words brushed against my ear. He let me go, brushing my hair from my face and tilting my head back.

I shook my head, trying to breathe. I couldn't let go of him, not yet. "I couldn't find you." I cupped his face between my hands. "*I couldn't find you.*"

He pulled me close to him but my canvas shoes stuck in the mud under our feet, and we went down—again. Somehow he managed to keep me from getting covered in mud, sort of, but he was coated from head to toe.

"He's here, Dad! Wyatt's here!" Dax was yelling. "With Allie…rolling in the mud." He sighed.

"Dad…" I said against Wyatt's neck. "Wyatt, Dad's looking for you, by the barn."

"Let's go." Wyatt took the hand Dax offered, pulling me up with him. "Thanks." His gaze was fixed on the barn.

"Glad you're okay, man." Dax slapped Wyatt on the back. "Dad's freaking out looking for you. Fireman made him go back to the truck now."

Wyatt nodded, his gaze bouncing from Dax to me to the barn. My hand captured his in a death grip. His eyes searched mine but he didn't say anything as he pulled me close and pressed a hard kiss to my forehead. He led us toward the fire truck at a fast jog.

Dad was standing by the hood, his face soot-smeared and dripping, and breathing hard and fast. His shoulders drooped, his eyes still scanning the area surrounding the barn. He looked so defeated.

Dax spoke up first. "Found him!"

"Mr. Cooper." Wyatt shook my father's hand but Dad pulled Wyatt into a strong, hard hug.

"Glad you're in one piece, Wyatt." The tone of Dad's voice said so much more.

"All clear?" the fireman asked.

"Nothing's in there," Wyatt replied as Dad's grip eased on him.

"Pecos and Daisy?" I asked, worried.

"They got out." Wyatt pulled me against his side, his voice rough. "I had to chase them down—no animal's fond of fire. Daisy got some burns on her rump."

"Mom'll fix her," I promised.

"Allie's right. June will take care of them," Dad agreed. "We need to take care of you." Dad's eyes swept Wyatt from head to toe, then he looked at the ambulance. When had an ambulance arrived?

"I'm fine, sir," Wyatt tried to assure my father.

Dad shook his head. "Wyatt…"

"Just to make sure you're okay. Please," I pleaded. I was siding with Dad on this one. I smiled up at Wyatt, wiping the last of the tears from my cheeks.

His gaze was warm as it traveled over my face. "Okay."

"Holy shit." Dax blew out the words. "Talk about a rough morning."

I didn't let go of his hand and Wyatt's grip never eased, even when the medic gave him the once-over. He worked around our joined hands, quick and efficient.

"He's fine. We'll be home soon—with two patients for you." Dad was talking to Mom on the phone. "No, no, Wyatt only mentioned some burns on Daisy. But you should probably check."

"Worst Monday ever." Dax sighed, hugging me with one arm. I nodded.

"Can't argue that one," Wyatt agreed, blinking as the medic used a flashlight on his eyes.

"I think it's safe to say you'll be excused from school today," the fireman teased, standing upright. "Well, hell, Wyatt, you got a bump on your head and, from what I hear, sounds like you need a chest x-ray—make sure you didn't damage your lungs. You went in there, didn't you?" He nodded in the direction of the barn...what had been the barn.

"Had to make sure he wasn't here," Wyatt answered.

He? Of course. His father...I froze.

I hadn't thought of him. It wasn't just the horses...of course it wasn't. I hadn't given a second's thought to Travis Holcomb because he was an ass who didn't deserve his son. The son who'd braved fire to make sure his dad was safe. I glanced at my father, swallowing back raw emotion, and moved closer to Wyatt. I wrapped my arms around him, holding him as close as I could. He turned into my chest, drawing in a deep, slow breath. His hold was fierce, easing after a few seconds.

My question was soft. "He wasn't in there?"

"No," he answered. "He wasn't."

I blew out a slow breath. "You hit your head?"

"I'm fine." He sat back, his hand gripping mine as I stepped out of his embrace. "Dirty, but fine."

I looked at Dad. *Help me,* I pleaded silently.

Dad looked at me, nodding once. "Wyatt, I know you're not a fan of hospitals and I can't make you go. But you should get your lungs checked out." It was hard to miss the meaningful look he shot me.

Wyatt didn't miss it. He sighed and nodded. I squeezed his hand.

"Oh, he's going," the medic said. "I didn't mean to make it sound like he had a choice. Concussion and smoke inhalation means monitoring him. And you're riding with us."

Wyatt arched a brow. "I don't need—"

"Boy, don't be stupid." The medic put both hands on his hips as he spoke. He looked at me, then stood as straight and tall as his five-foot-two frame would let him. "You want to start coughing up a lung in front of her? Or pass out? Get your ass in the ambulance and close your mouth."

I blinked.

"George Montgomery." The medic shook hands with my father. "My wife and Wyatt's momma, Joanna, were good friends."

Joanna. Joanna Holcomb. It was a good name.

"Come on now," Mr. Montgomery nudged Wyatt. He sighed when he saw how tightly our hands were linked. "She can come too."

I glanced at my father.

"Go with him, Allie." Dad helped me into the back of the ambulance. "Where are the horses? June and I will come back with the trailer from the clinic for them."

"In the south pasture." Wyatt's voice was hoarse. He coughed. "They'll probably be a bit jumpy. Might call Hank, see if he can lend a hand."

"Don't worry." Dad's voice was low and calming. "We'll be up at the hospital soon."

"What about me?" I heard Dax ask as the doors closed.

I watched them clip the oxygen thingy on Wyatt's fingertip. When Mr. Montgomery saw the number, he put an oxygen mask on Wyatt. Mr. Montgomery sat back and I leaned against Wyatt, sliding my arm around his waist and resting my head on his shoulder. Wyatt leaned into me, his cheek pressed against the top of my head.

"Feeling okay? Light-headed?" Mr. Montgomery asked.

"My head hurts, but that's about it," Wyatt answered roughly. He coughed again.

Mr. Montgomery asked, "Hard to breathe? Or talk?"

Wyatt shrugged.

"Don't shrug." Mr. Montgomery sighed loudly. "Yes or no."

"No," Wyatt said firmly, shaking his head.

Mr. Montgomery laughed. "Good."

By the time we made it to the small hospital, Wyatt was restless. He wanted to take off the oxygen mask. He wanted to walk inside, not sit in the wheelchair. He didn't see the point of an x-ray or getting any blood work done—he wanted to leave.

George Montgomery was smart. He found an older motherly-type nurse to hand Wyatt over to. Wyatt's philosophy of respecting his elders ensured he would do exactly as Nurse Lorene asked, even if he wasn't exactly happy about it.

I paced back and forth in the lobby while he was getting his chest x-rays.

"Anything?" Mom asked when they arrived.

"X-rays," I answered, relaxing into her embrace.

"Good. Want to be sure his lungs are free and clear." She used her most doctor-ly voice.

I nodded. "He wants to go home."

"If his x-rays are clear, we can take care of him at home," she agreed.

"And if they're not?" I dared to ask.

She shook her head. "One thing at a time, Allie. Right now, you need to be all smiles and reassurance for him."

I glanced at her. "I can do that."

"I know." She laughed. "I checked on the horses. They'll be fine. Daisy might have a little bit of a bald spot, but it's not too bad. Dad and Hank are getting them to the house."

"Dax?"

"School."

"Mom…" I couldn't imagine going to school after this morning.

"He wanted to go, Allie. Your dad and I didn't make him," she offered.

I didn't say anything. Why the hell would Dax *want* to go to school? Maybe he needed to avoid the drama? God knew we'd had more than our fair share recently. Not like there was much he could do now anyway.

"Could they save anything?" I asked her.

"I don't know, sweetie." She led us to some chairs. "Your dad wasn't optimistic about it. I think they were hoping to contain it more than stop it, since it was such a big fire."

Which made sense, considering how dry everything was. "Guess it's a good thing it rained last night." But it *had* rained last night and it *hadn't* stopped the fire from taking Wyatt's home.

Wyatt and a doctor walked into the lobby. His face was clean, a white bandage taped over his temple. With his almost healed multi-colored eye, he looked more like a bad boy than the cowboy he was. When he smiled at me, reached out for me, I was there, grasping his hand in both of mine. Apparently that wasn't good enough for him, because he pulled me in to his side.

The doctor smiled at me, then my mother. "Mrs. Cooper?"

"*Dr.* Cooper," Wyatt corrected.

"Ah, yes." The doctor nodded. "Sorry about that."

My mother smiled and shook her head. "No, no problem. So what's the news?"

"Wyatt's lungs look good. I've told him to take it easy for the next couple of days—which I know won't be easy for him."

I laughed, the worry I'd been holding at bay easing a little. I'd sit on him if I had to. I smiled up at him, studying his face. His arms tightened around me and I loved it. I rested my head on his chest, listening to his strong heartbeat.

"He's going to be short of breath, especially if he pushes too hard too fast. He has an inhaler, in case he needs it. He does have a concussion, so he needs to be watched for the day. Ice every twenty to thirty minutes every couple of hours until he goes to bed tonight."

"Anything else?" my mother asked.

"I've patched this boy up a time or two. He's a tough one." The doctor clapped Wyatt on the shoulder and added, "But some pain reliever might be in order."

Wyatt caught me staring up at him, his slow, easy smile chasing the last of my fears. I stood on tiptoe and pressed a kiss to his cheek. "I love you," I said, meaning it.

"I love you, Allie." His eyes swept over my face slowly.

"Well…on that note," my mother interrupted, "let's get you home."

The doctor grinned. "Here's my number—in case something comes up."

Wyatt held the door open for me and Mom as we left, which made me laugh. "What?" he asked as we walked out into the sweltering heat.

"You. Ever the gentleman."

"That's a bad thing?" he said, capturing my hand in his.

"Nope." I squeezed his hand. "Ironic, considering you're the one that's bruised and battered." My gaze wandered to the stark white bandage against his forehead.

"How do you feel?" Mom asked, opening the car door.

I pushed Wyatt to the front passenger door, but he shook his head and climbed into the back seat with me. I saw my mom smile in the rearview mirror.

"Honestly?" he asked.

"Yes, of course." She backed up and pulled out of the parking lot. "Please."

He rested his head back. "I'm hungry."

She laughed, and so did I.

I twined his fingers through mine. "You did sort of miss breakfast."

"Let's get you something to eat," Mom agreed.

We drove on in silence. I couldn't seem to stop staring at him, watching him…

"Horses okay?" he suddenly asked, his forehead

creasing.

"Fine. You don't need to worry, I promise, Wyatt. We took care of them," Mom assured him. "Pickett's going to be very happy to see you. Davis said he's looking for you everywhere."

"Poor Pickett." I saw him relax. "I couldn't do much for the horses, just penned them so they wouldn't run off. Animals are smart—have a strong sense of self-preservation."

Mom nodded. "That they do."

We pulled into the parking lot at Peggy's. Mom left the car running and went inside, leaving us—finally—alone.

He turned, instantly pulling me closer to him. "I'm sorry." His head rested on my shoulder, his nose brushing against my throat.

My arms wrapped around him. "For what? For worrying about your family?" I ran my hand over his head. "I'm just sorry I...I freaked the way I did."

He looked at me, his hands resting on either side of my face. Something in his expression made me pause.

"Talk to me," I whispered. "Please."

His eyes bore into mine.

"You'll feel better once you tell me."

His voice was low, gruff. "I'm not so sure about that."

"Try me."

His eyes searched mine for a minute. "My dad started the fire."

Speechless.

"The hay. The house." He shook his head, his hands slipping from my face.

"You...are you *sure?*" I asked.

"No. Yes." He paused. "The barn was mine. I kept it up."

I nodded. I remembered.

"A can of kerosene was missing." He ran a hand over his face.

"You think..."

"He doused the hay with it. He had to, with all the rain." His anguish almost made me lose it. I hurt, ached, for him. He was only eighteen, too young to be dealing with the piles of crap he kept getting.

"But your *dad?*" I couldn't believe it. Maybe I just didn't want to.

"He had the only other key to the barn."

My heart twisted. "What are you going to do?"

He looked at me. "I don't know if I can *do* anything. He's my dad."

I nodded, reining in the anger that washed over me. Travis Holcomb might be Wyatt's father, but he'd endangered his son. Or had he? Had he known Wyatt wasn't there? I almost didn't ask, fearing the answer. "Did he...did he know you were staying with us?"

Wyatt's eyes shut and I had my answer.

I rested my head on his shoulder. "It's going to be okay."

His arm captured me, his hand rubbing up and down my back. "I know."

"I love you. I haven't said it in five minutes so I thought I'd remind you." It was a lame attempt at humor, but I didn't know what else to do.

Mom hurried out of Peggy's, a brown paper bag in her hand. "I think I could have cooked your burgers on the concrete," she said as she climbed into the car. She glanced into the backseat. "Wyatt, honey, you can't sleep for a while. Let's get you home, get some food in your stomach and some ice on that knot. Then we'll decide what's next."

I squeezed his hand, drawing his gaze my way. "Sounds like a good plan," I murmured.

He nodded, but turned to look out the window as we headed out of town.

19 CHAPTER NINETEEN

Wyatt read for the rest of the day. From what I could tell, he stared at the same four pages over and over again. I knew he had a lot to think about, so I didn't push him. I did drop an occasional kiss on his temple, stroke his arm, or cuddle him whenever I had the chance. Pickett was glued to his side, following him from the couch to the bathroom and back again.

"Sit on the front porch with me?" I asked when he set the book down. He nodded.

"Take this." Mom handed Wyatt a bag of ice wrapped in a clean dishtowel and waved us outside.

Wyatt sat and I held the ice on his head while he leaned against me. The sun started to drop and a cool evening breeze blew in. If I hadn't known Wyatt was dealing with such a horrible life-changing debacle, I might have been blissfully happy. I wanted to do something—anything—to make this better. I just didn't know what to do. I pressed a kiss to his forehead. "Need anything?" I asked.

"I'm good." His voice was soft.

"Are you?" I leaned back, looking at him—our gazes locking. "Honest?"

His smile was a little sad. "Right now? I'm great."

I smiled back, happiness bubbling up. "Even bruised and sore and exhausted?"

"Even so." His eyes searched mine. "You're here."

I swallowed. "Wyatt," I whispered, "I want to tell you something."

He tilted his head, tensing a little. I didn't like the way his jaw locked, like he was preparing himself for bad news. "Tell me."

I trailed my finger along his jaw. "Coming here—to Black Falls, I mean—was hard. It wasn't what I wanted. But now I see that the move...everything...brought me to you. Or brought you to me." I felt a little flustered by the sudden intensity on his face. "It's just..." His fingers threaded through mine, giving me the courage to go on. "I might not deserve you, but I'm so glad you're mine." *Mine? Way to freak him out.* "I mean—"

"You had it right, Allie." He swallowed, his fingers brushing along my cheek. "Yours."

I leaned into his touch, soaking up his warmth.

We were a little too caught up in each other to notice the trucks headed up the drive. But then Dad came out on the front porch, effectively severing the building awareness crackling between the two of us.

"Guess school's out." Dad wiped his sweat-drenched forehead with a blue bandana. He'd been working on the barn since we got back from the hospital. Once he'd checked on Wyatt and eaten some lunch, he'd been back at it.

Levi was the first one out, running up the steps two at a time. "You look like sh—" He eyed my father. "Er...rough around the edges."

My father shook his head and walked back inside.

"Are you seriously here to pick on him?" I asked testily.

"Hell no, Miss Allie. We're here to finish that damn barn."

I saw the torn expression on Wyatt's face, how fidgety he became as more trucks arrived. I knew some of the people, and some I didn't. A Furman's Hardware truck pulled in, loaded down with lumber, metal roofing, and bags of other equipment. Levi winked and ran out to meet the truck, calling over some of the boys to help him unload.

"Wyatt," I murmured, feeling him tense to stand, "sit still." He looked so frustrated. "They want to do this for you. Let them."

Dax's truck pulled in, parking closest to the house. He winked in our direction and headed straight to the barn. Hank and Molly and some guy I didn't know drove up next, pulling a beaten-up horse trailer. I tried not to shoot Molly the evil eye as she walked up the steps of the porch.

"Hey." She smiled at Wyatt, barely glancing my way. "Hank and Cannon pulled some gear together. More's coming," she offered, glancing at me again. "Might take a few days, but I'm guessing you're not supposed to be doing much until then anyway."

Wyatt shook his head. "Y'all don't need to do this."

Molly shrugged. "Well, it's done." She glanced at me— nervous. "I'm not much use with a hammer. Anything I can help your mom with?" She tried to smile but her eyes shifted from mine, rather guiltily I thought.

"I don't know," I said, wishing I could like her. I wanted to, I really did. *But you messed with my brother, so you messed with me.*

Speaking of Dax... My poor brother was frozen at the bottom of the steps, his gaze pinned on Molly. He recovered pretty quickly, hopping up the steps. "How's it going?" he asked Wyatt. "Allie bossing you around yet?"

The look on Molly's face threw me. If she was with this Cannon guy, why was she looking at Dax like he was the most amazing person she'd ever seen?

Wyatt's arms slipped around me, pulling me close. "I don't think I'd mind if she did."

I smiled up at him. "You say that *now*."

He laughed. Dax did too, but it sounded forced.

"Gonna go check in with Mom," Dax murmured.

"I'll go with you." Molly sounded breathless. "See if I can help out."

I saw my brother's face, saw the hurt, and wanted to tell Molly to get the hell off my porch. But Wyatt's hold tightened on my hand. Looking at him I knew what he was trying to tell me. *They need to work this out.* I sighed and nodded.

Dax and Molly disappeared into the house, and I forced myself to relax. "Sorry," I murmured.

"Don't be. He's your brother."

I nodded. "And he's never been in love before."

"I know how he feels." Wyatt's hand slipped beneath my hair, his fingers slipping through my hair.

A new, wonderful warmth ran from the tips of my toes to the top of my head. *Who knew you could actually feel this way? How did I get so lucky?* "But you've got me." I rested my head on his shoulder, savoring this strange bond we now—irrevocably, I knew—shared.

"Damn right. And I'm not going to let you go." He spoke softly, resting his head on mine. We sat in silence for a while. His voice was low when he said, "Thought about that letter you got? Since today's been sorta slow and all."

I laughed. I'd known what I was going to do as soon as I'd opened the letter. "Not much to think about," I answered softly.

He stiffened a little. "Oh?"

"Free rent," I teased. *Which is true.* "Good roommate." I nudged him.

"You're going to A&M?"

"It has the best program." *Which is true.* I paused, feeling him relax.

"Nothing to do with me?" he asked.

I looked up at him. *Yes. Maybe. Is that wrong?* "Should it?"

His words were soft. "I'll go where you go. If you're

okay with it?"

I saw the love in his eyes, felt it in my heart. "I'm okay with it." My whisper was husky, strained. *How did I get so lucky?*

"I love you," he whispered.

I nodded, running my hand along his leg. "Good."

He laughed, pressing a kiss to my temple. And there it was—after a horrible, evil day, I was completely happy.

As content as I was to do nothing more than sit there, all wrapped up in him, us, and love, Wyatt was having a hard time with the whole not *doing* something. Every time someone walked by, lifted or carried something to the barn, raised a saw or hammer, climbed up a ladder, he sighed or shifted on the swing. "It's killing you to sit here, isn't it?" I asked.

"It's not too bad." He looked down at me, the look in his eyes surprising. Maybe he wasn't moping about the barn. Maybe he was thinking about me.

The front screen door opened and Dax re-emerged, looking more frazzled than when he went inside. "Need anything?" he asked.

I handed the bag of ice to him. "We're done with this for now."

He took it, turning it over in his hands. "Anything else? Wyatt?"

"A hammer. Or a nail gun." He leaned forward, rubbing a hand over his face.

"Ain't happening." Dax clapped him on the shoulder and went back inside.

Two agonizing hours later, Green's Bar-B-Q arrived with a van full of food for everyone working. Not that anyone really took a break. They grabbed food and went back to work. By then the barn was illuminated from inside with work lamps, while the outside was bright with truck headlamps.

"Looks good," Wyatt said, breaking the comfortable silence that had settled over us. He sounded strange, tense.

My hand rubbed his thigh. "It does," I agreed, hoping he'd talk to me.

He looked at me, a small smile on his gorgeous—tired—face. After a second, he added, "In the barn I had some of Hank's gear, Cannon left some bridles and bits, Molly had an older saddle... It wasn't just my stuff that burned up."

I wished there was something I could say.

"I hate him." His voice was low, but his eyes blazed.

"Wyatt." I slipped from the swing, kneeling in front of him. "You can't. Don't go there, please. You have every right to be angry—"

"Well, I am. For all he knew I was sleeping in my bed," he growled. "He...he didn't care. I don't matter to him."

I shook my head, pressing my lips tight. I didn't know Travis Holcomb. I couldn't say anything to make this better. Wyatt was only saying what we'd both been thinking. As much as I hated his father, Wyatt was better than that.

"Look at that," Mom said as she came out onto the porch. Her blue gaze traveled from the barn to us. Her smile faded. "Everything okay?"

"Wyatt's frustrated," I offered, hoping to leave it at that. "He wants to help out."

"Oh, Wyatt." Mom's voice was full of sympathy.

"Don't worry, Dr. Cooper, there's nothing to help with." Levi was back, looking more satisfied and cocky than ever. He waved Wyatt over. "Done. Come on, you big baby." He paused then, asking Mom, "He *can* walk, can't he?"

My mom laughed.

Wyatt stood up. "I can walk."

"Then check it out," Levi said.

The rest of the night was a blur. The barn was awesome—at least I thought so. On the wall hung pegs, just like at Wyatt's. Ropes and lassoes and bits of rodeo gear I didn't know the names of yet were already hanging there. I might not be a big people-person but that didn't mean I wasn't in awe over what Black Falls had done tonight. And the amazing generosity and kindness amongst them—even Levi—was really hard to get my head around. I couldn't think of a single person more deserving than Wyatt. He looked over every single thing, thanking each and every person that had come out to help.

I couldn't stop thinking about what Wyatt had said. Watching him shake hands, endure teasing, the odd playful pat on the back, I knew he was struggling. Anger was a powerful emotion, one that could get in the way. But I knew it'd be okay.

You'll do the right thing. I smiled when he glanced at me. He always did. But "the right thing" was his call—no one else's. I couldn't tell him what to do; this was his father we were talking about. As much as I wanted Travis Holcomb far far away, it wasn't my place.

When the last truck pulled away, the sky was black and the stars were out in full force. We sat on the porch, the five of us, talking, until Dad pulled rank and made us all get ready for bed.

"You're home tomorrow," Dad said to Wyatt. "Doctor's orders. But you two..." He looked at Dax and me and shook his head.

I knew he was right, but letting go of Wyatt, the hand I'd held all day long, was a lot harder than I'd expected.

***

Tuesday was weird. I didn't know most of these people, but that didn't stop them from asking about Wyatt, what he needed or how they could help. From the counselor to the coach, everyone was worried about him.

Coming home was the best part of the day. Wyatt was in the barn, talking to Pecos, Pickett nearby. I leaned against the solid wood doorframe, perfectly happy to stand there, looking at him. I'd never thought I was the boy-crazy type, but I was happy to be wrong. That he was here, safe, mine...I swallowed the emotion that threatened to

281

choke me. "How are they liking their new place?" I asked as I walked in.

He turned, his crazy-gorgeous smile almost knocking me over. "No complaints."

I smiled up at him, wanting to touch him but holding back. It was bad enough I'd thought about him through most of my classes—what a pathetic lovesick girly-girl I'd turned into. I wasn't going to throw myself at him. I'd lose all self-respect. "That's good."

The length of rope he'd been holding hit the dirt, and his warm hands tugged me against him. He smelled like sunshine and hay and…and Wyatt. I slid my arms around his waist, relaxing against him. His fingers tilted my face toward his. "Have a good day?" His gaze searched mine.

A hundred times better now. But I only said, "Everyone's worried about you."

He shook his head. "You tell 'em I'm good?"

I couldn't stop smiling. "I did. But that's not going to stop them from worrying about you. Lots of people love you, Wyatt. You make it kind of easy."

His gaze was fixed firmly on my mouth now, hot and brown and—making my chest tighten.

"Wyatt?" I whispered, hoping that look meant what I thought it meant.

His attention didn't wander.

"Are you going to kiss me now?"

He nodded slowly, leaning down to brush his lips over mine. A shiver ran down my spine, a wonderful, powerful jolt of pleasure.

"Have a good day at school?" My father's voice separated the two of us. Wyatt stepped back immediately, stooping to pick up the dropped rope at his feet.

Talk about a buzz kill. "Fine," I muttered, clearly irritated.

Dad was smiling, enjoying the way we shifted awkwardly. "Homework?" he asked.

I nodded, scowling at him. "Yep. But I was hoping to

do it after I spend some time with Wyatt—since I've been worr—thinking about him all day. I thought I'd try cheering him up."

Dad made a strange choking sound then laughed. "Sounds like a plan." He winked at Wyatt and walked out of the barn.

"Definitely cheered up," he whispered as our lips came together, our hold on each other a little tighter, a little closer than before the interruption.

Was it normal to kiss for half an hour? To almost stop breathing, get dizzy, and want more? To burrow against his neck and inhale his scent as deeply as I could? Something about being close to him made me ache. Like I couldn't get enough of him, get close enough…

His hand brushed through my hair, tilting my face back. "You're beautiful."

I shook my head, blind-sided—again—but this time it was his words that knocked me for a loop.

"You are," he murmured.

"Wyatt…" I took a deep breath. Now was probably a good time to ask him. If we weren't distracted soon, there was the serious possibility of my body exploding.

"What?" His smile faded a little.

"I guess… Well." I shook myself. "I know you've kind of been through a lot the last couple of days. And you've got a lot weighing on your mind and your really ripped shoulders." I paused, appreciating his smile. "And this is sort of stupid and definitely not something that's on your radar. But I was wondering if…" Was I really panicking over this? I spit it out, quickly. "Will you…do you want to go to the Homecoming dance with me?"

He was grinning like an idiot. My cheeks were blazing. "I was going to ask you," he said and stroked my cheek.

"You were?" How had a stupid high school dance become something so freaking exciting?

"Stuff just got in the way," he murmured, his smile fading again.

"I know." I waited, watching his expression darken. I squeezed his arm. "I'm here, okay? Talk to me, if you want to. I'm here."

And just like that he was staring at me, his eyes warm and inviting. "I know. And I'm grateful." His lips were feather-soft on mine before he drew back. His gaze followed his thumb as it raked over my lower lip.

I shivered. "Wyatt," I whispered before he kissed me again.

"Hmm?" he asked, his lips traveling across my cheek.

"You're making me...feel...crazy—" I bit off as his lips fastened on my earlobe. I pushed, gently, on his chest.

His eyes were narrowed, his breathing rapid.

"Keep it up and..." I scanned the barn quickly. "Well, we're not in my parents' house right now."

He wore that strained, barely-in-control expression that made him hotter than ever. His thumb raked over my lower lip again.

I groaned. "You said you wanted to go slow."

His smile was huge. "I do. We will. Didn't say I wasn't going to *think* about...things."

"So...you're thinking?" It was hard to get the words past the lump in my throat.

He nodded, that damn muscle in his jaw twitching.

Which only made me crazier. I swallowed. "Well...stop it...or you'll have to explain things when one of my parents comes in and I'm pulling your clothes off."

He swallowed, his attention wandering from my face to my chest. His in-control was slipping, his pained expression making my insides go hot and liquid.

I stepped back, taking his hand in mine. "Seriously. I can tell what you're thinking, and it's not helping my whole good-girl-who-won't-toss-her-hot-cowboy-into-the-nearest-pile-of-hay vibe." I was teasing. Sort of.

His hand slid under my shirt, pressing against my back. "There's no hay in the barn."

"It's a good damn thing," I whispered, his hand sliding

up between my shoulder blades. *Enough. Defusing sexual tension now…* "Oh, in case I forgot to tell you, I have your homework too," I said sweetly.

He laughed. "I thought you said everyone was worried about me."

"They are." I led him from the barn. "And they don't want you to get behind."

He let go of my hand long enough to put the length of rope on one of the wall pegs. His fingers laced with mine as we walked to the house, Pickett running circles around our legs as we went.

***

Things got easier when Wyatt got the green light to start doing everything again. He was the sort of person that needed to be busy. School, rodeo, work, they actually made him happy. And I made him happy. I was beginning to accept that—to love that.

I turned up the music coming from the computer my parents had let me have in my room. It was nice to know they were beginning to trust me again. And it was nice to listen to music, loudly, when I felt like it. Like now.

Homecoming was Saturday, two days away. And the only thing I had to wear was the sparkly gold sequin dress Lindie and I had purchased together. We'd matched—mine was gold, hers was electric blue. They had been the shortest, tightest, lowest cut dresses in the store—leaving nothing to the imagination. Likelihood of dancing in it? Slim. But we'd bought them anyway, intending to wear them to the prom and stir up all sorts of trouble. But prom had been two weeks after the accident.

I'd been under suicide watch—missing the dance, the parties, the tribute to Lindie and Zach the Student Council had put together. It was a good thing I hadn't gone. If I hadn't already been in the nuthouse, that would probably have put me there.

I held up the dress, looking at my reflection in the mirror. It wasn't a pretty dress. But it had cost a lot of money and I'd been in full do-whatever-it-takes-to-piss-Dad-off mode, so…it had been the perfect dress. And Lindie'd said I rocked it.

Honestly, that could be a bad thing. Her confusion over feminine versus slutty had always amused me. I had a feeling this was one of those situations, but decided to see for myself. I pulled off my school clothes and tugged…and tugged…and tugged it on.

I was a little out of breath when it was finally zipped up. *Oh yeah. Oh no. I look like a high-dollar hooker.* I turned, looking over my shoulder. *Huh.* Had I actually looked at my reflection wearing the dress before I bought it? Was I that clueless? *Yes. Yes, I was.*

The house phone rang but I ignored it, fidgeting with the zipper that was now snagged in the gold sequins. The phone rang and rang. "Dax?" I yelled. Nothing.

I ran out of my room and hurried down the stairs.

I picked up the phone. "Hello?"

"Hey sweetie, your dad and I were invited out. A little dinner and maybe a little dancing."

"Sounds fun." I still felt guilty over ruining their last attempted date.

"You three can handle dinner on your own, right?" Which was mom code for: Can you three behave, or should we stay home instead of having a night out?

"We'll be good."

"I'll have my cell phone if you need anything. See you later."

"Have fun," I said, hanging up the phone.

"Allie?" I heard Dax calling outside. "What's up?"

I walked out onto the front porch, shielding my eyes from the late afternoon sun. "Mom. She and Dad are going out tonight." By the time my eyes had adjusted to the sun, I realized Dax wasn't alone. Wyatt, Levi, and Hank were all gathered around an old tractor, the hood open and tools lying on the ground. Guess my music was a little too loud. How else would I miss the roar of Levi's truck?

But they were all here now, staring at me. Dax was shaking his head. Because I looked like a stripper.

"Okay then," I said, backing into the house. "Shit."

I spent the next five minutes trying to get out of the dress, but the zipper was stuck and there was no way I was pulling it over my head or pushing it past my hips. I spent another five minutes looking for a pair of scissors, which I finally found in a kitchen drawer. I heard the screen door and braced for another Dax lecture on needing attention.

"Hey." It was Wyatt.

I froze, scissors in hand. "Hi." I glanced at him. "I...I...Zipper's stuck."

"Some dress."

"Trying to find something for Homecoming."

His eyebrows went high. He opened his mouth, then closed it.

"I'm not going to wear it, don't worry." My face felt hot. "I can't...Where's Dax?" Maybe I could convince him to help. Instead of letting me wallow in total humiliation.

"He went to get some parts for the tractor," Wyatt murmured, shoving his hands into his pockets.

"Oh." I nodded. *We're alone? I look like this and he's looking at me like that...*I held out the scissors to him, jerking the zipper. "I can't..."

He blew out a slow breath. "Cut it?" His eyes swept me from head to toe before he gave up and closed his eyes.

"Not like I'm ever going to wear it."

He opened his eyes, approaching me slowly. He took the scissors from me, put them on the counter, and bent to look at the zipper. I glanced down at his dark head, then stared at the ceiling.

Besides the faint music from my bedroom upstairs, the room was quiet. Other than my breathing and my heartbeat, that is.

"Sequin in the zipper teeth." He sounded completely normal, as if seeing a problem that needed fixing removed the whole girlfriend-in-next-to-nothing issue.

"I couldn't get it out," I explained. "So, scissors."

Our eyes met. He sat back on his heels, his detachment disappearing. His jaw clenched and his breath picked up a little. He stood up, pulling me into the circle of his arms. I didn't care that he was covered in dirt, that his white undershirt was sweaty, that the stubble on his cheek was rough against my temple. All I knew was he was humming, his hands holding me close, as he moved us to the music.

I smiled, resting my head against his shoulder.

"My dad was arrested today," he murmured when the music stopped. He didn't let go of me, or tighten or loosen his hold.

I didn't move, but I did hold on tighter. "You okay?"

"Yeah. Sheriff Hodge was at the arena waiting for me. He told me Dad didn't put up a fight. And he doesn't want to see me."

I swallowed back angry words.

"He admitted what he did. Guilt, I guess. He told the sheriff he thought it was Saturday, thought that I was on the road, or he'd never have done it."

"Oh, Wyatt." I didn't know what to say. What his father did was wrong, but knowing he hadn't meant to hurt Wyatt helped—a lot.

"He's ashamed." He cleared his throat. "That's what Sheriff Hodge says. That's why he doesn't want to see me."

"Makes sense." I looked up at him, needing to see his face. "I'm sorry. But I'm also really relieved."

His brown eyes bore into mine, understanding. "I am too."

"What does this mean…for your dad, I mean?"

He frowned. "Two years in prison. Maybe longer, since he's had some trouble before."

His father would miss so much—Wyatt's graduation, going off to college, his rodeos, his life…

"I'm so sorry, Wyatt." My heart ached for him. I

brushed my fingers along his jaw, into his hair. "You okay?"

"I've been better. But I've been worse, too." He smiled, leaning into my hand. "Guess I'm just glad I didn't have to turn him in."

I nodded. I knew how much that had been weighing on him. No son should be put in that position. "I wish there was something I could do...or say. Something to make it better."

His gaze traveled over my face. "Tell me you love me."

"I love you, Wyatt," I said, stroking his cheek.

He covered my hand with his. "That's all I need." He tilted my face back, locking our gazes. "Knowing that is enough. *You* are enough." There was no doubt in his voice. What he said was simple fact. His smile, his dimples, had my heart thudding. "I'm here, with you, until you don't want me around anymore."

Not want him? "Never gonna happen," I admitted softly.

His laugh was gentle, maybe even a little relieved. "That's what I was hoping you'd say."

That was when I understood. He loved me the way I loved him—completely. It was necessary. It was right. We were right.

"You know," my voice was high, full of happiness as I slid my arms around his neck, "a kiss would be nice too, cowboy."

He smiled, his arms pulling me against him. "Yes, ma'am."

ACKNOWLEDGMENTS

Marilyn Tucker, Jolene Navarro, Joni Hahn, and Storm Navarro, you guys gave me the courage to write Allie and Wyatt's story. I'm so glad you told me to keep at it!

Grace Coronado, I love your keen eyes. Your enthusiasm over this book and your excitement over Dax and Molly's story is a fantastic motivator.

Stephanie Lawton – thank you for reading and putting your name on my first YA!

Thank you Inkspell Publishing! Melissa Keir and Shilpa Mudaganti, your belief in my stories keeps me writing. Deb Anderson – you rock the edits.

Thank you to my family—I am so blessed. Jakob, you make me laugh when I need it most. Kaleb, you give the best cuddles and encouragement—even when I know you'd rather being doing something else.

ABOUT THE AUTHOR

Sasha is part gypsy. Her passions have always been storytelling, history, romance, and travel. She writes fantasy, contemporary, sci-fi, and YA romance. Her first play was written for her Girl Scout troupe. She's been writing ever since. She loves getting lost in the worlds and characters she creates; even if she frequently forgets to run the dishwasher or wash socks when she's doing so. Luckily, her family is super understanding and supportive.

Enjoyed This Book?

Try Other

Sasha Summers

Novels

From Inkspell Publishing.

Buy Any Book Featured In The Following Pages

at 15% Discount From Our Website.

http://www.inkspellpublishing.com

Use The Discount Code

GIFT15 At Checkout!

She wasn't meant for movie stars, Hollywood, or happy endings. And then she met him.

All she wants for Christmas is for Hollywood to love her again. But once she meets him, her Christmas list changes.

Her secret will change everything. Will it destroy hope for a Hollywood happy ending too?

SASHA SUMMERS

"THE RED CARPET SERIES ARE ROMANCES AT THEIR FINEST...TRULY FANTASTIC STORY TELLING."
- PATRICIA W. FISCHER, AWARD-WINNING AUTHOR OF WEIGHTING FOR MR. RIGHT

HOLLYWOOD
Homecoming
RED CARPET SERIES - BOOK THREE

CPSIA information can be obtained at www.ICGtesting.com
Printed in the USA
LVOW06s1329060415

433459LV00004B/140/P

9 781939 590305